THE REALM OF SILENCE

JUDE KNIGHT

PG (one intimate scene, reference to violence)

Published by Jude Knight

Copyright 2018 Judith Anne Knighton writing as Jude Knight

Publisher: Titchfield Press

Thank you for your purchase. If you enjoy this book, please check with your favourite retailer for other books by Jude Knight.

All rights reserved.No part of this book may be reproduced in any form or by any electronic or mechanical means, including information storage and retrieval systems, without written permission from the author, except for the use of brief quotations in a book review.

ISBN: 978-0-9951101-1-3

❀ Created with Vellum

THE REALM OF SILENCE

"I like not only to be loved, but also to be told I am loved... the realm of silence is large enough beyond the grave." George Eliot

When Susan Cunningham's daughter disappears from school, her pleasant life as a fashionable, dashing, and respectable widow is shattered. Amy is reported to be chasing a French spy up the Great North Road, and when Susan sets out in pursuit she is forced to accept help from the last person she wants: her childhood friend and adult nemesis, Gil Rutledge.

Gil Rutledge has loved Susan since she was ten and he a boy of twelve. He is determined to oblige her by rescuing her daughter. And if close proximity allows them to rekindle their old friendship, even better. He has no right to ask for more.

Gil and Susan must overcome danger, mystery, ghosts from the past, and their own pride before their journey is complete.

To my beloved sister, whose name I borrowed for this heroine. Thank you, dear Sue, for being the friend I can always count on. I love you.

1

Gil Rutledge sat in the small garden to the side of the Crown and Eagle and frowned at the spread provided for his breakfast. Grilled trout with white butter sauce, soft-boiled eggs, grilled kidney, sausages, mashed potatoes, bacon, a beef pie, two different kinds of breads (one lightly toasted), bread rolls, a selection of preserves, and a dish of stewed peaches; all cooked to perfection and none of it appealing.

Two days with his sister, Madelina, had left old guilt sitting heavy in his stomach, choking his throat and souring his digestion. And the errand he had yet to face did not improve his appetite.

He cut the corner from a slice of toast and loaded it with bits of bacon and a spoonful of egg. He was too old a campaigner to allow loss of appetite to stop him from refuelling. He washed the mouthful down with a sip from his coffee. It was the one part of the breakfast Moffat had not trusted to the inn kitchen. His soldier-servant insisted on preparing it himself, since he knew how Gil liked it.

No. Not his soldier-servant. Not anymore. His valet, butler, factotum. Manservant. Yes, his manservant.

Gil raised the cup to the shade of his despised older brother.

"This is the worst trick you've played on me yet," he muttered. The viscount's death had landed the estranged exile with a title he never wanted, a bankrupt estate, a frail frightened sister-in-law and her two little daughters—left to his guardianship but fled from his home —and an endless snarl of legal and financial problems. And then there were Gil's mother and his younger sister. His mission in leaving Gloucestershire had been to avoid war with the first and make peace with the second.

With a sigh, he took another sip, and loaded his fork again. The sooner he managed to swallow some of this meal, the sooner he could be on the road.

Beyond the fence that bordered the garden, carriages collected their passengers from the front of the inn. Stamford was on the Great North Road, and a transport hub to half of England, with roads branching off in every direction. As Gil stoically soldiered his way through breakfast, he watched idly, amusing himself by imagining the errands and destinations of the travellers.

Until one glimpsed face made him sit forward with a start. Surely that was Amelia Cunningham, The Goddess's eldest daughter? No. This girl was older, almost an adult, though still dressed as a schoolgirl.

He frowned, trying to work out how old little Amy must be by now. He had last seen her during his most recent posting to England, before he was sent overseas to Gibraltar then on to the Peninsular wars. At the beginning of 1808. He remembered, because that was when he parted with the best horse a man had ever owned. More than four years ago. The Goddess who held his heart had been a widow these past two years and Amy must be— what? Good Lord. She would be sixteen by now.

He craned his neck, trying to see under the spreading hat that shielded the girl's face, but she climbed into a yellow post chaise with a companion—a tall stripling boy of about the same age. And the woman who followed them was definitely not The Goddess; not unless she had lost all her curves, shrunk a good six inches, dyed her golden hair black, and traded her fashionable attire for a governess's dull and shapeless garb.

No. That was not Susan Cunningham. Amy would have a governess, presumably, but the boy was way too old to be Amy's brother Michael. No. The girl could not have been Amy.

The door closed, the post boy mounted, the chaise headed north, and Gil went back to his breakfast.

Cambridge, England, 1812

Susan Cunningham fumbled for the chair behind her, her legs suddenly too weak to keep her upright.

"Missing?" she repeated, frowning as she tried to make the word mean something else. Anything else. "But where? How?"

Mrs Fellowes, the proprietor and headmistress, took the chair behind the desk, her lips pinched and her nostrils flared. "The school has been much deceived, Mrs Cunningham. The girls clearly planned this escapade very carefully. We could not have discovered their absence any earlier."

"I don't understand…" Susan frowned, trying to think through the panic that howled and gibbered in her mind. "How can she be missing?" Slowly, as if working in thick mud, her mind pulled some more facts out of the headmistress's complaint. "How long has she been gone? Who is she with?"

"We could not have known," Mrs Fellowes insisted. "The girls sent a note saying they were going to the art exhibition with Miss Foster, Miss Grahame's aunt, and that Miss Cunningham would stay with her friend for the remainder of the weekend. This is a common occurrence, Mrs Cunningham, and has your approval."

That was true. Patrice Grahame was Amy's dearest friend. Wait. The weekend? "This was yesterday?" she asked. Please let it be yesterday. Surely two sixteen-year-old girls could not travel far in one day?

Mrs Fellowes sniffed. "Not Sunday, no. The notes were sent on Saturday morning, Mrs Cunningham, and Miss Grahame and Miss Cunningham have not been seen since."

She unbent a little, "I was in the process of writing you a letter when you arrived unexpectedly." A slight edge to that last word. Mrs Fellowes did not approve of parents who arrived during term time, and without warning. But Susan had been passing on her way to London, with only a ten-mile detour between her and her daughter.

Not to the point. Susan reined in her skittering thoughts and pursued the question of how two girls could be absent from Saturday to Monday with no one the wiser.

"Did Miss Foster not report the girls missing?"

"She also received a note, in which the girls said Miss Grahame would be staying at the school with your daughter. I am very disappointed in them, Mrs Cunningham. They are not biddable girls, but I had not thought them liars." She sniffed again, jerking her chin upward as she did so. "You will wish to speak to Miss Foster. You have her direction, I imagine."

Susan was ushered firmly to the door before she could formulate a response and did not think to ask what measures had been taken to find the missing girls until she was halfway to Miss Foster's townhouse. She continued on, as more and more questions crowded her mind. Perhaps Miss Foster knew the answers. If not, she would go back to the school and demand explanations. Later.

Miss Foster looked more than ever like a crow: a long gaunt caricature of a female, dressed ten years out of fashion in unrelieved black, with a hooked nose that dominated her features. "I suppose you are here about your daughter and my niece," she grumbled when the maid showed Susan in.

"I have just come from the school," Susan explained. "What can you tell me, Miss Foster?"

Very little, and Susan felt her manners splintering with her patience when that little was delivered with many animadversions on the two girls, and dire predictions about how the coming scandal might affect Patrice's younger sister, Clementine.

"What does Clementine say about this disappearance?" Susan asked, cutting into the flow of criticisms.

"Clementine?" Miss Foster narrowed her eyes. "Clementine knows nothing."

Susan, who had three children and had been one of five, thought this highly unlikely. She took a deep breath, forcing her mind away from horrific images of all that might lie in wait for two gently-born maidens. "May I speak with her, please?"

Miss Foster grumbled, but sent the maid for Clementine, who confirmed Susan's instincts by sidling in the door and refusing to meet Susan's eyes.

Susan made her voice soft, though the strain of it hurt the throat that wanted to scream and wail. "Clementine, your sister and my Amy have been missing for two and a half days. They may be in great danger. Please tell us what you know so we can find them before they get hurt."

The girl looked at her aunt, who opened her mouth then shut it again at a peremptory gesture from Susan.

"Clementine?" Susan prompted.

"They were leaving me out. Again," Clementine whined.

"Leaving you out of what?" Susan could manage this. She would remain calm. She would not take the child by the throat and shake the story out of her, or collapse weeping.

"They always do it. Going off and whispering. It isn't fair."

"What happened on Saturday, Clementine?"

Bit by bit the story came out. Amy arrived at Miss Foster's house early on Saturday, as the other two girls were about to leave for school. Patrice and Amy sent Clementine on ahead, but she doubled back and followed the two older girls to an inn. Clementine did not see what happened after that, as she feared being late to school.

"What enquiries have been made?" Susan asked Miss Foster. "Has anyone been to the constables? To the inn?"

Miss Fellowes drew herself up, her eyes widening. "Certainly not. Just think of the scandal."

"Think of the scandal if they are found dead in a ditch and you have made no shift to look for them."

Clementine sucked in a sharp breath.

Susan must ask at the inn where Clementine left them. She

would not let panic overwhelm her and empty her mind as it had at the school. Someone must have seen her child; relatives of peers did not just disappear into thin air. She would think of the right questions to ask; the right places to ask them.

She stood. "Do you wish to accompany me to question the stable master at the inn?" she asked, not expecting Miss Foster to agree. But minutes later all three of them—Miss Foster, Clementine and Susan—made their way into the courtyard of the post inn nearest to the school, where a boy was soon scurrying to fetch the stable master.

"Did you rent a carriage to two young girls?" Miss Foster barked, before Susan could speak.

The stable master bristled at the accusation in her tone. "We run an honest business here," he protested.

"Just answer the question, man. Two girls have been missing since Saturday."

Susan needed to take charge of this interrogation. She touched Miss Foster's arm.

"If you would excuse me, Miss Foster."

Miss Foster glared but took a step back.

Susan smiled at the stable master, and if the smile was forced he did not seem to notice, visibly thawing.

"I am certain you have done your job admirably, Mr–?"

The stable master removed his cap and admitted to the name Ben.

"Ben," Susan repeated. "Ben, you will understand a mother's fears. We must hope that all is well, but a child is so vulnerable, as I am certain you know, and the close relative of an earl? Well, we must find her as quickly as possible. I would be grateful for any information you can give us." She shook her reticule. The coins within did not chink as she had hoped, but the movement caught the stable master's eye.

"Very grateful." Susan said again.

"Ah Missus, I do wish I could help, that I do. Saturday, you say? And probably in the morning? We was busy, like always, and I don't recall no little gels. They didn't hire a carriage or a horse; not from me. I'd remember that. And if not from me, then likely not from this inn." He appealed to the crowd. "Does anyone remember two gels? School gels, like? One with eyes like this lady? They'd remember the eyes," he confided to Susan. "Unusual, they are."

Susan added her plea to his. "Has anyone seen my daughter? Dressed similarly this young lady?" She indicated Clementine Grahame, in the school's signature blue skirt and coat, and straw bonnet. "I am offering a reward for information that leads me to her."

The buzz of conversation stilled when a deep voice announced, "I may have that information, Mrs Cunningham."

She knew that voice; vibrated to it at some idiot physical level that took no account of their mutual antipathy. The crowd parted to let her see him. Gil Rutledge, dusty from the road and dishevelled, but still compellingly handsome in the hard chiselled-granite sort of a way that had gifted him with the nickname Rock Ledge. How dare he look so appealing. It was an offence against decency when her daughter was missing.

She would be pleasant to Satan himself if it helped her find her daughter. "You have seen Amy, Colonel Rutledge? Today?"

Four years had passed since he last crossed verbal swords with Susan Cunningham, and she looked no older. Did the infernal woman have the secret of an elixir of youth? She had been widowed long enough to be out of her blacks, and back into the blues she favoured: some concoction that was probably the height of fashion and that both hid and enhanced her not insubstantial charms.

As always, she was perfectly dressed, perfectly coiffed, and perfectly behaved. And he undoubtedly looked every bit as if he had been travelling for weeks, apart from the brief stopover in Derby with his sister.

She was breathing quickly, fear for her child flushing her face. To one who knew her, and who watched her closely, she held her composure by a thread.

The crowd of onlookers leaned forward to catch his reply. "Is there somewhere we can discuss your business in private, Mrs Cunningham?"

That fetched a considering nod. "Miss Foster, may I present Colonel—no, Lord Rutledge? He and I grew up on neighbouring estates. Lord Rutledge, Miss Foster's niece Patrice is, we presume, with my daughter." She indicated the child shifting nervously from one foot to another nearby, with Miss Foster firmly gripping her shoulder. "Patrice's sister Clementine. But shall we seek privacy for our discussion?"

Until this moment, Gil had wondered if he was setting up a false trail. After all, he was not certain he'd seen Amy in Stamford. Why would The Goddess be hunting for her in Cambridge if she was a day's hard ride away? But the girl had been dressed like the child Clementine and was of the right age and appearance. Besides, if he were wrong he'd make it up by devoting himself to helping with the search. The interview in Essex with his reluctant sister-in-law would need to wait until The Goddess's daughter was safe.

He gave Moffat the signal to deal with their mounts and the packhorse, and followed Mrs Cunningham into the inn. Susan, he said silently, though underneath that silence earlier names sounded in his head. Joan. Athene. Boadicea. Just as her father had named his sons for battle-tried kings and emperors who led successful armies, he had given his daughter the names of female warriors: a saint, a Goddess, and a queen. The ten-year-old girl who followed the boys at their games demanded and won a more common name, but to his mind it had never suited her as well as those bestowed upon her before God, at her baptism.

He expected her to demand answers as soon as they were private, but she had never behaved like the other women he knew. She stood, seemingly at ease, one golden brow arched, and waited for him to speak. She took his breath away. She always had.

"How long have the two girls been missing?" Saturday, the ostler said, which would fit. But it seemed unlikely such a devoted mother would have so long delayed the search.

"Saturday," Susan confirmed, "though the school found out only today, and told me when I arrived unexpectedly." She seemed to think that required further explanation. "I was journeying back to London from Michael's estate in the north and diverted on a whim to visit Amy.

The girl could have been Amy, then. "What would she be doing in Stamford?"

"Stamford! I can imagine no reason why she and Patrice might go to Stamford, or how. I have been asking about carriages, but… Wait. You saw her in Stamford?"

"Yesterday morning. I did not see her clearly. She was dressed like Miss Clementine here. One of those bonnets. Black half boots. A skirt and coat thing. Both blue. Wool, I think."

"A pelisse, yes. In bishop's blue over a lighter coloured skirt. The Fellowes' Academy requires all its students to dress the same. And her companion would also have been wearing the uniform."

"She was with a boy. Or, at least, someone dressed as a boy. Thin face. Dark hair from what I could see under the cap. Tall for a girl, if it was a girl. Taller than Miss Cunningham by perhaps five inches. Their governess, or whoever it was, ordered them into the post chaise and they took off on the North Road."

"Governess." Susan's brows drew together as she thought about that.

"It must have been someone else," Miss Foster proclaimed. "Patrice would not dress as a boy. The very idea is ridiculous. This gentleman knows nothing." She turned a shoulder on Gil and glared at the little girl. "You have misled us, Clementine. They did not come here."

"I saw them," Clementine insisted. "I told you, Aunt Audrey. When Amy arrived at our house, Patrice told me to go straight to school, but I followed them here."

Gil looked to Susan for elucidation, and she did not disappoint, summarising what she had learnt from Clementine.

"You haven't seen them since?" he asked the girl, who flinched and shrunk in on herself, her shoulders hunched.

"No need to bark at her, my lord," Susan admonished. "He means no harm, Clementine. He is used to dealing with soldiers.

No, she has not seen them since, and before you ask, Clem did not tell the school or her aunt what she saw until the girls were found to be missing, which was only this morning."

"This morning?" That seemed unaccountably careless. To mislay two young ladies for two days and not notice.

"My daughter and her co-conspirator are to be congratulated on their planning, apparently." She explained about the art exhibition and the notes, her tone calm and dry.

Her white-knuckled grasp on her reticule and the lines around her eyes told a different story. She was holding her emotions in with great difficulty, the panic mounting behind.

Gil kept his own voice confident. "We have a place to start, then, and can question the stable master about a girl and a boy, or possibly about a woman with a girl and a boy. Perhaps other children at the school may know what set them running?"

His own memories of boarding school provided a number of reasons for running away, and he admired the young ladies' initiative in arranging such a strong lead over the inevitable pursuit. But boys on the road seldom faced the same dangers as girls. He shook off the horrifying speculations that tried to cloud his mind.

"Unless Miss Clementine has something else to tell us?"

The girl wouldn't meet his eyes, and the old crow was declaring her intention to cut the older niece off and take the younger one home. "I do not believe they have headed north, and if they have, then I wash my hands of them. Clementine? Come."

No. He needed to know what the child was hiding. He reached out a hand to stop her, and Susan caught his eye. A small shake of her head, a look at Clementine with widening eyes, and then a tip of her chin at Miss Foster.

Gil obeyed the unspoken command. "Miss Foster, a moment of your time, please." He took the woman's bony elbow and escorted her from the room, managing a farradiddle of questions about the authenticity of the note she had received. Was she certain it was from her niece? Could it have been from a third party? Did she have any idea who the governess-like escort might have been?

Gil was as quick to understand her now as when they ran wild over the lands around Longford. Susan made short work of discovering what Clementine didn't want her aunt to know, and re-joined Gil by the stables.

"This governess. Was she slightly built, of below average height, and dark haired?" she asked, then, at Gil's nod, "We need to find out whether a boy hired a post chaise, or possibly a young woman with a French accent. I have no idea whether there is a connection, but apparently the French music teacher is also missing, and she fits that description."

She had thought he would take over the questioning, but he seemed content to allow her to coax answers out of the stable master, confining himself to looming at her left shoulder.

Looming was unnecessary, however. The stable master remembered the French lady on Saturday morning. "Just the lady on her own, ma'am. She wanted a post chaise for Newcastle, but I told her we didn't go no further than York. She could get another there, I told her."

"What of other travellers that same morning? Was there a boy, perhaps around fifteen or sixteen? He may have had a young lady with him of a similar age? Perhaps also travelling to York or Newcastle?"

The stable master was shaking his head when another ostler spoke up. "I saw the boy. With a girl, he was, but I didn't see her proper. The boy came in and rented the post chaise while the girl waited out the front. It was while you was with that dook's party, Ben. For York, but they only took 'un as far as Stamford. Joe—he's the post boy, ma'am—he came back last night."

The stable master nodded once, a swift jerk of the chin. "Right."

"We will speak with the post boy," Gil decreed. But the post boy was out on a job. He would return within the hour, and the stable master would keep him against Susan's return.

"I will be back in one hour," she said. "Thank you for your

help." She repeated the thanks to Gil before setting off at a brisk pace for the school. The fear jittered inside, but she quelled it. She had a lead, which was more than she'd had half an hour ago. If the French lady was the music mistress. If the boy was Patrice in disguise. If the two young people the ostler saw were her runaways. The whole trail of 'ifs' depended on Gil's observation. If the girl in Stamford was Amy, the rest fell into place.

Merciful Heavens! If the girl in Stamford was Amy, Susan must have passed her on the road, one of a myriad of yellow bounders heading north and Susan's party headed south. If only she had seen… *No. No point in dwelling on might-have-beens.*

At the school, she would demand to see Amy's room and to talk to some of the other girls. She also had questions to ask the head mistress about the French music teacher.

The presence at her elbow impinged on her conscious mind. Gil, still looming, his long stride easily keeping pace with her rapid steps, would not leave her side apparently.

She stopped. "Did you want something, Lord Rutledge?"

Grave brown eyes met her glare; dark brows meeting above the straight aristocratic nose returned it. "I am helping." Not an offer or even a request. An obdurate statement. Arrogant male.

Susan fought to keep her irritation from showing. "You have been helpful. Thank you. I can handle it from here."

Gil lifted one shoulder and dropped it again. "Undoubtedly. Nonetheless…" A second shrug, as expressive as the first. She didn't have time to argue; not that arguing ever changed Gilbert Rutledge's mind once it was made up.

He had clearly decided his participation was a foregone conclusion. "What did the Foster chit tell you?"

She would be a fool to refuse him information that might make his help useful. "The Grahame chit," she corrected. "Clementine Grahame said that her sister and Amy were always whispering together and would not tell their secrets. When Amy arrived at their house before breakfast and she and Patrice went up to Patrice's bedroom, Clementine put her ear to the door to try to hear them or, failing that, spy on what they did next."

He did not ask the obvious question; just waited for her to continue.

"They talked too low for her to understand. But Patrice left her room dressed as a boy and she and Amy caught Clementine in the hall. They threatened her with retribution if she told anyone what she had seen and instructed her to tell the aunt they had left for the exhibition together. The rest of Clementine's story is true, or so she assures me. She followed them here, and actually waited until they left in the post chaise. She then went off to school and pretended the whole thing had not happened."

Exasperation coloured the last sentence. Susan understood the child's fear of her unyielding aunt, and her jealousy of the friendship between the two older girls. But if Clementine had spoken earlier, Amy might well be safe now.

"Oh," she added. "One other thing. Clementine found Patrice's chopped-off hair hidden in a window seat in her room. Which confirms she is disguised as a boy, Lord Rutledge."

Of course the child had searched the room for clues to her sister's secret. Any younger sister would have done the same. Gil made no comment. Just nodded thoughtfully, then waited.

Susan grimaced. "Come then, if you must. I am going to the school. You can question the headmistress about the French woman while I talk to Amy's friends and check her room." And if Susan weren't so worried about her daughter, she might be entertained by the thought of the coming confrontation between the haughtily disapproving educationalist and the grim uncompromising soldier.

An hour later they compared notes as they walked back to the inn.

"Not much except gossip," Susan reported. Her concern for her daughter made it easier than usual to ignore her inconvenient attraction to the oblivious Lord Rock Ledge. "Amy appears to have taken no clothes or supplies for a trip. Amy and Patrice have apparently been playing some secret game for weeks, and the other girls are bristling with speculation, but short on facts. Some suspect a romantic entanglement with students or soldiers; others think they are on a hunt for treasure, or possibly spies."

"French spies? The music mistress?"

"Or the cook, or three of the maids. The French language mistress. The music mistress is but one of the suspects. But only the music mistress is unaccountably missing."

"Not unaccountably. Your Mrs Fellowes says Mademoiselle Cornillac has a dying brother in Doncaster. A letter came on Friday night. She asked for, and received, leave to be with him. An *émigré* family."

"Doncaster, not Newcastle," Susan mused. Gil made no comment, but she could all but hear his thoughts. Mademoiselle Cornillac's family crisis did not explain why Amy and Patrice were with the lady, if Gil had indeed seen their runaways.

"Mrs Fellowes cannot explain the young gentleman who appeared on Sunday, anxious to retrieve a book of poems from the music mistress."

Susan could not see how the unknown gentleman factored into the already confusing situation. "On Sunday? Then surely he has nothing to do with our runaways."

"Probably." Gil shrugged. "One never knows. Mrs Fellowes assured me she does not permit her teachers to have gentleman callers, and Miss Cornillac will find her position no longer available when she returns. Oh. And the young gentleman insisted on retrieving the poetry book, but Miss Cornillac must have given it away or taken it with her, because it could not be found in her room."

Susan could not spare the energy to pity the music mistress or her suitor. Poetry books! If Gil wanted to help he should not be starting after hares. "Nothing of significance to our search, then."

"Probably," he repeated. "But as I was putting up my horse at the Bell in Stilton on Sunday afternoon, a young man meeting the description of the poetry hunter rode in from Cambridge and demanded a change of horse."

Susan stopped walking to give Gil her full attention. "The description? He has some feature that makes him notable?"

Gil shook his head. "Medium-height and build, brown hair, brown eyes. Perhaps mid-twenties. Spoke like a gentleman but not from the top drawer." As Susan turned to continue towards the inn, he added, "What sticks in my mind is that he was asking if the inn had changed horses for a French lady in a post chaise."

The post boy confirmed the identity of at least one of his passengers. "Yes, ma'am. Couldn't mistake those eyes. Same colour as yours. Never seen any so blue."

At first, the post boy had assumed he was assisting at an elopement. "But they weren't at all lover-like, the young gentleman and the young lady. Argued all the time, they did, at every stop. He was worried about his aunt, and she said they had to be prepared to sacrifice for the mission."

"The mission," Gil said. "That word?"

"Yes, sir. That's what she said. The mission."

"What happened in Stamford," Susan asked.

The post boy frowned. "I don't rightly know, ma'am. It were our last stop for the day, and I took the prods off to the stable while the gentry went into the inn. Then the young gentleman came out and said he would not require the chaise any longer and I could go home the next morning. Well, he'd paid up front for York. No skin off my nose if he didn't want what he'd paid for. So, I had a good kip and then came back to Cambridge." His shrug was eloquent with contempt for the incomprehensibility of the gentry.

Once they had asked every question they could think of in several ways each, they let the boy go. Gil had requisitioned a private parlour for their interview, but of course Susan could not remain here alone with him. Nor could she follow her burning urge to leave immediately for the answers that must surely lie in Stamford; not on a moonless night. She would thank Gil for his help and go up to her room.

As if he heard her thoughts, Gil turned from a low-voiced

conversation with the inn-keeper's stout daughter and said, "I've ordered us a dinner. No point in our leaving until the morning."

The urge to remain in the comfort of his presence surprised Susan with its strength and made her refusal less gracious than it might have been. "I cannot have dinner alone with you, Lord Rutledge."

A flicker of uncertainty before the granite face settled again. "Do you want to send for your maid? To protect your good name?" His voice was as calm and emotionless as ever, and it was unfair of her to read a sneer into that last remark.

"I do not have a maid with me. Just my groom. He has a room above the stables." She had sent her other carriages on ahead when she chose to detour to Cambridge, figuring she and Amy could have lunch together before Susan followed her younger children and her servants to London.

Gil regarded her gravely, and Susan waited for him to berate her for foolishness, impetuosity or arrogance in thinking she could run her own life as she pleased, without the interference of a man. But he merely nodded once. "My man is entirely trustworthy. So, if you sit down and eat, no one but you and I will know. And you need a good dinner. Have you eaten today?"

Susan was about to disclaim appetite when her stomach made her a liar by rumbling with considerable enthusiasm. Was that a twinkle in Lord Rock Ledge's eye? Surely not.

She surrendered, at least this battle, returning to the seat she had just vacated. "Very well. But I shall pay for my own meal."

Gil made no reply; just took his place in the chair on the other side of the hearth, as two maids carried in laden trays and began transferring their contents to the room's table.

While the servants set the dishes out, and laid a place for each of them, Susan made some commonplace remarks about the weather during her journey from Dirleton, just out of Edinburgh, where her son had his estate. Gil said nothing. Was he even listening? She seemed to have his attention; certainly he did not move his gaze from her; barely blinked. But what thoughts seethed under that still surface? Even as a boy, he had been grave and silent.

She had made a fool of herself when she was a debutante of seventeen, letting him know his courtship would be acceptable. He had left London immediately, and soon after changed regiments to be sent overseas. She had never again hinted at his effect on her, avoiding him if possible; keeping him at arms' length with snappish remarks when they found themselves in the same company. This last hour had been the most conversation they had had in years, and it had been entirely a monologue.

Mind you, even to his friends, he spoke seldom, though always to good purpose. He waited until the maids left the room, closing the door behind them.

"So, by now your other children are safely at home in London with their nurse and your father. I will go after Miss Cunningham and Miss Foster, of course, but you had better come with me."

"Come with you? I am going alone, with my groom. My missing daughter is not your problem to solve, Lord Rutledge." He might look like a stone carving, all hewn planes and angles, but he had never been a fool. Surely he must realise how impossible it was for the two of them to travel together?

Gil stood. "We should eat." He suited action to words by pulling out a chair at the table, standing with one hand on the back, waiting for Susan to take her place. It would be childish and counterproductive to refuse to sit, purely because he expected her to do so. She quelled but did not extinguish the spirit of opposition that consumed her whenever one of the men in her life tried to organise her. She would eat the dinner he had ordered, but he would not be coming north with her.

2

The Goddess fought him every inch of the way right through dinner and went up to her room still determined to do without his support. Gil's blood ran cold at the thought of her facing the perils of the road with none but her elderly groom to defend her safety and her honour. Especially a groom who would take bribes, as the man Lyons did when Gil found his room above the stables. Gil paid the old man to warn him when The Goddess ordered her carriage, and set his own man to watching the groom.

"Have a sound horse waiting for me when she is ready to leave, Moffatt."

"And one for me, Colonel? My lord, I mean?"

"Later. Catch up when you can. If we've left Stamford, I'll leave you our direction." Gil instructed Moffatt to find safe boarding for Gil's horses and to send some letters, which Gil would give him in the morning. He had advised The Goddess to write to her male relatives, but would do so himself in case she decided to ignore him.

And he needed to send a note to tell his mother he did not know when he would be home. He grimaced at the thought of her reaction as he headed upstairs to do that task first.

His Goddess looked as if she had not slept, the dark smudges under her eyes only making the blue more intense as she glared at him from the seat of her cabriolet-phaeton.

"Lord Rutledge, where do you think you are going?"

Was he expected to answer? He was going wherever she went, of course, as he had told her last night.

She didn't wait but gave the horses a light flick to get them moving, and Gil mounted and followed, easily catching up with the cabriolet-phaeton. It was a sweet equipage: four wheels with the body suspended low between them on elliptical springs. The calash top was down, but could be raised to shelter the driver and whoever was with her. The main seat would take two with ease, and three if none were large. Another seat behind allowed room for a groom, but currently had luggage strapped to it. Gil rather approved of the dark blue paint with the thin gold stripe, and the cheerful red hubs to the black wheels made him smile. Typical Susan to add style to practicality.

Had the elderly groom chosen the two horses? If so, he had done well. They responded sensitively to Susan's hand on the reins, as she threaded her way through the early morning traffic. The horse Moffat had selected was up to Gil's weight and had an easy motion that would easily eat the miles between here and the next change. Gil could only hope for as suitable a mount at the other inns along the way.

The traffic thinned as they left the town, crossing the bridge into the country. Gil held his horse to the rear of the cabriolet-phaeton, giving silent thanks for the rain in the night that had laid the dust. He had little hope that staying out of Susan's sight would lessen her ire.

He would not revisit, even in his own mind, his reasons for insisting on escorting her. He'd spent long enough in the night cross-examining himself. Duty was reason enough, and the rest was irrelevant. Any *man* would understand that he could not let a female relative of his oldest friends wander the roads of England on her own.

A female would not understand the duty a man had to his friends. And The Goddess—her appeal in no way dimmed today by the carriage coat covering her curves—was very much a female.

It was true that, for twenty-seven years, since she was a child of ten and he a mere two years older, he'd been prepared to move heaven and earth to be near her. It was also true that his heart lightened as he rode further from the confrontation in Essex. Not relevant. He was her brothers' friend and her cousin's, and therefore he would keep her from harm and help rescue her daughter.

And avoid spending too much time close to her, as he had for the past nineteen years. She had made her opinion more than clear since his brother's villainy had prevented him from courting her. His longing for her was no less hopeless today than it was yesterday.

They changed horses at Huntingdon. Susan ignored Gil and waved away the ale that he sent with a pot girl. He didn't bother to approach her, but in Alconbury he ordered coffee and a large slice of pie, and took it to where she waited for the new team to be hitched. He knew for a fact she had not eaten today, for he had abandoned his own breakfast to join her when she'd rushed straight for the stable on waking.

"Eat and drink. You will not serve your daughter by falling ill before you reach her."

Her eyes shot sparks at him and she pressed her lips together until they whitened. Her pride and her common sense warred, and common sense won. She took the pie in one hand and the mug in the other. She even, as he turned away, managed to choke out a short, "Thank you."

Gil acknowledged the thanks with a nod and returned to his horse, where a maid waited with his own refreshments. He made sure, too, that Susan's groom Lyons was looked after. The old man needed fuel to keep up the pace they'd been able to set so far, travelling roads in good repair with only light traffic. Particularly since he seemed to harbouring an ague.

As soon as the fresh horses were in the traces, The Goddess was anxious to be off again. They'd have one more change before Stamford, which he expected to reach by three of the clock. Good. The runaways had a a strong head start. Perhaps today they could make up some of that lead.

At the third change, Gil brought Susan another ale. "A fresh brewing, Mrs Cunningham. Quite palatable."

Susan's initial irritation at his arrogance had worn itself out in the hours since they left Cambridge. Whatever his motives for barging into her affairs and trying to take over, he was here, and could make himself useful. She took the earthenware mug with a smile and her thanks, hiding her amusement at the wary sidelong look he gave her.

"After Stamford, I would like to travel on for as long as we have the light," she told him.

He nodded, laconic as ever.

"If we divide tasks, we can accomplish our questioning more quickly," she added. "At Stamford, will you question the stable hands while I speak to the innkeeper?" That garnered another nod.

"If you ride with me in the carriage, we can discuss our strategy." It would be a tight fit. Gil was a large man, and Lyons was broad, if not tall. Still, they could move some luggage so that Lyons could go up behind. But Gil was shaking his head.

"No room. And your man won't last half an hour on the footman's perch. He should be retired, Goddess."

"Don't call me that!" He had made her childhood a misery with that nickname. One long summer of it, anyway. At ten, she had still worn the ridiculous name her parents had bestowed. Not just Athene, though that would have been bad enough. Joan Athene Boadicea. Long before that summer, her brothers had picked up on the initials and dubbed her Jab. But then Gil, a newcomer to the neighbouring estate, came home from school with Susan's brothers, her cousin Rede and two other boys. Gil dubbed her 'The Goddess', and it had quickly become Jab The Goddess. She'd been forced to take stern measures to win back the space to be herself, adopting a version of her mother's name and refusing to answer to any other.

She glared at him. To be fair, he had not been part of the tormenting; had even tried to stop it. But she had never forgotten it was his mocking remark that set it off.

He bowed, ever so slightly, a mockery in itself. "Mrs Cunningham. His hands shake, and his knees buckle when he walks." No hint of disapproval coloured his voice or his expression, but the mere statement showed he thought she hadn't noticed.

Susan had offered Lyons a cottage and a small pension when the shaking became too obvious for him to hide, but had given in to his pleadings and allowed him to continue as her personal groom. In effect, his only role was to sit beside her while she drove or beside one of the family grooms when she and the children used the town coach, or the larger travelling carriage.

Lyons had little to do and was still part of the bustle of a working stable, surrounded by the horses he loved, and friends with whom he could share a beer and a yarn when the day was over.

Colonel Rock Ledge remained impassive under her glower. Susan was sure he would never allow sentiment to divert him from his course. If Lyons had served the Rutledge family faithfully for more than five decades, since he was a mere child, the poor man would have been put out to grass will he, nil he.

Though, to be fair, she trusted Rutledge to at least make sure any such dependent was given a pension, which was more than his older brother would have done.

Beyond the colonel's shoulder, Lyons was eating a slice of pie while watching the new horses being put in the traces, pausing from time to time to sneeze. He hauled out a large handkerchief to blow his nose. Had he contracted a cold? He would tell her if he could not continue, surely? "Thank you for seeing to his comfort, my lord. And mine."

She meant only to turn the subject, and to show, however grudgingly, that she appreciated his support, but something in her remark displeased him. The signs were subtle, but she had known him for twenty-seven years. His nostrils twitched in the minutest flare, his lips stiffened, and he turned his intent gaze away to look over her head.

"Gil, if you would, or Rutledge, if you must. Even Rock Ledge would be better than being my lorded by one of my oldest friends."

Susan couldn't possibly call him Gil, not out loud. And she was certainly not going to address him as Rock Ledge. Perhaps only she and Gil in the whole world knew she had invented the name in retaliation that long-ago summer. The boys had gleefully adopted it and taken it back to school with them, where it stuck. Even his soldiers had, apparently, called him Colonel Rock Ledge.

But he had never expected nor wanted the viscountcy, and if a tenth of the gossip was true, his brother had left it bankrupt both financially and morally. No wonder the honorific was a burden. The least she could do to repay him for his help was to avoid using it.

"Very well, Rutledge. And you may claim the privilege of long acquaintance and call me Susan. It appears your new horse is saddled and my carriage is ready. Shall we go?"

Susan settled back in her corner of the carriage, watching the countryside as they sped along, thinking about her lost daughter and then about her younger two children. They would be safe in London with her father who was their legal guardian. It was a fiction; he was content with the role of grandfather, and trusted Susan to be guardian in all but name, since the law denied her that privilege.

Lyons' sneezing increased as the horses consumed the miles to Stamford. By the time they pulled into the stable yard at the Crown and Eagle, he was wheezing with every breath, and failing in his attempts to subdue paroxysms of coughing. His flushed face indicated a fever, which was probably lower than if they had not been driving into a chilly wind for the past hour.

Gil handed his horse into the care of a stable boy and came to help her down, stopping when he looked across her at Lyons. The groom leant forward and swayed, paling so alarmingly that Susan clutched at his arm and pulled him back into his seat. "Stay where you are until Lord Rutledge comes around to help you," she commanded.

Gil was wearing his granite face again. If he hadn't donned the expression to hide the urge to say 'I told you so', her instincts were completely at sea. She gave him credit for being gentleman enough not to crow. "Lyons is wretched, Rutledge. We must get him inside."

The groom protested, but weakly, letting Gil help him to the ground. He leaned against the much taller man, his eyes shut. Gil wrapped a firm arm around him to keep him upright. "He's burning with fever, Mrs Cunningham. Come, Lyons. Let's get you into a bed."

"I'll deal with the horses," Susan offered. "Will you ask the innkeeper to send for a doctor?" Lyons was so sunk in misery he didn't respond. Gil supported him through another spasm of racking coughs then half carried him into the inn, and Susan turned to give her instructions to the stable hand.

She followed a servant upstairs fifteen minutes later. Another trailed behind carrying Gil's saddle bags over his shoulder and a valise from the curricle in each hand, Lyons' bag and her own overnight things. Susan was not fool enough to think they'd be moving on tonight. She was unsurprised when the innkeeper greeted her as Mrs Rockingham and told her that her husband had reserved a suite upstairs and was even now with the doctor. Rockingham indeed. She could only hope Lyons recovered quickly.

A servant let her into a nicely-appointed sitting room, with chairs upholstered in a sturdy chintz, patterned with purple chrysanthemums. A door on either side led, presumably, to bedrooms. Yes. As she crossed to the warm fire, she caught a glimpse through the open door; the corner of an iron bedstead, part of Gil's back and one strong leg. She could hear the murmur of voices, but none of the words.

The servant hefting the bags took them through to the other room. "Will there be anything else, ma'am?"

Susan's mind had returned to her missing daughter. She recalled it to those in her care here in Stamford. "Can your cook make a soothing tisane for my groom's throat? And Mr Rockingham and I would appreciate a pot of tea, please. Perhaps some bread and cheese?" Gil had a prodigious appetite.

They hurried away and Susan sat to await the doctor's verdict and to fret about her daughter, another day's hard travel away in Doncaster.

180 miles north, in Newcastle

"No dawdling," Mam'selle Cornillac commanded, setting a rapid pace through the busy market. For the first time on their travels, they had stopped for the day in the middle of the afternoon, and Mam'selle had taken full advantage of several used-clothing vendors, determined to reclothe her two unwelcome companions.

"Which is further evidence that she is up to no good, Amy," Pat insisted as they hung back as much as they dared. "She thinks we are being followed and wants to disguise us." They had been sharing a coach with Mam'selle during the day and a bedchamber at night, limiting their opportunities for conversation.

"I'm sure you're right, but I will be pleased to have something other than school clothes to wear." Amy shot a glance at her friend. Pat made a pretty boy: she was tall, even lanky in schoolboy pantaloons, and the hair left after she'd sacrificed her heavy mop for the mission had sprung into a thousand curls. "Don't you want to wear a dress again?"

Mam'selle had reached the inn where she'd taken a bedchamber and was waiting for them on the step.

Pat was shaking her head. "Not really. You have no idea how much easier it is to walk, and people treat you differently, as if you have half a brain. I may still be a child, but I'm a boy child, or so they think. I am to be encouraged, not stuffed into a box and tamped down, with all the bits that don't fit to be worried at until they drop off."

They had caught up with Mam'selle. "Come." She marched up

the stairs from the main hall and along the labyrinth of halls and passages to the little room they'd been assigned. She spoke to a maid they passed on the way, and not long after they'd spread their purchases out on the shared bed that took up most of the room, hot water arrived.

Mam'selle clapped her hands. "First, we shall turn Master Pat into Miss Patrice again, *n'est ce pas?*"

Mam'selle had an eye, no doubt about it. The lilac figured-cotton dress was of a grown-up length; only the tips of Pat's sensible boots showed. With her lanky calves hidden, she suddenly looked willowy rather than coltish, the ribbon under her breasts hinting at a womanly shape that the straight lines of the school uniform had obscured. Mam'selle took scissors to the hair Amy had butchered and finished with several lengths of ribbon whose colour matched the flowers on the dress. In a few moments the curls framed Pat's face.

Amy loved Pat but had always rather pitied her for her long face, square jaw, and decidedly prominent nose. Suddenly, with the new hair style, all of these features fell into new proportions, and Pat looked almost pretty.

"There." Mam'selle's satisfied smile grew broader at Pat's reaction when she looked at herself in the music teacher's small hand mirror. She stood and twisted to try to take in her new finery.

"You look lovely, Pat," Amy told her, looking forward to her own turn in Mam'selle's magical hands.

The dress Mam'selle had chosen for her to wear was light green with narrow cream stripes. "It is a little long, Miss Amelia," Mam'selle acknowledged, "but we three shall repair that fault, and meanwhile pins shall do for this evening, *oui?*" She deftly plaited and twisted Amy's hair, pinning it high on her head with some of Mam'selle's own pins.

"So pretty," Pat declared, and from what she could see in the mirror, Amy had to agree. "Thank you, Mam'selle."

Mam'selle waved her away. "Now be seated, if you will, while I repair my own *toilette*. I have commanded a private parlour for *le diner*."

"We could await you downstairs, Mam'selle," Amy suggested, unsurprised when Mam'selle refused with uplifted brows and a sardonic curl of the lips. Amy and Pat had sought help several times, most recently in York while Mam'selle was hiring a post chaise to take them on to Edinburgh. They had approached an officer and insisted that they were being kidnapped by a French spy. The result had been the same as before. He had laughed, and taken them back to Mam'selle, sympathising with her for the imaginations of her charges. Since then, her close watch had sharpened, extending even to joint expeditions to the water closet.

Before long, Mam'selle had also changed her clothes. At Doncaster, she had abandoned the severe, plain, dark dresses that Mrs Fellowes mandated for her teachers. In a light floral print with her hair caught up in a simple knot of cascading curls rather than a tight bun under a white cap, she looked not much older than Amy and Pat, and certainly nothing at all like a teacher.

Each wrapped in a soft shawl against the cold, they descended the two flights of stairs to a large room lined on both sides with doors. In the centre of the room, several groups of men sat in quiet discussion on soft chairs and couches set around low tables. While Mam'selle stopped at the desk for directions to the private parlour she had requested, Amy and Pat crossed to the opposite wall, beckoned by the mirrors between each curtained window.

They examined their reflections in silence. The schoolgirls they saw each day had disappeared, replaced by two young ladies. The cheap cotton dresses, enhanced by the trims Mam'selle had chosen, seemed richer in the lamplight.

"None of this makes sense," Amy complained. "She is so nice to us, but she will not let us go, or explain what she is doing. And when we said we would go back to school on our own, she told us she would have us beaten or worse."

Pat disagreed. "She didn't, Amy, and you know it. She said two girls alone on the road were likely to be beaten or worse."

Amy acknowledged the point with a shrug. "Anyway, if she is a spy, it is our duty to stay with her and see what she is up to." She turned her attention back to their reflections. "Mama says I can put my hair up and my skirts down when I am seventeen. I look seventeen now, do I not?"

Pat smoothed a hand a quarter of an inch from her curls, being careful not to touch. "If I had known I could look like this, I would have cut it all off long ago." She sighed. "When we get home, my aunt will lock me up until it all grows again."

"It is very pretty," Amy agreed. "I wish mine curled."

"Yours is pretty, too." Pat linked her gloved arm through Amy's. "We do look grown up. Aunt Audrey would say 'Fine feathers do not make fine birds', but we are very fine, are we——?"

Amy interrupted. "Look. Isn't that the man Mam'selle meets in Cambridge?" Behind their reflected selves, they could see Mam'selle, still at the desk. She was being watched. A gentleman had arrested his decent of the stairs and was staring at her from behind the concealment of the newel post.

The girls turned for a better look. "It could be," Pat ventured. "He is a very ordinary looking man, but so was the one in Cambridge."

"We will know if he talks to her."

But as Mam'selle turned away from the desk and beckoned to the two girls, the man on the stairs turned and retreated the way he had come.

3

———————

*S*tamford to Doncaster

Lyons was too ill to continue, so Susan arranged lodgings and nursing, which meant it was ten of the clock before she and Gil were crossing the stable-yard to the readied carriage.

"I feel guilty about abandoning him," Susan said, as they pulled out into the road.

Gil didn't take his eyes from the horses, which were fresh and inclined to take offence at swaying bushes and innocuous puddles. "You have left him well cared for. You have no need to feel guilty."

He had his own reasons for not wanting to leave Lyons behind. Handing Susan down from the carriage yesterday was torture enough. Riding in the cabriolet-phaeton with her was a mix of Heaven and Hell beyond anything he could have imagined. Even when she sat decorous inches away, every particle of his body stood to attention. And when she leaned into him as they took a corner, her shoulder brushing his arm, he went rigid with the effort of keeping that arm on its appointed job, and not wrapping it around the appetising bundle beside him.

His arm was not the only part of him that was rigid. Only the fact she never gave him the least encouragement allowed him to maintain a facade of gentlemanly behaviour.

From the corner of his eye he could see Susan turn towards him, saying nothing, examining him for so long that Gil had to quell the urge to shift under her inspection. "I thought you were going to demand I let you go on alone," she admitted, after a very long silence.

"I need you for when we catch up with Miss Grahame and your daughter." Young Amy hadn't seen him in four years, and Miss Grahame didn't know him at all. Gil didn't want to imagine the fuss the two girls or the woman with them might make if they objected to his attempt at a rescue.

"I cannot make sense of it, Rutledge," Susan complained. "Why did they join forces with Miss Cornillac? And who is the young man?"

"If it is Miss Cornillac," Gil cautioned. "We know only that she is French and bound for Doncaster. A pity no one observed the first meeting between her and our two runaways."

All the inn could confirm was that the two parties—one a French lady calling herself Madame Duval and the other a very young couple who claimed to be brother and sister—had arrived in separate post chaises and commissioned separate rooms, but had breakfasted together and left in a single post chaise. And yes, the mysterious pursuer had put in an appearance the day before yesterday, notable only for his questions about his French cousin, who was travelling north alone.

The Goddess worried at the few threads they had as they passed Burghley Park and trudged up the steep rise to North Witham. Gil listened with half an ear while planning their stops on the day's journey. The horses were still stepping out well enough, and from here the road was easier through to Grantham. They'd change at the Angel; order fresh horses and something to eat and drink. They'd make Grantham to Newark the next post and lunch at the Saracen's Head. Gamston or Bawtry for the next stop, arriving in Doncaster late afternoon or early evening. With luck, they'd find

Miss Cornillac and her brother tonight. With more luck, the two girls would be with them.

They had no news at the Angel, but the post chaise could have changed at the town's other posting inn or in another town altogether. Susan was worried they'd miss their quarry if they didn't ask at the George, but Gil pointed out that stopping at every posting inn on their route would add hours to the trip and could prevent them from reaching Doncaster tonight.

"If we don't find any trace of them at Doncaster, we'll need to retrace our steps," he agreed, "but Doncaster was the destination our quarry told her employer, she asked for the name of inns in Doncaster, and if she has gone on to York, or to Newcastle, she must pass through Doncaster. We should find trace of her at one of the posting inns there or within ten miles either side."

Susan stopped arguing, but he could measure her agitation by her anxiety to return to the chase. She had given the ostlers an extra fee to set the new horses to as quickly as possibly, and now she watched them carefully, as if they would all disappear if she took her eyes off them.

As they crossed the stable-yard to return to the cabriolet-phaeton, a voice called Susan's name.

Susan? Susan, it is you." The speaker hurried towards them with hands outstretched, and in a moment, she and Susan were embracing.

"Ella, what are you doing here? Is Alex with you? The children?"

It was Lady Renshaw, Susan's sister-in-law. Gil had met her four years earlier when he sold the Renshaws his favourite stallion.

"They're at home. I am returning from a trip to Nottingham, to the lace factory that is buying our village lace. But what are you doing here?" Lady Renshaw's glance at Gil was full of speculation. He bowed. "Lady Renshaw."

She gave a small bob. "Lord Rutledge. What does one say in

such circumstances?" For a moment, Gil thought she referred to finding him and Susan travelling together, but she went on, "From all I've heard, the death of your brother was a mercy to his family and his tenants, so expressing my condolences seems inappropriate. If you grieve him, I am sorry for your grief."

Another refreshingly straightforward woman. Gil smiled despite the topic. "I do not. He was a blight on his family and the world."

Lady Renshaw returned his nod and turned back to Susan. "Do you have time to take a dish of tea with me and tell me why you are here and where you are going? If you wish to, that is. I would not interfere for the world."

"Oh, Ella. Amy has been kidnapped! Rutledge and I are on her trail, or at least I hope we are."

"We know they are heading to Doncaster," Gil reminded her, soothingly.

"Ah. Then I will not hold you up. What can I do to help? Should I send for Alex? Contact Father?

A truly admirable woman. No fuss about propriety and no panic.

Susan assured her sister-in-law they would be two days ahead before her brother Alex could reach them and that she had already written to her father. She outlined what had happened and promised to keep the Renshaws informed by letter.

With a final hug and the promise of prayers, Lady Renshaw waved them away, standing in the stable-yard to watch them out of sight.

They picked up the trail earlier than they expected, at the Saracen's Head in Newark, where the French governess and her two charges, a brother and sister, had changed horses and asked about the best inn for an overnight stay in Doncaster. Just a stay, so it seemed that York or Newcastle was their destination after all. And the young man was also still in pursuit, for when Gil asked if anyone else had enquired about the French lady, he received the same description as at the school.

Rain set in after lunch, and once they left the well-drained causeways through the marshland beyond the Trent, their travel was slowed by deeply rutted quagmires instead of the dust that had plagued them the day before. They put up the calash—the oiled canvas roof—and kept mostly dry, except when the road turned into the wind. Even then, the waterproofed lap rug Susan produced from under the seat repelled the worst of the wet.

The going was slower than Gil would have liked, and Susan's anxiety a palpable presence, but Gil did his best to distract her—and himself, since his physical reaction showed no sign of wearing itself out—by asking after her brothers and sisters, starting with the Renshaws. The doings of the couple and their stud farm beguiled the miles to Luxford.

"The horse you sold Alex and Ella," Susan told him, "has sired the Renshaws' next generation of mares, now rising three years old. Alex is very proud of them and assures me that the horse world is beginning to sit up and take notice."

"I'm glad. A much better fate for Trooper than more war, and perhaps death on a foreign battlefield." Gil had sold Trooper to Alex to keep his stallion from that fate when Gil had been posted overseas.

"What of that rundown estate that came with his title?" he asked. The buildings were half ruins, but the land was good.

"You should see it now, Rutledge. They've repaired the stables, of course, and the house, which is lovely. Just as well, since Alex seems to be in a competition with Trooper. You know they have two babies in their nursery? And, just between you and me, another on the way."

From Luxford to Gamston, where they changed horses again, and up to Barnby Moor, Gil heard about Susan's cousin Rede, another schoolmate and now the 8th Earl of Chirbury. Gil kept to himself the fact that Rede's wife Anne owned the estate at which his brother's wife and daughters had taken refuge after they fled his mother.

They passed through Scrooby to news about the oldest of Susan's brothers, Major Harry, serving with distinction in Spain. The second brother, Captain Rick Redepenning, had gone to sea at fourteen, and Gil didn't know him as well as the others, but listened cheerfully to stories about him, his ship, his wife Mary, and his three children, which took the hour from Scrooby to Bawtry, along a good level road to the River Torne and the Rossington Bridge, and up a gentle rise to Doncaster.

Newcastle and beyond

Mam'selle had insisted on an early night, brushing off Amy's suggestion that their room had been searched while they were at dinner.

"I see no signs of a search, Miss Amelia. And even if it is true, I do not care. I have nothing to hide, though you do not believe me. I will not allow you to delay while we speak to the landlord, who may wish to call the authorities. And who knows if you will find someone to support your foolish notion that I am a spy? The English; they do not love the French."

Amy and Pat exchanged glances. They had no confidence they would be believed. The officer at York had thought their story hilarious. At Stamford, when Mam'selle had first seen them and then insisted on them going with her, the servant they had begged for help had told them not to be silly. At another inn along the way, a plea to a pleasant-looking woman had been rewarded with a scold.

"But there," the woman had said to Mam'selle. "They will do it, these foolish girls. And what would become of them if we listened to their nonsense?"

"Nothing good," Mam'selle agreed, which made Amy shiver.

"But the room was searched," Amy whispered to Pat. "My brush is not where I left it, and the other new dress was on top of my new chemise, and not below."

Mam'selle hissed at them to stop whispering, but when she

closed her eyes, Pat waved to silently catch Amy's attention, then nodded agreement.

Amy was sure she wouldn't sleep, but in no time at all Mam'selle was calling her to rise, wash, and dress. The cold grey light showed the sun was not yet up, but by the time they'd descended the stairs to the stable-yard, the sky was streaked with pink and yellow, and the eastern sky flamed red. To the north, heavy clouds hinted at rain. Mam'selle had refused to answer any questions about their destination, but she'd booked the post chaise as far as Edinburgh, and Amy knew that road well. Gorburn Hall, the estate her little brother inherited from their father, was 25 miles from Edinburgh on the sea coast at the mouth of the Firth of Forth. Despite the early start, in rain they'd do well to make Dunbar tonight, some miles south of the Hall.

A maid carried out a tray with mugs of hot tea and steaming hot savoury pastries. Mam'selle waved them forward. "This is breakfast, young ladies. Take what you wish and let us be on our way."

Amy held back, letting Pat choose then hanging over the tray asking the maid about fillings while Pat drifted towards the rear of the post chaise. "Hurry along, Miss Amelia," Mam'selle urged, then responded when Pat called. "Mam'selle, is this rope fraying?"

Amy had the note they'd prepared hidden in one hand, and swiftly slipped it to the maid with one of the last coins from the small store she'd brought on this adventure. They were almost out of paper, too, having used up the last few leaves of Amy's notebook and surreptitiously torn the blank leaves from the back of Mam'selle's poetry book. They would need to find some more, but meanwhile they'd managed to leave notes at Doncaster and at York. And now Newcastle.

"Hide the letter," she told the maid, "and once we've left, give it to the innkeeper to be called for by the people who are following us." She hoped. Soon, anyway, someone would come looking. They would have been missed yesterday morning, but it would take time for the school to send to London to notify her mother, and her mother to dispatch someone to Cambridge to make enquiries.

The maid tucked the letter and the coin inside her bodice.

Behind Amy, Mam'selle berated the post boy and the ostler for the condition of the rope tying the luggage. Well done, Pat, for finding a real problem to distract their captor!

Amy made way for Mam'selle to choose her own pastry and hot drink, and clambered into the post chaise, with a wink and a grin at Pat. One more clue left behind them and one kidnapping French spy lulled into thinking they would help her. A very good start to the morning.

At Doncaster, the Ship and Anchor rewarded Susan with the information she and Gil sought. It was possible that a French governess and her charges had stayed the night, and did Madam by any chance know the name of those charges?

"Why do you ask?" Susan wondered.

The clerk, an earnest young man with thinning hair and a face set in lines of anxiety cast his gaze around the room, as if for inspiration. He nodded to an older man, who cut short his conversation with an aproned maid and limped over to speak to them. This man was altogether more prosperous looking, in neat clothing of higher quality cut, fabric, and stitching.

"Is there a problem, Clemowes? May I be of service, madam? I am the proprietor, Mr Withers."

"I am seeking some information, Mr Withers," Susan explained.

"This lady was asking after the French lady, sir, and the young lady and gentleman."

Withers pulled his spectacles down his nose to regard her over the top, then appeared to make up his mind. "Clemowes, you have the helm. Madam, would you be so good as to step into my office.

Gil came in from ordering the next change of horses and followed them as she and Withers crossed the inn's entry hall through a door hidden in the panelling.

The office was small, with barely enough room for the desk, shelves neatly stacked with file boxes and books, and three upright chairs; one behind the desk and two in front.

"If you would be kind enough to be seated, Mrs– Er–, I will explain." Withers squeezed between the desk and wall of shelves, and faced them with his hands on his own chair, standing until Susan had selected her chair and lowered herself into it. Like the man himself, it was serviceable but not ostentatious.

Gil ignored the remaining seat to stand behind her, his silent presence an unaccountable comfort to Susan.

Withers tidied an already neat stack of papers then more perfectly aligned an ink pot on its tray.

If he would not begin the conversation, Susan would. "I asked your clerk about the French woman and her two charges, Mr Withers. In return, he asked me an impertinent question. I trust you do not intend to follow that example."

Mr Withers grimaced. "It is an odd circumstance, madam, but I could not be easy in my mind if I did not follow the instructions I was given, as Mr Clemowes has followed mine."

"And those instructions are?"

"First, madam, would you indulge me by naming at least one of the young people? Even just a first name? I would not insist, but yours is not the first enquiry, and the previous fellow did not appear to be aware of… But never mind."

Susan glanced up over her shoulder, and Gil nodded his agreement. "I am seeking Amelia, known as Amy, and Patrice, known as Pat. Pat is travelling as a male."

Mr Withers let out his breath in a sigh and opened a drawer to his right. "Then you are the rightful recipient of this note, madam, left for me by one of the young ladies. I might add that the note was wrapped in another, addressed to me as innkeeper. Before I hand it over, I must ask for the full name of one or both of the young ladies."

"Amelia Susanna Elizabeth Cunningham and Patrice Grahame," Susan told him. Mr Withers passed her the folded piece of paper, and another that he said was the note to him. Gil reached over her shoulder to pluck that one from Mr Wither's hand.

Susan recognised her daughter's neat schoolgirl hand on the single sheet, clearly torn from a lined notebook, with some commonplace about the weather written in ink at the top and crossed out in pencil, and a pencil-written message taking the rest of both sides of the paper.

"*To our rescuer,*" she read.

"*We suspect Mlle Cornillac of being a French spy. She caught us following her and has forced us to go with her. We don't know our destination, but the post-chaise is booked for Newcastle, and she has inquired about accommodation in York. We will be staying at The White Rose. Ask there for a further message.*

"*Look for a lady with a French accent accompanied by a girl in the costume of our school, and a boy. Amy is the girl and Pat is the boy.*

"*Please let Amy's mama and Pat's aunt know that Mlle has not hurt us, and we are both quite safe. But she is very clever, so when we seek help, she turns it so people do not believe us. If we get the chance, we will escape.*

"*Yours faithfully, Amelia Cunningham and Patrice Grahame.*"

Susan handed Gil the letter with a hand that shook slightly, and took the note addressed to Mr Withers.

"*To the innkeeper. Please keep the enclosed note safe and give it only to someone who asks after us and who knows our names. This is not a game. Our lives could be forfeit if you fail.*"

Like the other note, it was signed with both girls' names.

"Clever girls," Gil murmured, making Susan smile.

"It is true, then?" Mr Withers flushed a little. "I must beg your pardon, Mrs Cunningham. I took the liberty of reading the enclosure in order to be certain I was not caught up in some child's prank. It is Mrs Cunningham, is it not? The eyes. One cannot mistake the relationship. And you would be Mr Cunningham, sir, I take it." He bowed to Gil, as well as he could while still remaining seated.

Gil accepted supposed relationship without demur. "Why York? It is but four or five hours away."

"A delay with the post chaise." Mr Withers colour deepened as he explained the post chaise lost a wheel not thirty minutes after leaving Doncaster, and the passengers had been left in a farm cottage while the post boy rode back for an alternative equipage. With nothing available but Mr Withers' own gig, he had himself gone to bring them back to the Ship and Anchor to wait for either the repair of the broken wheel or the next post chaise to return from its travels. The note had been discovered after the party's second departure from the inn.

Gil nodded at the conclusion of the saga. "So, they did not leave until early afternoon. Good. That helps us, Susan. Now, Mr Withers, we cannot delay. We have but another three hours of daylight and I wish to be as close to York as I can before we stop for the night. We will take some refreshment, and will you join us, sir, to answer some further questions?"

Within thirty minutes, they were on their way, warmed as much by the news of the girls as by the hot stew and the pint of ale inside them. Thanks to the accident with the post chaise, they were catching up faster than they'd hoped. The girls seemed in good spirits and not in immediate danger.

The mysterious young man was still in pursuit, but not, it seemed, of the girls. He did not even realise that the one dressed in boys' clothes was a girl, and mentioned them only as accessories to identify the French woman who was his real quarry.

And they would not be delayed by searching every inn a half-day's journey from here for the runaways' next stop. The girls had made certain they knew to ask at The White Rose in York.

The next stage was flat and lonely; a broad wet landscape cut by myriad drains and not improved by the persistent rain.

"Kidnapped, Gil!" Susan exclaimed. "Were the girls right, then, about Mlle Cornillac being a spy? They must be. Should I send to London for my father, or for an enquiry agent?"

"We are not far behind them and can catch up long before help arrives from London. But write to the Brigadier-General at the next stop. He will be anxious to hear, in any case, and will almost certainly know who to ask whether Mlle is a known French spy."

"Surely not! Left by our government in a girl's school? But it looks suspicious, Gil. No sick relative, and Doncaster is not her destination, and why kidnap the girls?"

After Susan had milked all the comment she could from Mlle Cornillac's perfidious lies about a sick relative in Doncaster and the girls' cleverness in leaving a trail, she fell silent and Gil, glancing sideways, could see she was slipping back into a fever of worry.

"You haven't mentioned young Jules. When last I was in England, I met his young wife, while he was on the other side of the world." Julius was the youngest of the Redepenning brothers and not long out of the nursery when Gil ran in a schoolboy pack with Susan's brothers and cousin.

As it transpired, Susan had quite a lot to say about Jules, or rather about his irregular conduct, prefacing it with: "I do not hesitate to tell you, Rutledge, for I know you are as silent as a clam and in possession of more of our family's secrets than anyone else besides. Indeed, you have proved yourself a true brother to me these last few days."

Gil should not find that irritating, since he had kept his far-from-brotherly thoughts to himself for more than twenty years. Indeed, perhaps he should regard it as a compliment. Her verbal barbs whenever they met had given him to understand she didn't like him, but if she thought of him as a family member, perhaps he could take a more optimistic view. Not that his relationships with his own family gave him cause to hope for a warmer friendship. His mother despised him, his sisters barely tolerated him and his brother hated him. Gil had every reason to hate the devil-spawn back.

She failed to notice his preoccupation, saying, "I expect you have heard that Jules married in haste years ago, to a girl still in the schoolroom."

Gil nodded. That much, he knew, and that the new Mrs Redepenning had been absorbed into the family, who closed ranks around her and dared anyone to gossip.

"Did you know how it came about, Gil?" Susan asked.

"Alex said they were imprisoned together by ruffians, and that Jules had done the best he could for the lady." Gil shrugged. He felt sorry for the young wife, who had been left almost from the church while Jules returned to his naval duties.

"Smugglers," Susan explained. "Jules was investigating the gang when they captured him. Mia and her father had run afoul of them and her father was killed."

Jules had felt impelled to wed Mia to protect her name and give her a home, but not to seek leave from the navy to spend any time with his new wife. He re-joined his ship before it returned to its post at Madras in the Far East, where his native mistress awaited him.

He raised his eyebrows when Susan explained that Mia had known about the mistress from the first. "She and Kirana have been exchanging letters these past seven years, if you can believe it, and now Mia is on her way to Cape Town, where Jules is currently stationed."

"Whatever for?" Gil wondered, envisaging the mistress cast out into the street, or perhaps some kind of an oriental menage with the two women sharing the one man.

"She is dying; not Mia, Kirana. Consumption. And Mia says she wants to be with her friend in her last days, and to bring Jules' children back with her. I must say, I see no other course, Rutledge. With their mother dead, and their father likely at any time to be posted back to England, what else will become of them?"

It wasn't Gil's place to comment, but it seemed very untidy to him.

"The same mistress all this time?" he asked. At least the boy was loyal. The man, he supposed. Jules was five years his junior so would turn thirty-four before the end of this year. Which meant he had been twenty-seven and his bride fifteen when he had deposited her with his father and returned to his posting in the Far East.

He had to obey orders, his bride belonged still in the schoolroom, and his mistress and children needed him. Looked at like that, it almost made sense.

"This is Brayton," he said. "We shall stop for the night in Selby, since it is growing dark. We'll be perhaps another fifteen minutes, Susan."

"How much further on is York?"

"Not twenty miles. We can order a fresh team of horses for sunrise, if you wish and breakfast at the White Rose while we make our first change."

Dunbar

As Amy had expected, the rain slowed progress north, and the post boy they'd picked up at the border would go no further than Dunbar that night.

Mam'selle wanted to continue, but: "Nay, lassie, 'tis not safe," the post boy insisted to Amy, whose familiarity with the local accent had come in handy when Mam'selle's frustrations strengthened her French intonations, leading to mutual unintelligibility.

And the ostler at the inn where they'd stopped continued to unbuckle the horses from their harness, while Mam'selle lapsed into French to insult the parentage of everyone from the post boy to the innkeeper.

Amy looked longingly north, where the darkness hid the way home, tantalisingly close, but still a three-hour ride in daylight. Even if she and Pat could escape while Mam'selle was distracted, and hide and stay hidden, they would then have the problem of convincing strangers that two penniless maidens should be allowed to borrow horses on a promise. Twenty-five miles was too far for anyone to recognise Miss Amelia Cunningham of Gorburn House, just west of Dirleton.

Amy had a better chance of meeting acquaintances in Edinburgh, where she had briefly attended school and where her family had relatives and friends. Pat had an uncle in Edinburgh, too, though she'd not seen him in years. And they would be in Edinburgh tomorrow.

Mam'selle grasped her arm, and Pat's, too. "If we must stay in this place, let us order a room and some *diner*." But as she marched them towards the doors that let into the inn from the coach-yard, a rider clattered into the yard, pulled up before the stables, and called, "Mademoiselle Cornillac? Is it you?"

Mam'selle let Amy and Pat go as she turned, a smile dawning and broadening as she recognised the man. In a moment, he had paid his vail to the ostler and was hurrying towards them, slowing his stride as he approached. It was Mam'selle's suitor from Cambridge; the one they thought they'd seen in Newcastle.

"Monsieur Griffin!" Mam'selle's voice was very different from the crisp bark with which she addressed Amy and Pat; softer, somehow deeper. "Monsieur Griffin, but this is wonderful. How do you come to be here, in this… this wilderness?"

"My employer has sent me to Edinburgh, my dear Mademoiselle. But of all the people I never expected to see in an inn so far north of Cambridge… Not that I… That is, how delighted I am to see you!" He looked over her shoulder at Amy and Pat, waiting by the door. "You are escorting girls from the school to their families, perhaps?"

"Yes," Mam'selle agreed, then glanced from the girls to Mr Griffin and back again, biting her lower lip. "That is…" She took a deep breath and let it out. Suddenly, her voice was brisk again. "I will tell you everything, Mr Griffin, but not here. Let us wait until we can be private."

4

———

Y*ork*
Susan and Gil left Selby before the sun was fully above the horizon and made good time to York, where they suffered a setback. The innkeeper at the White Rose, fresh from his bed and unhappy at being woken, denied all knowledge of a note, the girls' names, or even guests fitting the descriptions of the French woman and her two hostages. A stern command from Gil and the promise of a gold guinea from Susan induced him to be slightly more cooperative. He promised to make enquiries while they broke their fast in the private parlour Gil had hired, and trudged off on that errand, yawning, while a maid showed them to the parlour.

"A big rally against the government last night, see," the maid explained. "And all sorts here till all hours of the morning. None of us are at our best, like."

But the cook had managed a creditable spread, and before Gil and Susan had washed the repast down with their second cup of tea, the innkeeper returned with a maid and a man in the casual garb of a stable worker.

"These two remember the parties about whom you enquired," the innkeeper said. "But I am sorry, madam. I have checked the correspondence basket in my office and asked the duty clerk, the housekeeper, and the stable master, and I have found not one trace of a note."

The maid had taken hot water up to the French lady's bedchamber. "A governess, I thought, ma'am, attending the young lady and gentleman; sister and brother, though he was too old to be sleeping in the same room as his sister, I thought, but there, the servant that was on the night before had made up a pallet for him on the floor, and put up a second screen for privacy, for washing and such."

"Did you hear any conversation to suggest how the young people regarded their governess?" Gil asked, but the maid said the three were very quiet, "People usually are in the morning, sir, and it was early they asked to be woken. They didn't stop for a bite to eat, neither, but just took some cheese between slices of bread, though cook makes a wonderful loaf of bread, she does."

The man was the ostler who readied the post chaise on Tuesday morning. The French lady asked about the condition of the road through to Newcastle. And he remembered the other pursuer; a fellow, he called him, confirming the impression they'd had from others that the unknown man was not quite a gentleman. "An ordinary sort of a geezer. Nothing to make him stand out, see?" Notable only for asking about the French lady and her charges, he had hired another horse and headed north.

"What of the passengers with the French woman?" Gil asked, but the ostler shook his head.

"Two o' them, sir. A young lady and a young gentleman, you say? I'm that sorry, sir, but I don't recall." He bit his lip, frowning. "It has been a busy week, see."

A knock on the parlour door heralded a post rider in the inn's red and yellow livery.

"Ah, Harvey," said the ostler. "Ma'am, sir, this is Harvey. He was the post boy as took the French lady to Newcastle. The lady and gentleman have some questions, Harvey." Harvey hovered in the doorway, his thin face anxious.

"Come on, boy," the innkeeper urged. "Come in properly and shut that door."

He wasn't a boy. Narrow-shouldered and slender, and barely taller than Susan's shoulder, he was a young man in his twenties, with the strong thighs of a rider and alert dark eyes. "Tell us about the passengers you took to Newcastle on Monday," Susan said.

"The French governess and the two young ladies." Harvey was not asking. He was making a statement and watching Susan for her reaction.

The innkeeper spoke before Susan could. "A young lady and a young gentleman, you fool."

Without looking away from Harvey, Susan held up a hand to halt the innkeeper. "What makes you say 'two young ladies'?"

"I stayed overnight in Newcastle, didn't I, ma'am? I saw them come back from the market, and I saw them leave the next morning. The tall one with the dark curly hair? A girl, no question."

"Here," said the innkeeper, his brows dipping to a double crease over his nose. "What's going on? Young ladies dressed as boys. People chasing others up the Great Road. Mystery notes, if a note there was. I don't like it."

Susan straightened her back and lifted her chin, silently fixing the man with a frosty glare until he shifted from one foot to another. "I mean no offence, ma'am. But I have to think of my inn."

"Your inn," Gil said, his voice lethally soft, "harboured a kidnapper and the two young ladies she stole from their school."

"We are grateful for your help in finding where they went," Susan added. "The sooner we can follow them, the better our chance of recovering them safe and well."

Harvey had paled. "I thought they was just having a lark, ma'am. The one dressed as a girl—your daughter, is she?—she told this officer in the stable yard that the Frenchie was a spy and had abducted her and the other young'un, and I thought she was yarning him. The officer did, too. He and the Frenchie had a right laugh about it."

Susan faltered at the thought of her daughter begging for help and being denied, then stiffened her resolve and asked her next question. "Did you hear anything more from any of them that might help us, Harvey?"

Dunbar

Pat was looking on the bright side. "At least Mam'selle had them bring up our dinner." She had worked her way through a heaping plate of fish stew and was now helping herself to slices of chicken. "Eat something, Amy. If we manage to escape, we may go hungry."

Ever since Mam'selle had locked them in their bedchamber so she could have her dinner in private with Mr Griffin, Amy had been trying to pick the lock with one of her hairpins. "It's no good," she complained. "No one ever teaches girls anything useful."

Pat giggled. "Madame Cunningham's Elite Academy. All young ladies instructed in Pianoforte, French Conversation, How to Open Locked Doors, and How to Pick Pockets."

Amy acknowledged the joke with a fleeting smile. "I have always given everything back, Pat." Pat was most impressed with the skill Amy had taught herself after listening to her uncles' stories. She wished she had spent the time on learning to pick locks instead.

She gave the recalcitrant lock a jab with her hairpin. "I know it can be done. But I have no idea how."

She got up from her knees, giving them a rub before she straightened.

"I did not even know such things were possible," Pat commented. "It must be exciting to have an uncle who is a thief taker, but I will never feel safe in a locked house again."

"You must bolt a door if you want it to stay locked, or wedge it shut with furniture or a bar. But we want this one to open." She began to serve herself some of the dinner, piling vegetables, fish stew, and chicken onto the plate.

"Amy!" Pat protested. "How can you! You will get all the tastes mixed up."

Amy was tempted to swirl her fork through the food to annoy Pat still further, but her irritation was with Mam'selle and the door, not her friend. Besides, while she wasn't as finicky as Pat, who could only bear to have one dish on her plate at a time, she had carefully positioned her helpings so she could enjoy each taste separately. Annoying Pat wasn't worth spoiling her dinner.

"I wish we knew what they are talking about down there."

"They are probably making love," Pat guessed, and giggled.

"Ew. No. I think they are in this together. We did see him in Newcastle, Pat. I'm sure we did. So that whole scene downstairs was for us." She took another mouthful. The fish stew was nice, and the chicken skin was beautifully crispy.

"We should search Mam'selle's luggage," Pat suggested, and Amy stopped with her fork halfway to her mouth. Why had she not thought of that?

"Of course we should." And there was no time like the present. She grabbed another mouthful of dinner before joining Pat on her knees in front of Mam'selle's band box and valise.

They went through the band box, lifting each item carefully and setting it to one side so they could replace things exactly as they found them. Nothing.

Amy opened the valise, but Pat put out a hand to stop her. "We should repack the band box first. We'll have more room, then, to lay out the things from the valise, and no risk of forgetting where things went or mixing them up."

So they did that, arguing a little over the precise position of the hair brush and the small jewellery case. They had just put the last item into the box and replaced the cover when they heard voices outside the door, then a metallic scrape as someone put the key in the lock.

By the time the door opened, the two girls were back sitting at the table under the window, forks in hand, trying not to giggle with relief that they'd not been caught. They rose and bobbed a curtsey to their teacher. They'd argued the etiquette of being polite to a kidnapper several days earlier, and agreed that Amy's mama and Pat's aunt would insist that girls of their age showed deference to adults, even when those adults were arrant villains.

Mr Griffin glared at them suspiciously while Mam'selle opened her valise and took out the book they had been reading from in the evenings: a small volume of sentimental poetry.

"Young ladies, have you finished your diner? The maid comes to fetch your plates." Sure enough, Mr Griffin moved to one side to allow the maid into the room, and then watched as she collected the remains of the dinner onto a tray.

"I'll bring up some hot water for thee, ma'am," she told Mam'selle, but Mam'selle shook her head. "*Non.* Not yet, thank you. I return to the parlour downstairs. I will ask you for water for myself and the young ladies when I come up to our room again, yes?"

The maid shrugged. "Certainly, ma'am."

Amy took a step towards the door. "Are we to go downstairs, then, Mam'selle?"

But Mam'selle lifted a hand to silence her until the maid was gone, then cast a glance at Mr Griffin, her lips curving. "Mr Griffin and I still have much to discuss. In private, young ladies. You shall remain in this room. You have your own books, and," again she turned her eyes to Mr Griffin, looking up sideways at him from under her lashes, "Mr Griffin and I are going to read one another our favourite poems from the book he gave me."

Mam'selle had allowed them to explore a book stall in Newcastle, and to purchase a book of improving stories, an illustrated memoir of someone's travels in Italy, and a copy of the Ladies' Almanac only two years out of date. Even as she closed the door on Amy and Pat, Amy was fetching the memoir and laying it out on the table. By the time the key had turned in the lock and footsteps had faded away along the hall, both girls were back on their knees in front of the valise.

Once again, they made neat piles on the floor, emptying the bag so they could check the lining. Mam'selle had a purse of coins hidden in a concealed pocket on one side, and some small items of jewellery on the other, but nothing suspicious. Not that Amy knew what she'd hoped for. A book of instructions for spies would have been helpful, or an arsenal of weapons. Mam'selle didn't even have a gun or a knife.

"Unless she carries them on her person," Amy suggested, when Pat pointed out the lack didn't seem very spy-like. "I would."

They returned every item as near as possible to where it had been. The coat Mam'selle had hung on a hook by the door had nothing in its pockets, and the neat bag for the purposes of her toilette, containined only her soap, her brush and comb, and the cream for her hands.

Amy looked carefully around the room but could not see anything else that Mam'selle had brought with her. Pat, though, lifted the pillow on the side of the bed Mam'selle claimed for her own, then moved aside the nightshirt placed ready, and triumphantly held up a bundle of papers tied with a ribbon. "Letters, Amy."

But before they could examine their find, they heard the rush of feet outside and the scrape of the key.

By the time the door opened, they were both back at the table, bent over a page opened at random. Amy was reading aloud the first sentence she saw. "In the hilly terrain, the villages tumble down the hills and are built of their clay, so they seem to have grown from the earth into suitable habitation for humankind."

Mr Griffin jostled Mam'selle in the doorway and reached them first. He had been sour before, but was now in a tearing rage, his lips white and his eyes burning. "Where is it? What have you done with the page you tore from the back of the book?"

Thirsk to Lovesome Hill

Susan and Gil made it to Thirsk before darkness forced a halt and started again as early as they could in the morning, despite the pouring rain. As they headed further north, the rain thickened, turning the road to mire where it strayed from the old Roman remains. But Gil pushed on, determined that they'd reach Newcastle and the place the girls stayed. At least the discomfort and the need to pay careful attention to the hired cattle subdued his raging lust. Somewhat.

Even the oiled coverings were not enough to fully protect them from the rain, sweeping in gusts across the moors and seeping into every crack until they were wet at neck, wrist and ankle, and damp almost everywhere else. Talking was impossible, every comment a shout over the drumming of the rain on the canvas roof and sides.

When they changed horses for the second time, at Lovesome Hill, Gil ordered a private parlour and a bed chamber. "And take hot water up to the room as soon as you can, with plenty of towels," he ordered.

"We cannot stay here, Rutledge," Susan protested.

"We can stop long enough for dry clothes and a hot meal, Susan. Go on up and I'll bring in our bags." They'd not help Amy and Pat by falling sick themselves. Besides, they'd be in Newcastle in a little over thirty miles. If they found answers to their questions quickly, they could make at least one more post before nightfall, perhaps Alnwick, or even Heferlaw Bank. They'd travel all the faster if they started warm and dry. Yes. Taking an hour for a meal was good strategy.

He was halfway back to the cabriolet-phaeton to fetch their bags when he stopped in his tracks, oblivious to the rain that ran in rivulets off the brim of his hat. He'd explained none of his reasoning, but Susan had not argued. Had she figured it out, too? Or was she beginning to trust him?

5

D *unbar*
Had it not been for Mam'selle, Amy whispered to Pat as they stood in the stable-yard the next morning, she was sure Mr Griffin would have strangled them.

"All that fuss over a couple of blank sheets of paper," Pat whispered back.

"Not quite blank. I've been thinking. Those doodles on the back of the page? What if they were the key to a code?"

"That list of numbers and letters? Do you…"

Mam'selle interrupted, having finished farewelling Mr Griffin. "Young ladies, what are you plotting now? You are sly, is it not? Not to be trusted."

Amy resisted the urge to snort. Not to be trusted, indeed! They weren't spies and kidnappers. But Mam'selle was cross enough about the notes Amy and Pat had left, and even crosser that Mr Griffin insisted on retracing their steps to see if he could retrieve them before any pursuers found them. The worst of it was that Mam'selle had introduced them by their proper names, so even if the innkeeper followed instructions, he would hand the note over to Mr Griffin.

"Come, come," Mam'selle commanded, and Amy and Pat could see no choice but to obey, settling themselves in the post chaise without complaint. Perhaps, if they behaved perfectly, they could lull Mam'selle into dropping her guard once they reached Edinburgh, where Pat could contact her uncle or Amy could find them sanctuary with her father's cousin.

Newcastle and beyond

Despite the rain and the mire, Gil and Susan arrived in Newcastle in the early afternoon, and Susan's enquiry about notes met with an instant response. Again, she was handed over to the manager and ushered into his private sanctum. Again, she disclosed the girls' names and was given a note very similar to the one in Doncaster.

She and Gil questioned the maid who had received the note, and everyone else who could tell them anything about the party, and also about the mysterious man. He was in Newcastle the same night but didn't join Mademoiselle Cornillac. "'E were interested in 'un, though, think on," said one of the maids, and the desk clerk agreed. Both recognised the description as that of a man who asked questions about the French woman and her two charges.

And the stable servants confirmed that both the post chaise and the single rider had headed north, their horses hired for Edinburgh.

"Edinburgh," Susan said to Gil, once they were on their way again. "What does Mademoiselle Cornillac want in Edinburgh?"

"We will be there tomorrow," Gil assured her, "and not more than a day and a half behind them. She will not expect pursuit to be so close on her heels."

Susan was not comforted. "But she will expect pursuit. She must know that, by now, the school will have reported the girls missing. We cannot expect her to stay in Edinburgh, Rutledge."

"Then we will follow. Take heart, Susan. As recently as yesterday morning, the two girls were alive and cheerful, and we have more than halved their lead."

The sun came out as they climbed from the Tyne valley. They still had more than five hours of daylight, so if the weather remained clear, they might make Belford before they needed to stop. And from there to Edinburgh was an easy day's journey.

Susan hoped that her husband's second cousin, who lived in Edinburgh and was one of her son's trustees, would not hear about Amy's kidnapping. He had been indignant that James's will named Brigadier-General Lord Henry Redepenning, her father, as guardian of James's heir, and not him, and would take any opportunity to prove her and Lord Henry unworthy of the responsibility.

"Dare I offer a penny for your thoughts," Gil asked.

She blurted the truth, comfortable in Gil's presence as she hadn't been since they were children. "I was wishing Amy were not headed for Edinburgh. My husband's cousin lives there, and he does not approve of me."

Gil was too sharp by half. "Will he use her kidnapping to make trouble?"

Susan shrugged. "He will if he can. He thinks he should have charge of the heir to Gorburn House, though he would leave me my daughters."

"He would separate young Michael from his family? What an idiot. I imagine your family would have something to say about that!"

Again, she expressed her doubts with a lift of her shoulders. "He is a lawyer. He will build a case if he can. And it will be ten years at least before Michael can ignore his wishes; thirteen before he will be of age."

Gil took his eyes off the horses long enough to cast her a sharp look. "Do you fear his care for Michael might be coloured by ambition for himself?"

"Oh, no." Susan had never considered such villainy, and even now that Gil had raised the question, she did not believe it. "Hamish Cunningham is a rigid traditionalist with a jaundiced view of women, but I acquit him of wishing Michael ill. He came close to approving of me when I finally gave James his heir after nine years of marriage."

"He could hardly blame you for having daughters first. Amy was born within a year of your wedding, after James had been posted to the far side of the world and left you to raise her alone. And when he came back, Christina was born less than a year later."

Gil knew all of that? He had been out of the country himself for most of that time, so who kept him informed, and why did he care? Susan hid her reaction to his knowledge and said, "Girls don't count with Hamish. He thinks I would have had a son first, had I only tried harder."

Gil expressed his opinion in a pungent noun that consigned Hamish to a sewer, then apologised for his language.

Susan suppressed a giggle and composed herself to give a serious response. "I do not suspect Hamish of harbouring evil intent. He is a warm man on his own account and has no need of Gorburn House or its incomes."

"He is not the only trustee?" Gil asked, clearly still suspicious.

"No. James also named my father, who is the children's guardian, and my cousin Rede, whose financial acumen James much admired. Hamish is unhappy the Redepennings have so much authority over the estate, but the will was clear and his challenges so far have all been by way of suggestion. And Rede says he manages the Scottish holdings well."

Conversation lapsed while Gil negotiated a particularly rutted stretch of road.

"I miss Michael and Chrissie," Susan confessed. "We have seldom been apart. Indeed, that is one of Hamish's complaints. He thinks Michael old enough to go to school. He is only eight, Gil. I try not to baby him, but he is still so little. And Chrissie is not yet eleven. She stays overnight with her friends, often, but that is her leaving me, not me leaving her." She sighed.

"Tell me about them," Gil suggested. "I remember them as little more than babies."

Susan was reluctant, remembering how bored James used to be when she talked about their children, but Gil asked questions and soon she was deep in a discussion about the right kind of tutor for a little boy who loved to take things apart to see how they worked.

They made their next change in Morpeth. At first, the fresh horses required all of Gil's attention, but they soon settled to their work and Susan broke the long silence.

"We have talked for two days about my family, Rutledge. What of yours? How are your sisters?"

The horses startled, and tried to sidle sideways, and Gil realised he'd tightened his grip. He relaxed his hands calling, "Steady, there. Steady," and they settled back into the swift walk suitable for the gentler terrain on this plateau.

Susan waited until he had the horses back under control before she said, "If your family is off limits, Gil, I will respect that. But I am a safe pair of ears if you need someone to listen. I was acquainted with your brother, remember. Your sister-in-law, too, though not well. And Mina and Cal were friends of mine once."

He had almost forgotten. He was accustomed to thinking of the Redepenning boys as school friends, but it began before that, when he and his mother and sisters had moved to West Gloucestershire, just under the Cotswold Edge. His grandfather had died a few days after his father was killed in a carriage accident, and his much older brother Gideon, the new viscount, had taken off for London and its myriad entertainments, but not before ordering their mother and her three children to his new estate.

The three younger Rutledges had fallen instantly in love with the family on the neighbouring estate, where Lord and Lady Henry were raising their own five children and one of their nephews.

Gil had gone gaily off to school with the boys and returned only for holidays until Gideon bought him his colours.

But Susan's words filled his head with images of three little girls at the Longford Whitsunday Fair and the Longford Harvest Festival and numerous festivities during the twelve days of Christmas: Calanthe and Susan, just a year apart in age and arm in arm, watching over Madelina, who was four years younger; none of the three confined to the schoolroom, but made free of the house and grounds of Longford Court, where Lord and Lady Henry ruled in the Earl's absence.

He bit hard on his upper lip and blinked rapidly to chase away liquid that clouded his eyes. "I had forgotten. They were happy then, weren't they? My sisters? Before?" Before he embraced school life, throwing himself into the friendships he forged there, and forgot his self-appointed responsibility to protect them from Gideon.

"We all were. I loved having neighbours of my own age just a short ride away." Susan gave a soft snort of amusement. "Even if my mother did hold them up as models of decorum every time I slipped out of the house to run away with you boys."

Gil hadn't known her mother disapproved. He had thought Susan perfect, just as she was. "I used to wish they were more like you. But they never would step outside of my father's rules. My father had firm views about how ladies behaved."

"I never met your father. Did he not die before you moved to Thornbury Hall?"

"Yes. Killed in a drunken race with his son and heir. But his memory still controlled my mother and sisters."

He'd said more than he intended, but it was true that he trusted Susan; perhaps even more than he trusted her brothers and cousin. Not that he could tell her the whole. He would go to the grave keeping his sisters' secret. He could, perhaps, share a little, though. She was a wise woman, was Susan. No one could absolve Gil but talking to her might ease the burden a little. "If you knew Gideon, you know what he was like."

"He was a dissolute, vicious monster," Susan said, decidedly.

"He was the image of our father," Gil admitted.

"I never knew your father, but I know your mother and sisters were terrified of Gideon, and I know what he did to Cal, and why she ran away with William Byrne."

This time, the horses stopped, responding to a signal he was unaware of giving as he turned to look at Susan, his mouth gaping. "She told you?"

"Of course not. I was only fifteen, then, and still in the school-room. I knew she became withdrawn and unhappy when your brother returned to Thornbury for the summer, and then she disap-peared. I never even knew she had eloped with Byrne until I heard the servants talking about how Byrne had ruined your sister and your brother was going to kill him."

"Walk on," Gil said to the horses. He had to control himself better. He was confusing the beasts. "Then..." He didn't know how to ask what she thought she knew without disclosing the scandal at the heart of his family's misery. Perhaps she had heard of the beat-ings; the cruel punishments. But not the other.

"Papa told me all when your brother thought to court me. He had it from Byrne when Byrne asked for his help to get Cal away."

Gil didn't know what question to ask first. When had Gideon courted Susan? Did Lord Henry help the fleeing couple? Was it him Gil had to thank for getting them on a ship for the Americas so secretly that Gideon never found a trace of them? And what, exactly, did Lord Henry tell his daughter? Did she know Gideon had paid a gambling debt by allowing the scum he owed a night with his sister? And had done worse to Mina, which Gil should have prevented, since Calanthe's experience should have forewarned him.

They were approaching West Thurston on one side of the River Coquet, and the steep drop and sharp turn to the bridge, followed by another sharp turn and steep climb to Felton on the other side. He'd need to pay all his attention to the horses. Gil promised himself they would continue this conversation later.

But in Felton, when they stopped to change horses and snatch a bite to eat, an overheard conversation pushed such ancient history to the back of his mind.

"Look, Pat, that's Edinburgh." Amy had her nose almost pressed to the window of the carriage as the road descended from Tranent, giving them a view over the Firth of Forth to the city, or at least its upper reaches, ten miles distant. "We should be there in an hour or a little more."

"We are not going to Edinburgh," Mam'selle told them.

Both girls turned from the window to stare at the French woman. "Then where are we going?" Amy ventured. "Further on?"

Mam'selle started to respond. "To..." She closed her mouth, regarded the girls steadily, then said, "You shall see. I wish you had not followed me, *mesdemoiselles*. I wish you had not." She turned her face to look bleakly out of the carriage window, her face drawn and her mouth pinched. She had dark circles under her eyes. Amy fought an impulse to comfort her. The woman was a spy, a traitor, and a kidnapper, after all! But she looked so unhappy.

"What do you think she means?" Pat barely breathed the words into Amy's ear, but Mam'selle heard enough to say, without heat, "No whispering, young ladies. Not, I suppose, that it matters. Oh, I hope we are in time! How slow these horses are?"

She lapsed into silence, leaning forward a little in her seat as if to urge the carriage to go faster. But it was quite another twenty minutes before the post boy drew them to a halt in the little village of Musselburgh, half an hour out of Edinburgh.

At Mam'selle's command, they descended from the post chaise. Musselburgh had started as a fishing village, and fishing was still the primary activity on the other side of the Esk, but on the eastern side of the bridge, High Street was a bustling marketplace and Amy had accompanied Susan when she played in the first women's golf tournament last year on the Musselburgh links to the north of the town.

She looked around, hoping to see someone she knew, but Mam'selle instructed her to hurry up and fetch her bag, because they had some distance to travel yet today, and Mam'selle needed to hire a cart or some other conveyance to take them the remaining distance.

They had no sooner retrieved their luggage than the post boy turned the horses and returned the way they'd come. Mam'selle set off at a brisk walking pace, with the girls trailing behind her, and was soon in discussion with the ostler at a small inn just off the main road. Amy, listening keenly, heard her negotiating to hire a buggy and driver to take her and the girls to Penicuik, some eleven miles inland. What was at Penicuik?

Felton

They spent the night at Felton and took advantage of a fine morning to break their fast in the small garden. Susan was already seated at a table and was pouring the tea with more anxious concentration than it warranted when Gil arrived back from ordering the horses put to in thirty minutes.

He sat and accepted the cup she passed him, briefly covering her hands with his own. "We have made good time, Susan."

She gave him a small smile before turning her attention to preparing her own cup. "I know. I cannot help but worry, though. They will have arrived in Edinburgh last night or this morning. We will get there tonight, will we not, Gil?"

Gil removed the cover from the large tureen on the table. Some sort of vegetable and meat stew. "If the weather continues fine and the road is not in poor repair." He gestured with the ladle towards Susan's bowl, and filled it at her nod.

"And the horses do not break their legs or their wind, and I manage not to fall out of the carriage," she replied, casting her eyes up as if seeking help from Heaven. Then, dropping the irony, "If they stay in an Edinburgh inn, we'll find them easily enough, even if their real destination is further on. But if they are going to a private house… Rutledge, what if we cannot find them? What might she do to them?"

He put down the ladle and took both of her hands. "She has not hurt them. You must hold to that." Susan sighed, but the small anxiety creases around her eyes relaxed a little. Gil stroked his thumbs soothingly over her hands, his own physical reaction to his Goddess subsumed in the need to soothe and reassure. "Remember, that they followed her. What a shock she must have had when she saw them, but she didn't… She took them with her, Susan."

Susan got his point and made it without mincing words. "She did not kill them." A single decisive nod. "Yes, a ruthless villain would have removed the nuisance. You comfort me."

The clatter of pottery shifting on a metal tray alerted them to the approach of a servant, and Gil released her hands and sat back. Just in time, because he had been on the point of leaning forward a few extra inches to steal a kiss. He was a cad even to think of taking advantage of Susan's anxious state.

The servant had brought several different varieties of pastry plus the two large tankards of ale Gil had ordered, Susan being one of the few ladies he knew who enjoyed ale with her lunch.

For a few minutes, they focused on their food, but with part of his mind Gil was still evolving a strategy for the next few days. Or at least thinking about the information he would need to make a successful plan. As soon as the servant left, he asked the first of his questions.

"Can we expect help from your husband's cousin, or should we avoid him altogether?"

Susan did not answer immediately but considered while finishing her stew. "Involving Hamish is not my first preference," she said, as she put her cutlery and empty bowl onto the tray that had held the pastries. "He will fuss. But he knows all sorts of people, and he will help if he is asked. He is not a bad man. Just entirely confident that women were one of God's few mistakes."

Clear enough. Gil had known any number of men like that. "Well, then, we will hold him in reserve."

Susan selected an apple turnover and transferred it to her plate as she considered the implications. "Which means we cannot stay at my townhouse. Michael's, I should say. Hamish has chambers there."

"Best we take rooms at the coaching inn our runaways are headed to," Gil agreed. "If Mademoiselle Cornillac follows her usual practice, she'll talk about the next day's destination to the ostlers, and we'll know where to head."

"Unless Edinburgh is her destination."

"Even so. Someone at the inn may have overheard something, or your clever daughter may have found a way to leave a message. We start at the inn." The pie Gil had chosen was filled with eggs and cubes of ham, potato, and carrot. He savoured the flavours then took another bite, relishing the crispness of the pastry.

Susan was washing her turnover down with a swallow of ale, shifting impatiently as her hands inched towards the knife and fork she had placed on her plate between mouthfuls, as proper table etiquette required. Her inclination to rush the meal and be on her way was clearly at war with her training in manners.

"Relax, Susan. A few minutes will make the world of difference to your digestion, and very little to our arrival time."

What a valiant creature his Goddess was. She managed a smile, though it didn't reach her eyes. "I know you are right, you annoying man. I will try not to worry and to be patient.

"You are thinking I have no notion what you are suffering, and you are right. I have never been a father and have never had to wait and worry about a child of my flesh." Gil almost left it at that, but then he took a deep breath and spoke the rest of his thought. "But I have been an officer with men I loved and who loved and trusted me, and I have had to send them into danger knowing that some of them will be killed and others wounded. That perhaps gives me a small inkling of your feelings, Goddess." He winced as the last word slipped out. She hated when people called her that, but it was how he felt. He had worshipped her from the moment he met her as a boy; carried a candle before her image in his heart since that day; held her as a beacon of the best of English womanhood through a thousand engagements on four continents and any number of islands.

She was oblivious to his preoccupation, considering what he had said. "I had not thought about it like that. Yes. I imagine you were a father, or at least an elder brother, to your men. My brothers are the same. It is similar, Gil. So, you know how hard it is."

Susan called him Gil, he noticed, when she was moved, just as he slipped into calling her Goddess. He did not call her attention to the slip, but when he moved her chair back to help her rise, and she stepped to one side almost into his arms, he could not resist wrapping them around her.

He had intended a brief peck on her hair. She lifted her mouth as if she had been waiting for just such a move, and he was lost. She was all that existed. The elusive scent of her saturated his nostrils, her yielding curves filled his arms, and her lips and mouth consumed all of his thoughts as he tenderly explored them.

How long the kiss lasted he had no idea, but when she stiffened and pulled away, he let her go immediately, sense rushing back into his brain and berating it for the most arrant stupidity. She didn't comment—wouldn't even meet his eyes—but led the way out of the garden, almost running in her hurry.

6
___

They had to wait in the stable-yard while the groom assisted a man in a hurry; a rider who spurred his way out of the yard without leaving a gratuity, much to the groom's disgust.

"Didn't give me nothing day afore yesterday, neither," he grumbled to Gil as Gil helped him with the horses for the cabriolet-phaeton. "Silly fool. What's he want to go dashing up and down to Scotland for?"

Gil looked after the disappearing hooves of the horse. "He's come down from Scotland? Did he say how the roads were?"

The groom shrugged. "Bit of a slip at Grantshouse, but he said he was ready for it, seeing as how he passed it on the way up yesteren. So what does he want to turn around and come back for, I says? He had business in Scotland, says he, and now he has business in Newcastle. Silly fool."

Gil backed the horse in his charge into the traces. It seemed a steady sort and moved without complaint or resistance.

The groom was doing the same with the other horse, but he suddenly stopped. "Hey, I just thought me. You was asking 'bout the man what was following the French lady? That was him there, what just rode out of this yard. Got as far as Dunbar then turned around and come back. Must be mad."

He had a ten-minute lead. It would be fifteen at least by the time Gil could get a horse saddled and be after him. Time for the man to disappear if he had a mind. Besides, how could Gil abandon Susan in an inn yard?

"What's at Dunbar?" the ostler mused.

Amy and Pat, perhaps. That news would take Susan's mind off his impudent kiss. If that was their mysterious pursuer, then they might be closer than they thought. Gil pondered the implications while his hands went ahead with the familiar tasks of buckling and fastening. The man was heading back to Newcastle in haste. Had he finished the task that sent him north? And if so, what did that mean for Amy and Pat?

Years in combat had taught him not to fret overlong about what he couldn't know and couldn't change. He thanked the groom and gave him a tip a dozen times the size of the despised measly offering from the pursuer.

"If that fellow comes through again, delay him, will you?" he suggested, and the groom laid a finger alongside his nose and winked. "Right slow, I expect I'll be, sir," he said.

Soon, they were rolling north, and Gil told Susan what he'd learned, and what he had concluded.

"Will we find them at Dunbar?" she asked

"We will be there by late afternoon. We will know then."

She was silent again, probably worrying about her daughter, though Gil was finding it near impossible to think about anything but that devastatingly beautiful kiss. It was dawning on him that The Goddess had kissed him back. What was he to take from that? He could reasonably conclude she wanted to be kissed. Wanted to be kissed by him? She was a chaste and respectable lady; one, furthermore, who had managed her own affairs and those of her household and her husband for close to twenty years. She kissed him back, and he couldn't believe she gave her kisses lightly.

It was the situation. She needed comfort. He dare read no more into it than that.

She was still silent, which bothered him more than he expected. He was used to her chatter by now. No. Enjoyed it. She was always intelligent, often insightful. She could spin a good story, and he loved listening to her voice.

Hoping to get her talking again, he said, "You never asked how I came to be in Cambridge."

"I did wonder. I thought you were at home, in the southwest." She slipped a hand into his arm and gave it a friendly squeeze. "And then you arrived at my elbow, with news of Amy and a direction for me to search, like an answer to my prayer."

Remembering her prickly reaction to his intervention, Gil suppressed a smile. "I had been to Derby to visit my sister, Madelina."

"Mina? How lovely! I have not seen her in years, and we have not kept in touch. How is she?"

Mina was quiet, contained, distant. They were strangers, having seen one another on only a couple of occasions in two decades, and then but fleetingly. They had last spent time together when Mina was little more than a frightened broken child.

Gil had written in the intervening years; very occasionally, as he had to Cal in Conneticut. Short, stilted letters that received short, stilted replies. Polite but unrevealing.

He had stayed with Mina and her family for two weeks, avoiding any topic that might make her uncomfortable, striving to make the acquaintance of her children; two daughters still in the schoolroom, and a son in the nursery. And her two grown step-sons, one a former friend of Gil's from Eton, both cautiously friendly and very protective of their 'Mama'.

By the end of his stay, all of them seemed less wary, but he left feeling tired and discouraged. Mina, despite the odds, had created a strong and supportive family of her own, and he was not part of it.

"She seems well enough. Her husband left her comfortably circumstanced, her and the children. I think she is happy. She said she is happy." He feathered a corner, and Susan pressed against him as the carriage swayed. Rascal that he was, he took comfort in her nearness. She had still not admonished him for the kiss, and he was certainly not going to mention it.

Susan resettled herself on her side of the seat. "She is widowed? I did not know."

"Five years widowed. He was much older, of course. You knew that?"

"Yes." She grasped his arm again and he turned his head to look down into her lovely eyes, gazing earnestly into his own. "Gil, she was content with him. Blessed, she said."

"She said? You saw her?" Could it be true? The marriage had been necessary to keep her safe, and she had agreed, for what that was worth. But given she was barely of legal age to marry and with child to an evil lecher with three times her years, her choice was no choice at all. Ever since, he had been sure he should have found a better solution.

"In Buxton, it would have been. Perhaps seven years ago? Mr Featheringham was there to take the waters and they made a family holiday of it. So lovely to bump into her, and of course I stayed an extra day so we could dine together and catch up. Mr Featheringham was a dear man. He doted on Mina and the children, and the little boy was just like him. And his children by his first marriage adored her. You did well for her, Gil."

Gil couldn't believe that, but nor could he prevent the hope that lightened his heart. "Really? Do you… Did she say so?"

Susan nodded again, and her voice was firm as she told him, "She said she owed you her life and her happiness. Has she not told you? She is shy of you, of course. Her brother the hero."

He turned his gaze back to the horses, ashamed to meet her eyes. "I'm no hero. You shouldn't think it."

Susan was having none of his disclaimer. "You are to Mina. She told me you rode in, the day before her wedding to that awful Lord Carrington, shouted down your mother, and carried her off, swearing to see her safe. And you managed it, too."

He was silent for a while, considering the days spent with the Featheringhams. "None of it was Mina's fault."

Susan made a sound between a snort and a huff. "I know that. She was what? Thirteen?"

"She turned thirteen just before the wedding to Featheringham." Old enough, the law said. But not old enough, his heart screamed.

Susan knew far more than he'd ever realised. "And you took her to the father of a boy you were at school with."

He had never explained to anyone before. "I didn't know what else to do, Goddess. Mother was all for the wedding with Carrington. Gideon had brokered the whole thing, from start to finish. Mother kept saying 'she will be a baroness,' as if Mina's suffering meant nothing. She said the marriage would remove Mina's disgrace, but it wasn't her disgrace!"

He waited in silence for absolution or condemnation as they rounded a corner and climbed a hill, then trotted smartly down the other side.

"No, Gil, Mina is right," Susan said at last. "I cannot imagine what else you could have done. And look at the results! You saved your sister and her baby, gave them a respectable and happy life, and helped a bereaved father and his sons and daughter. And you did it in the face of your family's anger. You are a hero."

It wasn't true, but the burden he had carried all his life was lighter because his Goddess believed it. He glanced at her again and she leaned closer and kissed his cheek.

"You are a good man, Gilbert Rutledge. You must be the only person in the world who doesn't think so."

He shrugged, uncomfortable with the undeserved praise. "I do my duty," he said.

Susan took pity on him and changed the subject. "The girl, Gillian, she must be nearly out."

He accepted the change of subject with gratitude. "Yes, young Gillian's brother's wife plans to present her next year."

"She was named for you, of course," Susan mused. "She looks very like you, too."

Gil was horrified. "She isn't mine!"

"I don't think it," Susan reassured him, "though I wouldn't have put it past Gideon. It wasn't him, either, was it? Carrington would only have offered to wed her if the child was his, and your brother was completely in thrall to him. After what he did to Cal, he probably felt quite virtuous about his arrangements for his second sister."

Another shock. Mina had not told even him the name of the father of her child. Though he had not asked. The letter from Calanthe that sent him at speed from London had spoken of her own experiences and of her fears for Mina. And Carrington's obsession with very young girls was well known in the neighbourhood, as was his determination to produce a second male child. Mina's very obvious condition when he arrived was all the confirmation he needed. "She told you?" But no, she was shaking her head.

"We did not discuss it. But by then I knew why Papa had supported Cal's elopement, so it seemed obvious. Your brother really was a monster, wasn't he? Your mother would have blamed everyone but him. She always thought he could do no wrong. He must have been furious that Mina escaped him."

"You don't know the half of it," Gil told her. "He would have killed me if he could, but I was already bigger and stronger than him. So, he bought me out of my regiment and sold me into another that was going to India. He told me he'd find her, wherever I had hidden her, and I wouldn't be around to steal her away a second time. And with luck the Marathans would get me."

Susan's sudden stillness attracted his attention back from the horses.

"He is dead, Susan. And I am not."

She waved his remark away. "That's why you transferred? Left England? I thought… Never mind." She took a deep breath. "How far to Dunbar now?"

He ignored the change of subject. "Nothing but my duty could have kept me from London and you. Did you not know that?"

She was shaking her head. "Oh Gil, I feel so selfish. You were saving your sister and facing down your brother and I had my hair out of curl because you left London instead of…" Her voice trailed off again, but he could finish that sentence.

"Dancing attendance on you? Believe me, I would have been

one of your court if I could. I always felt so privileged to be one of those permitted to attend you, Goddess. Sorry. Susan, I mean." She had been so lovely, the anointed Beauty of that year, lighting the room with her smile and her unconventional delight in the pleasures of the Season.

He was not the only man smitten, but he was one of the few—and the others all friends of her brothers—that she favoured. He had bribed a maid in her father's household to keep him informed about the entertainments she would attend and made sure to be at every one his regimental duties allowed, and in return he often had the privilege of taking her into supper or sitting beside her at dinners.

He had carried the image of her in his mind to India, hoping but not believing he would have another chance to court her. And then the news came she had married. He threw himself into his career as a soldier and tried to forget his Goddess. But he never succeeded.

Dancing attendance on her? That's what the stupid man thought she had wanted?

The next post change brought the conversation to an end, as he handed her down to sit on a seat outside the inn while they changed the horses. It was a pleasant country inn, and the courtyard bustled with activity as a coach pulled in, and another pulled out.

Susan paid little attention. She didn't know how to react to the revelation that Gil saw himself as just another admirer. Did he have no idea she had been waiting for a proposal?

Even at seventeen, she had known she might have to be patient. Though he seemed much older than the other boys with whom she flirted—serious and more responsible—he was still only two years her senior and not yet of a rank that would allow him to afford a wife. That said, Susan had money of her own, from her mother's family, and nothing to prevent her giving him as much time as he needed to realise they were meant to be together. Even after he left

England without a farewell, she continued to hope, and to refuse all other offers. She was a few weeks from her twentieth birthday when she accepted James and would have happily waited longer on a word from Gil.

Did he really not know? She thought she had made her preference clear, though modesty, pride, and fear of rejection kept her encouragements subtle.

Dear Lord. All these years she'd held a small bubble of resentment that he'd left London and then England without a note or a message. She should have thrown caution to the wind and written to him before she agreed to marry James.

She snorted at the thought. A fine letter that would have been. "Dear Lieutenant Rutledge, a fine young naval officer has asked me to marry him, and before I give him my answer, I just wish to enquire whether you have any interest in having me instead."

Regrets and might-have-beens were stupid. She had been happy with James, at least in the beginning, until he proved to lack the gift of fidelity. Even after he made it clear that he would not give up his other women, he did not flaunt them in her face. He was courteous and friendly, respected her abilities and supported her decisions, gave her control of his estate and his income, expected little from her except his nominated allowance and the occasional public appearance. She had been content in her life, if not her marriage, and she had the three most wonderful children in the world.

Accepting Gil's hand back up into the cabriolet-phaeton, she composed herself for the next stretch of the journey. Knowing he admired her still, at least enough to kiss her, set all of her body singing. She needed to be realistic, and smother the foolish dreams creeping from her memories. She was thirty-seven, and he was a viscount. He would need to find a young wife who could give him an heir, and she would need to smile and be glad for him.

A less personal subject than family was needed for the next part of the trip. "What think you of the situation with the United States, Rutledge?"

The weather stayed fine, and the roads were drying. With careful driving, Gil avoided the remaining mires and they made good time, crossing into Scotland around noon and reaching Dunbar in the early afternoon.

Their quarry's chaise would have made post at the George. Susan patronised the New Inn for a meal stopover on her way north or south from Edinburgh or her son's estate, so there was a chance she might not be recognised, but the innkeeper greeted her by name as soon as she entered the building.

"Good day, Mrs Cunningham. Welcome to the George. How might we help ye?"

"Mr McGregor, good afternoon. I am looking for three or possibly four people who may have changed horses here the day before yesterday. I would like to question your stable master."

His brow creased, and he looked up into the corner of the high ceiling as if he did not wish to meet her eyes. "The Mistress of Gorburn will have all th' help this establishment can provide, ma'am." He chewed on his upper lip and then seemed to make up his mind.

"Mrs Cunningham, is one o' those folk a relative of yours? Perhaps yer daughter?"

Susan clutched Gil's arm, grateful for his silent support. "You have seen my Amy? She stopped here?"

The innkeeper exhaled on a puff of air, nodding his head slowly. "So it was her. She and her companions bided the night, ma'am. I am so sorry, Mrs Cunningham. I thought I recognised th' eyes, and it has been botherin' me this past day. When you walked in just now I remembered where I'd seen them before. She hasna been with ye the last few times ye've stopped, ma'am, and if that lassie was wee Miss Amelia; well, she has grown a bit since I last saw her."

Gil intervened as Susan started to comment. "Do you have an office or a private parlour where we can hear your story, Mr McGregor?"

He was right. They must not put Amy's reputation at risk by speaking where anyone might hear. Susan closed her lips firmly to pen her questions in and followed Mr McGregor into a small but comfortably furnished business room.

The French lady, as Mr McGregor called her once he began his story, had arrived with the two girls two evenings before, "And a rare wild night it was, as ye must remember. She wanted to travel on, but th' post boy wouldna risk th' horses in that rain and wind at night."

They heard about the arrival of a man on his own, who exclaimed at the chance of meeting the French lady, and how pleased she seemed to see him.

"This Pendragon, as he called himself, had dinner with th' Frenchie in a private parlour." The innkeeper shook his head at the impropriety. "Sent a meal up to the lassies with a maid, so I didna see much of Miss Amelia, ma'am, or it might be I would have remembered earlier."

"They were friends then," Gil said. "Tell me your impression. Were they romantically involved or working together?"

"Or both, perhaps," Susan suggested. Didn't women and men who worked together become romantically involved? Father had given that as his reason when he suggested she always chose other women as her team mates for the many charitable projects she supported. And look how this journey with Gil was turning out? For a moment, she let her mind linger on the kiss, and the prospect of more. But McGregor was answering, and she needed to put all of her mind to getting Amy home and safe.

"I would say the lady thought they were romantically involved. Not so sure about yon laddie. He was an odd body. Sharp enough to cut hisself, as they say. Anyway, they didna stay downstairs for long. Somethin' upset him, and he stormed up to th' Frenchie's room and started shoutin' at th' girls; somethin' about a note an' a page torn from a poetry book. Fit to kill, he was. Called them young ladies all sort of names, and fair put about th' Frenchie was."

"With the young ladies or with this fellow Pendragon?" Gil asked.

"I don't rightly know, sir. She wis affronted with his shoutin', but she wasna happy with the young misses, either. She was still cross when they left west oan th' Edinburgh road. Min' ye, she was sweet oan th' chappie, mah missus says, an' he went south, so mabbe that was it."

They spoke to the maid who had served the girls in their room, and another who took the meal to the couple in the private parlour. Amy and Pat had been in good spirits, and Miss Cornillac and Pendragon had been reading poetry together.

"But 'en he got aw radge, and up the twois ay them went tae the bed chamber. Shoutin', an' th' Frenchie trying tae calm him doon."

The maids both told the same story. The young ladies had torn a page from a book that Pendragon had given to the French lady, and he wanted it back.

"Fit tae commit murder, he waur, Ma'am," one maid said with an artistic shudder that had Susan discounting the dramatics. Or, at least, so she hoped. And certainly, Mademoiselle Cornillac had not permitted murder, so Susan could be grateful for that. According to the stable master and his ostlers, they'd parted in the morning, two very subdued girls in a post chaise heading for Edinburgh with their supposed governess, and the angry Englishman on horseback returning south.

The innkeeper was more than helpful, giving them a private parlour for their interviews and fetching one servant after another. So much for gossip. The whole of East Lothian would buzz with stories of the kidnapped girl and the widow with the silent forbidding 'friend'. Susan could only hope the stories would not rise through the classes or would be discounted if they did.

Ah well. She and her family were good at ignoring scandal. If enough people of high estate pretended strongly enough that no questionable activities had occurred, sooner or later the rest of Society would believe them.

Gil left most of the questioning to her, as the known local, but after the last of a long succession of servants left the room he called a halt. "We have spoken to everyone available, Susan, and have a three-hour journey to make while the light lasts."

He was right, of course. Even as she demurred, Susan stood and began collecting her reticule, bonnet, and coat. "I would like to speak to the post boy, but he is based in Newcastle and has gone home, McGregor says."

"McGregor also says he will find out on the post rider's next trip where he left Mademoiselle Cornillac and our two runaways, but we might well have found their trail—perhaps the girls themselves—before the man returns, and I do not fancy a two or three-day return trip in the wrong direction to chase him down."

"Especially since he may have been sent days away in the other direction." Susan couldn't help her sigh, but at Gil's worried frown she reached up to kiss his cheek.

"Edinburgh, then, Gil. We are close behind them and they were safe yesterday." She hardly knew whether she was reassuring him or herself.

7

———————

From the locked room of the apartment Mam'selle had rented in a house in Penicuik's High Street, Pat kept watch on the road. Mam'selle had been gone most of the day, leaving them with food and drink, and the necessities for hygiene behind a small screen. But the food was all gone, the slop bucket nearly full, and the water jug close to empty, and still she did not return.

Amy threw down the hairpin she had been manipulating unsuccessfully in the key hole, then scrambled after it when it skittered across the floor. "When I get home, I am going to demand that Uncle Wakefield teaches me how to pick locks," she declared. "Mama and Grandfather must see what a useful skill it is."

"When you get home, they will probably lock you up until you are thirty," Pat predicted. "I know that is what my great-aunt will do."

Amy ignored the provocation, coming to peer over Pat's shoulder. "I wonder who she is meeting."

"Do you think she is breaking someone out of prison?"

The pair looked doubtfully at the tall brick chimneys of the Valleyfield paper mills, visible above the trees between the village and the river. The owners of the mills had sold them to the government a year ago to house prisoners-of-war, and Amy and Pat could not doubt that Mam'selle's errand had to do in some way with those incarcerated there.

This was perhaps the seventh or eighth time today they'd had this conversation, but with no further information all they could do was worry at the same speculations again and again.

But wait. Was that Mam'selle, turning onto High Street a few buildings down? The light was failing as the sun set, and Amy could not be sure.

Amy pointed. "Is that her?"

Pat put her face closer to the glass, crushing one cheek against it for a better view along the street. "Yes, I think so."

As the slowly trudging figure approached and came into focus, they could see her slumped shoulders, but not the lowered face, obscured by the bonnet, until she stopped and looked directly at the house, squared her shoulders as if preparing for a challenge, and came on more briskly. Amy felt a sudden pang of sympathy. "She looks sad." As she should be. Amy needed to remind herself that Mam'selle was the enemy.

Pat's softer heart clearly gave her no such conflict. "I wonder what went wrong?"

Mam'selle disappeared beneath them, and a few minutes later they heard her steps on the stairs and then the rattle of the key in the lock.

Mam'selle entered, and with her the house's servant, who bustled behind the screen and came back carefully carrying the slop bucket.

Mam'selle wrinkled her nose as the maid passed. "I apologise, *mesdemoiselles*. I was longer than I expected. You are well, you have not lacked?"

"Only our freedom, Mam'selle," Amy challenged.

Mam'selle did not respond, taking off her bonnet and pelisse, and sitting down in one of the chairs by the fire as if her legs could no longer support her. The maid had left the room, closing the door behind her, before Mam'selle spoke.

"Ah. Freedom. How beautiful a word." She unlaced one half

boot and extracted her foot, picking it up to rest on her knee so she could massage the arch. "What am I to do with you, *mesdemoiselles*? I may be here for days. Weeks, perhaps. There is a doctor, they say, who might advise me, but he is away from the valley."

Amy glowered. "Advise you on what to do with us?"

"*Non, non.*" Mam'selle glared back. "This is not about you. You two should not be here at all, you and your spy stories and your interference. I did not ask you to follow me."

As if Amy could believe that. Mam'selle had been denying her guilt from the start, but look at the evidence! "If you are not a spy, Mam'selle Cornillac, what are you doing here? Why did you run away from the school, and why did you kidnap us?"

For the first time, Mam'selle answered the challenge. "I could not leave you on the road, could I? Or hand you over to strangers? Quite apart from the danger to two gently-born maidens abandoned to every ruffian and scoundrel, what if someone believed your fantasies?" She turned her attention to the other foot, her voice dropping again, as if she spoke to herself rather than Amy. "Or even the truth, which would be bad enough in the eyes of some. An émigrée with a brother who is an enemy soldier? At the very least, I would have been detained for questioning, and even now I am afraid I am too late."

With both feet back on the ground she leant her head against the back of the chair, eyes closed. "Mrs Fellowes would not allow me to continue in my employment. Though I suppose by now she has received the note I sent from Doncaster, and I shall lose my position in any case. But as I said in the note, I had to bring you with me, for your own safety if nothing else. And now I do not know what to do." A tear leaked from under her closed lids and spilled down her cheeks, followed by another and another. "I do not know what to do," she repeated, and began to cry in earnest.

Pat was the first to kneel beside the Frenchwoman, putting an arm around her and murmuring condolences. Amy put her suspicions to one side, at least for the moment, and patted Mam'selle's shoulder. "Tell us, Mam'selle. If you are not an enemy of England, we will help you."

"Ah *demoiselles*, I am undone. It is my brother, my Armand, my only family. How could I not come? How could I delay on the journey? He is not dead, they tell me, but they will say no more. Talk to the doctor they say, but the doctor is not home, and they do not care, at the gate or in the village. What am I to do?"

Amy tried to extract some sense from that. "Your brother is in the Valleyfield Mills? He is a prisoner? But I thought you grew up here in England?"

"Yes, from when we were children, but Armand returned to France in the Peace of Amiens and was trapped when the war began again. For nearly seven years, I have had nothing but a few smuggled notes to know he was still alive." She drew in a breath that shuddered with unquenched sobs.

It sounded plausible. The brief peace with France long before Amy began to take an interest in politics or war had led to many English visitors being detained for the duration of the war. She knew that. Her honorary uncle and aunt, David and Prue Wakefield, had stories to tell of the detainees they'd helped when in France years ago.

And many French citizens who had fled the revolution for England had taken advantage of the Peace to visit family or sell property. Those too slow to read the signs that war was about to break out again found themselves forced to declare their support for Napoleon and France or be charged as traitors.

"So, when he wrote to say he was in Scotland, you came to see him?" Pat prompted.

Mam'selle shook her head. "Not Armand. Someone from the prison camp wrote. An officer. To say that Armand was very sick with a fever, and if I wished to come, he would arrange a pass so I could see my brother. But the officer is not on duty, and they said I must first speak with the doctor, for only he can tell me if Armand lives or is dead."

"Then we must find the doctor," Amy decided. "And we must find out all we can about the prison and how it works, so we know what to ask the officers. They cannot disobey their orders, Mam'selle. My father was in the navy and I have uncles in the army, and I know they must follow their orders. I am sure, though, they will surely wish to help a sister who wants only to see her sick brother. Especially a pretty sister. It is too late tonight, but tomorrow we will ask the woman who owns this house, and all the servants, and up and down the street at all the shops and houses. The villagers will know. Mama says the villagers always know."

The grief eased in Mam'selle's face, and she caught Amy's hand and kissed it. "You will help me, though I kidnapped you? You are so good." A watery chuckle. "Naughty and stubborn, but good."

Pat and Amy exchanged glances. Yes, Pat, too, was still suspicious, but if Mam'selle was telling the truth she deserved their help for the extra worry they had caused. And if she wasn't, appearing to help would give them the freedom and the information they needed to stop whatever she really planned.

Susan and Gil arrived at the White Swan in Edinburgh as the sun was setting and, almost before she was out of the coach, Susan was questioning the ostler who arrived to tend their horses.

The man disclaimed all knowledge of a French woman accompanied by two girls, but he was only one man, so Gil was not concerned. The stable master would be a better source of information, but he had finished his work day and was out for the evening.

Susan tapped her foot and shifted impatiently.

"It is nearly ten of the clock," Gil pointed out. This far north and so close to midsummer, the days were long and the nights short. "We can ask at the front desk, but if they did not take rooms, we may need to wait until morning."

At Susan's insistence, he asked all the stable hands still on duty, then repeated the questions to the inside servants with the same negative results when she finally consented to go inside the inn. He ordered rooms, hot water, and a private parlour where a light meal could be served. Something quick that would not delay them seeking their beds. He had no doubt they would be making an early start in the morning.

The morning brought no better news. The French woman had not stayed or changed horses at the White Swan.

Gil had ordered breakfast in the parlour he had commandeered for interviewing the servants, and he now filled a plate from the dishes on offer and set it before Susan.

"Eat. You'll do Amy no good if you fall ill."

She obediently picked up her knife and fork. "They could have stopped anywhere. Or gone on; they left early enough yesterday morning. I wish we'd been able to question the post rider at Dunbar."

"It is frustrating, I know. But we will pick up the trail again, Susan, even if I have to backtrack a little." Gil brought his own plate to the table and began to efficiently refuel for the work ahead.

Susan was eating mechanically, with little attention to what was before her. "I was so certain they would at least change horses here. But perhaps at one of the other inns?"

"We will try them all," he assured her.

They had no success. At one coaching inn after another, they used cajolery, authority, charm, and gratuities, working smoothly as a team to find out whatever they could about the travellers of the previous two days. Nothing. The French governess and the two young ladies, whose trail they had followed so easily since Cambridge, had disappeared as if they had never been.

They were coming back along George Street discussing which of the inns outside of the town to investigate first when a voice hailed Susan.

"Cousin Susan!"

The speaker was a tall thin man, soberly dressed, with the combination of pale skin, bright—almost orange—hair, and pale blue eyes that appeared so often among the Celtic races.

Beside Gil, Susan stiffened, then consciously relaxed and turned to the speaker with a smile. "Hamish. Lord Rutledge, may I present Hamish Cunningham, my cousin?"

"Your servant, my lord. Cousin Susan, I had no idea you were planning to return to Edinburgh. Are the children with you?"

Susan looked a question at Gil, but it was not for him to answer. It went without saying he would support whatever story she told, but the story must be hers.

"I had not expected to be here, Hamish, but Amy has gone missing from school, and Rutledge and I have followed her trail as far as Dunbar. We are now trying to find a trace of her here."

So, it was to be the truth. Gil had long since schooled his face to show no reaction, but inwardly he smiled. Of course, she did not send up a smoke screen of excuses, and he had already known she would not lie. His Goddess was true to the core and would scorn to dissemble.

Cunningham lifted his chin and his eyes widened. "Missing? Cousin, I am at your disposal. What can I do to assist?"

Susan eyed him with her head tilted to the side. "Rutledge, Hamish knows Edinburgh far better than I do."

"Then certainly better than I," Gil agreed. "Cunningham, can you suggest a private place where we can tell you the whole story, and make a plan?"

"My chambers are in the next street. Follow me."

Gil appreciated a decisive man and warmed to Cunningham even more when he stopped Susan's self-recriminations for choosing the school in the first place, for delaying in Scotland instead of arriving in Cambridge a few days earlier, and for not being on the road north the moment she found Amy missing. "Before you knew which direction she had gone? You did the right thing, Cousin. And nothing is to be gained by wishing you had been able to predict the future." In the next moment, he lost Gil's sympathy again by adding, "Though I could wish you had left the chase to Lord Rutledge, here, or sent for one of your brothers, or written to me. It is most improper for a lady to travel all this way on such an errand." And with a man not her husband remained unspoken, though the words hung in the room.

Gil ignored Cunningham's pointed look and took up the story

where Susan had left it, explaining their discovery at Doncaster, the post boy's observations at York, and the note left in Newcastle.

"She is a brave, clever lassie," Cunningham observed. "Be easy, Cousin. Whatever this woman's intentions, she hasna hurt our girl, and Amy has a rare head of good sense, if too much spirit for our comfort. And the note sent you to Edinburgh?"

Susan agreed. "They stopped overnight in Dunbar, but this was where they were bound when they left there. We have been to all the coaching inns we can find within the town, however, and none of them recognise the description."

"We shall have to extend our search then." Cunningham had sent for pies and ale so they could eat while telling their story, and now he cleared the leftovers out of his way and began spreading out maps; one that showed the streets within Edinburgh's walls, and others of the surrounding hamlets.

Susan argued the advisability of involving Cunningham's clerks. They would cover more ground more quickly, but how would Amy's reputation be affected? Cunningham dismissed her concerns. "First, from what you say, the young lady has been in the care of this Mademoiselle Cornillac, who may be a French spy and is certainly a kidnapper, but has also made sure that both girls are with her at all times. There is no impropriety there." He put a slight emphasis on the last word, then caught Gil's frown and hurried on, "Second, my clerks know better than to gossip about confidential business. No one works for me unless they are trustworthy."

"It shall be your decision," Gil told Susan, "but extra people to cover the ground would speed our work." He looked at the maps, now marked with dozens of pins. "I had no idea Edinburgh had so many inns.

In the end, they split into three teams, each taking a clerk and heading in a different direction. Cunningham tried to insist that Susan wait at the office or go home to the townhouse, but Susan refused to lose her part in the search. "I shall go mad if I am forced to wait and do nothing, and Rutledge and I have had practice at questioning people."

Gil supported her, and Cunningham reluctantly agreed, sending her off with his oldest and steadiest man, and the office boy for extra protection.

Gil stood for a moment in the street with his own assigned clerk at his elbow, watching the others as they walked to the next crossing and then split, Hamish and his clerk going left and Susan and her two supporters heading straight along the street.

After five days constantly in her company, seeing her walk away left him bereft. He shook his head rapidly to disperse the maudlin mood. He had work to do. "Come along," he told his companion, and set off for the first place on his list.

8

Susan refused to allow her shoulders or her head to droop as she walked briskly towards her son's townhouse. She was tired and discouraged, but that was no reason to be slovenly.

"There he is again, Mrs Cunningham," said the office boy who trailed at her elbow. "I saw him too," the clerk confirmed, "but he has slipped out of sight again."

The man had appeared in the distance several times, always watching them, never approaching, and running away when he thought himself noticed.

There he was again, running from a side street not far ahead of them, casting a frantic glance in her direction and another over his shoulder, then darting across the road in front of a carriage, and diving down an alley. Susan's two companions hesitated. "Go," she urged. "I am twenty yards from my own front door. Try to catch him."

They needed no further encouragement, racing into the alley as Gil appeared from the direction the watcher had first fled. He saw the heels of the office boy disappearing down the alley, and then Susan, standing alone on the footpath.

His own clerk arrived beside him, and then carefully crossed the road between the traffic before starting to run again to chase the others.

Gil strolled towards her as if he had not just been in hot pursuit.

He didn't bother with a greeting. "You saw him? That's the man we missed in Felton; the one who has been after our girls and their spy. Pendragon, if that is, in fact, his name."

"Go after him," Susan urged, but Gil shook his head.

"He has Cunningham's finest on his heels, and I have no intention of abandoning you unescorted on a city street. Cunningham thinks me a barbarian as it is."

Susan huffed. "I would not want you to suffer the displeasure of my cousin Hamish," she said, but he merely smiled and offered his arm.

McMurdo, her—no, Michael's—butler opened the door, his face too well schooled to show any of the curiosity that must be burning him up inside. "Your room has been aired, ma'am," he said, "and a maid assigned from the household, since yours was unable to travel with you."

"Thank you, McMurdo. And a room prepared for Lord Rutledge." It was not a question. She had sent a note from Hamish's chambers when both men insisted she would be more comfortable in the townhouse. Indeed, she was looking forward to sleeping at least one night in a bed of her own, and the only reason for avoiding the place had been to keep Hamish in the dark about her carelessness in mislaying her daughter. Too late to fret about that now.

McMurdo had not answered. Did she detect a trace of concern?

"McMurdo?"

The butler stared at a spot above her head, his voice carefully calm? "Mr Cunningham's orders were to prepare a guest chamber for Lord Rutledge in Mr Cunningham's apartments."

Susan quelled the impulse to countermand the order and assert her authority as mistress of the house. Which would merely promote the very gossip in the household that Hamish was, with an admittedly heavy hand, trying to avoid.

She nodded, instead. "Thank you, McMurdo. And has Mr Cunningham returned?"

"He is in the library, ma'am. With another person."

"There will be three more persons at the door in the next half hour, I have no doubt, perhaps with a fourth. Show them to the library, will you, McMurdo?"

The other two parties had had no more success than Susan and her escorts. Between them, they had visited every coaching inn within the city walls as well as those within an easy ride. They had also visited livery stables in case Mademoiselle Cornillac had chosen to hire riding horses for the next stage to her destination.

The clerks who had chased Pendragon returned to admit he had escaped them. "Disappeared," the older one reported, gloomily.

Susan gave them all a crown in consolation for their disappointment, and they went off amiably arguing; the clerks taking the position that a mere office boy should not be paid at the same rate as an articled clerk, while the office boy held chasing criminals was not covered by the usual rules, and he was as qualified as them to perform such duties.

Dinner was a gloomy meal, the disappearance of the girls and their kidnapper the only topic they could settle to. Had Mademoiselle Cornillac gone somewhere else, or was she hiding in Edinburgh in a private house? They needed to go back to Dunbar, to the last known appearance, and check all the way along the road until they knew the route that Mademoiselle had followed.

Susan didn't linger after the meal. "I shall go early to bed, if you will excuse me, gentlemen. It has been a long week."

Hamish and Gil both murmured their wishes for a pleasant night, and Hamish suggested that he and Gil would retire, also, and take their nightcap in the apartment. The apartment took up one half of an upper floor, closed off from the rest of the house and accessible only by a locked door on that floor or by a door to the street which let onto a narrow stair leading up four flights to a modest front door. Hamish had taken him by way of the street on each of their trips between the house and the apartment, explaining that the internal door was never used.

In a small but efficiently appointed study, he poured Gil a brandy, and invited him to take a seat. "Thank you. I shall have to ask you to excuse me soon, though. As Mrs Cunningham says, it has been a long week."

But the brandy was excellent, and Gil had warmed to Cunningham's company during the day. It was obvious the man genuinely cared about Susan and her children, even if he was an ass about the abilities of women.

"You have known Susan a long time?" the ass asked. So, it was to be an interrogation, was it? Cunningham was a lawyer of course, and a good one, Susan said. But Gil figured he could hold his own.

"Most of my life." He kept his voice mellow and amiable. "I met her when I was twelve."

"An old friend, then. Were you friends with James, her husband, I wonder?"

Gil shrugged. "I knew him to speak to, but I would not say we were friends. I have spent most of the past twenty years on overseas postings, as did Captain Cunningham. We were seldom in England at the same time, and our paths never crossed elsewhere."

Cunningham held up the decanter and poured himself another glass when Gil declined. He didn't sip, though, instead rolling the glass between his hands. "What did you think of him?"

Gil tired of the game. "I thought he did not appreciate the treasure he had married."

Cunningham surprised Gil by agreeing. "You are right. He did not."

"She is one of the finest women of my acquaintance, Cunningham." The very finest. In twenty years without her, he had never found her equal. "She is strong and capable, brave and loyal, clever and loving. And a dedicated and devoted mother."

Shrewd pale eyes met his, and Cunningham gave a wry twist of his mouth that was not quite a smile. "My cousin has told you that I want to challenge her father's guardianship of Michael and raise him myself."

"You would be wrong to try to take the boy from his mother." Gil didn't bother to disguise the hostility in his voice. Let the man know that The Goddess had more champions than her immediate family, though they were formidable enough.

Cunningham played with his glass, twisting it in his hands and holding it up to see the lamplight through it. "If my cousin were married, Lord Rutledge, perhaps to a landowner who could train the boy in the skills he will need, I would not be concerned. But her father is a career army officer who lives in London and whose money is all in investments. I cannot like it."

"Her brother, Renshaw, and her cousin, Chirbury, will gladly fill that role for the boy, Cunningham. I can vouch for their tutelage, having profited from it myself. I was a career officer myself, until my brother died, but they have ensured I know my duties and can carry them out to the benefit of my people and my land." Or at least he would be able to if only he could find a better source of income than the land his brother had run close to ruin.

"That is all very well, my lord, and I do not mean to disparage your friends." Gil saluted the sentiment with his brandy and waited for the disparagement. "It is not the same. Lord Chirbury was a merchant before he inherited from his cousin, and Lord Renshaw an army man like yourself. I am sure they do very well, but they have not been trained from childhood as a landowner should be." Cunningham leaned forward and waved his glass to emphasise his point. "Besides, the lad needs to learn on his own land; to learn his own people."

As he had been doing. As The Goddess would ensure he continued to do. "Has Michael not recently been staying at Dilburton? Mrs Cunningham gave me to understand that she visits regularly so that he is not a stranger to his estate."

"That is true," Cunningham conceded the point with a slow nod. "That is true. My cousin's widow is devoted to her children and means to do her best by them. I cannot deny it and would not wish to. She is a good woman. But she is a woman, Rutledge, you must agree."

"She is, but I don't see how that causes you concern." Stupid duffer. "Indeed, one might suggest that her motherly devotion is an asset in raising the boy to be a worthy holder of his father's estate."

"Ah. But there we are not in accord, Rutledge." Cunningham put his glass down and sat back in his chair, his fingers steepled under his chin. "No woman should have the raising of a boy child, especially one who might have inherited his father's unsteadiness. I have my own family's example to inform me. James was not a bad man, but his father died when he was a mere boy, and his mother raised him. My father did not like to interfere with a grieving widow, but he always regretted that he stepped aside and allowed my aunt the spoiling of the heir. I cannot reconcile it with conscience to do the same, my lord. I cannot do it. Petticoat rule is not good for a boy. Everyone agrees on that."

Had Gil's mother turned Gideon into a monster with her devotion? He had been twenty-two when Gil's father had died, so Gideon had not been without male influence, but from all accounts their father had been a careless rake and a bully who spent little time with his heir until the boy was old enough to partake of the father's less savoury interests.

Other babies had died in the ten-year gap between Gideon and Gil. Was it those repeated losses that left the dowager Lady Rutledge unable to deny Gideon anything he wanted; uninterested in her three younger children?

Gil could not imagine any force, any experience that would sour Susan's love for her children, and her firm commitment to raising them as moral and responsible adults.

"I do not agree," he told Cunningham. "Women are not all the same, just as men are not all the same. Had Michael been raised under the tutelage of his father, I would still place my faith in Susan to counter his influence. As it is, Michael could not be in better hands. She is nothing like her mother-in-law, and has, besides, the advice of her father and four brothers to provide the male influence a boy needs. I think your concerns unfounded, Cunningham."

Cunningham nodded, but more as if agreeing with a thought of his own than with Gil's statement. "You admire her."

Of course he did. "There is much to admire."

Cunningham unfolded himself from the chair. "We will have a busy day tomorrow. Shall we seek our beds, Rutledge?" He picked up the glass and tossed back the remaining thimble full of brandy, then held out his hand to shake Gil's. "Thank you for indulging me with conversation."

"I trust I have given you a different view of the matter," Gil said, with no particular conviction. The man seemed set in his ideas.

They traversed the short hall in silence, but as Gil opened the door to his bed chamber, Cunningham replied. "You give my heart ease. I have no desire to disturb James's provisions or to upset Susan, but I am concerned for the boy. Marriage would be the thing. To a steady man with an estate, if Susan could be brought to consider it. Good night, Rutledge."

Mam'selle and the girls found the doctor's direction easily enough, questioning the landlady, Mrs Geddes, over the oatmeal she served for the breakfast meal in the little dining parlour downstairs. She was happy to talk about the prison camp, which the town regarded with mixed feelings. And when she heard that Mam'selle had a brother in the infirmary, she was all sympathy, though since that took the form of listing the men who had died of the ague, Amy wished she had stayed silent.

They hurried to the doctor's residence immediately, only to find that he had been called out in the night and was not expected home until afternoon.

Mrs Geddes nodded wisely when they returned to her house to decide what to do next. "That will be Molly McInnes. First birth, and her right up in th' hills. Or maybe Jessie McGuiness. She's near her time, too. But no, she drops them like lambs, th' sweet wee ones. She has had four, ye ken. She wouldna even call on th' doctor except her Donald worries."

When Amy asked her about the best people to advise Mam'selle on what the camp was like and how to get into it, she changed her apron and fetched her bonnet and led them forth to introduce them up and down the street.

Though no one could tell Mam'selle how her brother fared, they all assured her that Dr McAllister would help her, and that he was an excellent doctor. "Those poor lads. Not their fault their government an' ours are at war, he says," one of the doctor's admirers said. "They need medical care same as th' next body, he says."

Some of the women they visited were locals; some the wives of guards in the camp. "If I were in France looking for my laddie, I hope some woman there would help me," said one of the later. They were standing on her doorstep when one of the other women with them noticed the vehicle making its way down the hill behind the town. "Is that th' doctor comin' home?"

The gig, if it was the doctor's, was tiny in the distance, and half obscured by the dust kicked up by the horses and the gig's wheels. "Probably is," one of the others agreed. "On that road. Gang wait for him, dearie. He can tell ye how yer brother is. I'll pray that it's good hearing."

So Mam'selle, Amy, and Patrice made their way back to the doctor's residence, warmed by the good wishes of the women. Mrs McAllister declared they were too early but agreed to let them in to wait when Mam'selle explained the gig had been seen coming down the hill.

Sure enough, not ten minutes later, they heard Dr McAllister greet his wife, and it wasn't long before she ushered him into the small neat parlour in which they were waiting. He was a spare-framed man in crumpled clothing, with tired but keen eyes that surveyed the three of them and fixed on Mam'selle.

Mrs McAllister was crisp. "Malcolm, this lady and her charges wish to talk to you about one of the French soldiers. The lady is his sister and has had a letter saying that he is ill. Mademoiselle Cornillac, my husband is fatigued and hungry. You will please refrain from keeping him overlong from his wash and his dinner."

Mam'selle nodded. "Of course, Madame."

"Cornillac. Cornillac." Dr McAllister was gazing at the ceiling rose, as if for inspiration, which clearly arrived because he lowered his gaze and fixed it on Mam'selle. "Yes, I know. Adjutant-Chef Cornillac. He is in the infirmary."

Mam'selle grasped her hands together, clutching them to her chest. "He lives? Armand lives?"

The doctor nodded. "He is still weak, but I believe him to be past the time of highest risk, Mademoiselle." He pursed his lips, considering. "A sight of his sister would be medicine to him, I think. Lisette, is it not? He spoke of you in his fever. Let me write you a note and we will see if I can get you a pass to see him."

"Malcolm, you need to rest," Mrs McAllister protested.

"It will take but a moment, Fiona." He crossed the room and sat down at a small writing desk. "You do not seem to have any of my paper, dear." He complained.

Mrs McAllister cast her eyes upwards and left the room, returning a few moments later with a tray of supplies: quills, ink, paper, and a blotter. "There. Now write your letter and let Mademoiselle Cornillac go on her way."

In five minutes, it was done, and they were hurrying down the street to the prison camp. "I should take you back to Mrs Geddes," Mam'selle fretted. "I cannot think that visiting such a place is what your mother and aunt would like."

"It is getting late, Mam'selle," Amy pointed out. "They are surely more likely to agree to a visit in the day than in the evening."

"That is also what I think," Mam'selle agreed, "and so we must hurry. But you will stay together? And if I am allowed inside you will sit somewhere safe and wait for me to return?"

Amy and Pat agreed, but it was not put to the test. The guard read the note from the doctor, but declared any visitors were against his orders. Amy and Pat stood several yards away where Mam'selle had told them to wait, but they could hear the whole conversation.

Mam'selle protested. "But the doctor…"

The guard, who had not bothered to stand at Mam'selle's approach, continued polishing his gun stock, looking out of the corner of his eyes at Mam'selle, a small smirk playing around the corners of his thin lips. "I have to obey orders, Miss. Keep th' prisoners in and all th' folk else out. That's my job. Can't help ye… Except…"

"Yes? Except?" Mam'selle asked eagerly.

"I could maybe send th' doctor's note to my officer," the guard said, reluctantly, then held up a hand. "I could get into trouble, mind."

"But if you could…" Mam'selle pleaded.

The guard pursed his lips and then smacked them together. "I would do it for a friend," he suggested. "A good friend."

Mam'selle frowned, her brows drawing together over her eyes. "I do not understand."

"I am off duty in an hour. Come back then and be very friendly, and I will see what I can do for ye." He stood and leered suggestively at Amy and Pat. "Bring th' lassies back with ye if ye wish. I wouldna mind a piece of th' body with th' yellow hair."

At that, Amy gave an indignant huff, and marched up to the guard post. "You are an utter disgrace to your uniform, you horrible man. What will your commanding officer say when I tell him you are prepared to take bribes to let people into the camp? Or will he be more angry that you are failing to oblige the doctor? Or making salacious remarks about young gentlewomen?"

He made a threatening move towards her with his rifle. "Now look here, missie. Ye just watch yer mouth. I could lock ye up."

Amy had a much bigger gun than his. "Then you would be obliged to describe your actions to my grandfather, and I recommend against that." Straight to the top, though she still had her uncles in reserve.

Her undoubted upper-class accent was beginning to penetrate the man's thick skull. "And who might yer grandfaither be when he is at home?"

"Brigadier-General Lord Henry Redepenning of His Majesty's Horse Guard," Amy replied, smiling sweetly. "Would you like to reconsider your position?"

"He isna here, though, is he?" The guard was rallying.

"Not right at this moment, no," Amy replied.

"I have me orders." The guard straightened into the first military posture they'd seen from him. "Not a body in wi'out a pass. Not a body out unless they have th' right papers. Get out of here, the lot of you. I don't want to see ye around here again."

Mam'selle protested that she had a pass, and Amy glared, but in the end they had to leave.

By now, Amy was repenting her temper. "I am sorry, Mam'selle. I may have made things worse."

"That *couchon* had no intention of letting me in, Miss Amelia. You did no harm. But how frustrating to be so close to Armand and unable to see him!"

"I expect the doctor will not be happy about what happened," Pat suggested. "Shall we send him a note and ask to try again tomorrow, this time with him?"

The doctor was asleep when they arrived at his house, but his wife allowed them in to write a note and declared herself disgusted at Amy's brief summary of the guard's behaviour.

"He should have sent the note to an officer for a decision. But to make such an improper suggestion to a lady! And in the hearing of two young gentlewomen! I am shocked, young ladies, and I am confident my husband shall have a word in the right ears."

"I do not wish to make trouble, Madame," Mam'selle protested. "Who knows what such a man might do to Armand if he is angry?"

"Hmm. I take your point. I will speak of it to Malcolm, and we shall see what might be done. In the meanwhile, Mademoiselle, you should go home and have something to eat and a good night's sleep. Nothing more will happen before morning."

9

Susan startled awake at the sound of a crash, followed by more crashes and bangs. The sound of a fight? She would swear it was within the house, and not far away. She lit a candle, steadying her hand so it didn't shake in her hurry, and dragged a robe over her night dress. The sound of a shot had her racing to the door. Another crash, definitely just the other side of the wall she faced, the one between the main house and Hamish's apartment.

Candles approached her from the servants' stairs: McMurdo with the housekeeper, Mrs Anderson, behind him, and further up the stairs two of the footmen.

"Mrs Anderson, fetch me the key to Mr Cunningham's apartment. The shot came from his side," Susan commanded, and the housekeeper hurried back up the stairs to her room.

The locked door was a little further down the hall. Before Mrs Anderson could return, it opened, and Hamish put his head out into the hall, blinking a little at the sight of Susan and the three men hurrying towards him.

"Send someone to fetch a doctor, Cousin. Lord Rutledge has been shot."

For a moment, Susan felt a rushing in her head and the world swam, but she took a deep breath. No time for nonsense. "He is not...?"

Hamish looked surprised at the half-question. "A glancing shot. He is not badly hurt, he says." He disappeared back into the apartment, leaving the door open behind him.

He says. So, he is not dead. She gave the order for the doctor and hurried after Hamish.

Gil was sitting on the edge of his bed, being helped into a pair of trousers. Susan hastily averted her eyes and turned her back, but not before seeing a pair of long muscular legs marred on the left by a ropy scar. The man had clearly been naked when he was shot. Did he sleep that way? The brief glimpse she'd had of his masculine equipment was etched into her brain.

"Susan, you should not be here," Hamish fussed.

Susan ignored him. "Where are you hurt, Gil?"

"You can look if you wish; now I have my trousers on." She would also ignore the infernal man's amusement at her embarrassment, especially when he went on to assure her, "It's just a scrape. It knocked me backwards for a moment, or I would have had him."

"Let me look." The wound was clear, even in the candle light and from across the room. The bullet had struck the fleshy part of his upper arm, which seeped a trail of blood down towards Gil's elbow.

Gil stood as she approached, and Hamish stepped in her way.

"We should wait for the doctor, cousin Susan," he insisted. "And it is most inappropriate for you to be in a gentleman's bed chamber."

Susan had no time for such nonsense. "Gil, sit down before you fall down. This is no time to fuss about propriety, Hamish."

She moved her cousin to one side and examined the arm Gil presented for her inspection. "Hmm. Yes. It seems to have missed anything vital, but the bullet is still in the wound and will need to be removed. What happened?"

"I could do with a brandy. And some more clothes," Gil prevaricated.

Hamish clearly sympathised, since he gave the order to the

manservant. "Pass Lord Rutledge his robe, Mendles, and then fetch him some brandy." The manservant obeyed, fetching a brightly coloured banyan from where it lay on a chair.

Susan capitulated, reflecting that Gil's naked chest a few inches from her face was not conducive to focus.

"Oh, very well." She stopped Mendles before he could hurry out of the room. "I'll need a clean cloth to cover the wound before that robe goes over his arm." She turned back to Gil. "My sister-in-law Ella swears keeping wounds clean reduces the risk of infection. It is fortunate you were unclothed when he shot you, Rutledge. No dirty pieces of cloth in the wound."

Gil managed a facsimile of a smile. "My manservant would be offended to hear you imply my clothing is unclean, Susan."

Mendles passed her a pad made from clean handkerchiefs and then several strips of linen to bind it in place, and Susan bent to the work.

"There," she said, after several moments. "That should be comfortable enough until the doctor arrives. Do you feel well enough to tell us what happened?"

Gill shrugged. "Not much to tell. I woke to find someone searching through my satchel. I called out, and he turned a gun on me. He wanted the note from the girls; the one they left at Newcastle. I told him I had thrown it away, but he didn't believe me. He said he'd shoot me if I didn't hand it over."

Susan made her displeasure heard on a huff of air, which Gil correctly interpreted.

"I didn't tell him you had it, Susan, and I'm glad he was the sort of idiot that thinks men can't trust women, because if he'd tried your room first..."

Susan was having none of such typical wrong-headed male gallantry. "I would have given him the note and would be perfectly well. I suppose you tried to assault him, you foolish man. And him with a gun."

"A weedy idiot with a big voice, so frightened that his hand shook." Gil's voice was laden with scorn. "Of course, I lunged for him. I was as like to get shot by mistake, the way he was trembling. But he pulled the trigger and had better aim than I'd calculated."

Susan blinked back tears and could not resist taking Gil's hand. "Foolishness," she told him, her voice soft.

The moment was broken by Mendles, who returned with the brandy. Susan stepped back and allowed Mendles to help Gil settle against his pillows. He looked much as usual. Perhaps a little paler, and with his jaw slightly more rigid. But it was just a minor wound, was it not?

Hamish broke into her thoughts with a question. "So what in the note is so important? I thought you said Amy wrote it?"

"She did," Susan agreed. "Or she and Patrice did. The note was in two hands. I'll fetch it, shall I?" She exchanged a glance with Gil, who nodded and smiled.

In a few moments, she was back with the note, which they spread out on the bed beside Gil so they could all look at it together.

"I can understand him wanting to stop us from receiving this," Susan said. "But I don't see why he should want it back now that we have read it."

Gil turned the sheet over and ran his finger down the marking on the other side.

"What is that all about?" Hamish asked. "It makes no sense."

"I think this might be what he was after," Gil told them. "Susan, they said at Dundas that he was shouting about a book."

She agreed. "A page torn from a poetry book, yes. But, Rutledge, it is just some letters and numbers."

Hamish stabbed the paper with his finger, an excited light in his eyes. "A code! I've heard about such things. A message is coded using substituted letters, hidden in some way in correspondence that sounds innocent. The person who receives it has a key that tells them which letters substitute for which, so they can decode the message."

"There is your list of the letters," Susan acknowledged, "but each letter only has numbers after it."

Gil nodded. "That's the clever part of this coding method. The numbers refer to somewhere in the book. Perhaps a page and then the number of letters through the page. For it to work, the person coding and the person reading need the same book."

"I see." Hamish picked up the copy of *Mountville Castle* Gil had on his bedside table. "So, if it were this book, and I was looking for a letter to substitute for T, I would find page 34. There. And then count 57 letters." He ran his finger along the lines, then looked up triumphantly. "And my letter would be A. T is A."

"Yes," Gil said, "Exactly. Of course, we don't have the book, and we don't know precisely what counting method they use, but that is the idea."

Susan frowned. "So, it is a code? And the book from which this was torn would have been the key?" *Oh Amy, what have you done?*

"I suspect Lord Henry would be very interested." Gil picked up the sheet and waved it. "Susan, do you mind if I send this to your father?"

"You must, Gil." *Father would know what to do.* If such things did not come under the purview of the Horse Guard, he would know who in the Home Office to send it to. "Oh dear. They really are spies, are they not? I have been hoping it was all some kind of silly mistake, though I could not imagine how."

Gil took her hand and enfolded it in his large one. "We will find her, Susan. They haven't hurt her so far, and there's no reason why they would now. I won't rest till you have her safe again."

Susan composed herself. She would do Amy no good by falling apart. Nor should she be leaning into Gil's strength when he was wounded, though she could not deny his words were a comfort. "You will rest right now," she told Gil, tartly. "For if I am not mistaken, here comes the doctor."

Sure enough, he entered from the main house, escorted by McMurdo, and immediately tried to evict Susan from the bed chamber.

"The bullet must be extracted, madam, and I do not have time for vapours."

"Nor senseless argument," Susan retorted, standing firm next to the bed on Gil's uninjured side. "I shall not have vapours, I shall not faint, and I am not going."

Hamish added his protests to the doctor's, but Gil slipped his hand into hers and did not ask her to leave, and that was good enough for Susan.

The doctor gave up the lost cause and demanded water to wash his hands before examining the wound. "Were these rags clean?" He barked.

"Yes," Susan assured him.

He grunted, not taking his eyes from the wound, into which he was probing while Gil turned pale and compressed Susan's hand in his own. "If you saw to that, you may be of some use," he conceded. "The bullet has missed anything vital, but we will have to watch infection."

His examination finished, he laid out the tools he would need on a clean cloth he brought from his bag. "This should not take long," he assured Gil. "Try not to cut off the lady's circulation."

Gil shot a guilty look at Susan and dropped her hand. "I beg your pardon."

"Not at all." In truth, her hand felt bruised, but she was bereft not to be providing that support.

"Here." Hamish handed over a cylindrical wooden column—a candle stick. "Squeeze this."

Gil murmured his thanks, Hamish and Mendles positioned themselves as the doctor instructed them to hold Gil down, and Susan rested her hand over Gil's on the candlestick.

The probing and digging seemed to take forever, until the sweat stood out on Gil's white face and he was unable to suppress the occasional fragment of a groan, hastily smothered. But at last, the piece of lead that had done the mischief clanged into the doctor's bowl, and he set about sprinkling the wound with basilicum powder and replacing the dressing.

He spoke to Susan while he performed that task, explaining how often to change the dressings, and what danger signs to watch for. No one questioned her right to give the necessary care. Because she was a woman? Or because they accepted her role in Gil's life?

She was not going to challenge their assumptions, whatever they were, because she would trust no one else to make sure that Gil healed. She had almost lost him, and her heart still pounded at the mere thought.

By the time the doctor left, the sun was up. "Another day," Gil said, his voice remarkably alert given how weak he looked. "What are our first steps?"

"Your first step is to go to sleep," Susan suggested, but Gil shook his head.

"We need to find where Amy went. I think we must return to Dunbar, Susan, and talk to the post boy, or at least the stable master if the post boy is not there."

That was precisely what Susan intended. "Yes, I agree. We can find out where he took Mademoiselle and the girls, and whether he noticed anything. But you cannot go, Gil. You are to avoid anything that might strain the arm, the doctor said. I will go."

Gil and Hamish both looked alarmed at that, and Gil spoke for both of them. "You cannot go on your own. It is dangerous. And not a good idea anyway, here where you are likely to meet people you might know."

Men could be exceptionally irritating. "I will take a maid." Susan conceded. "You need not be concerned, Rutledge."

"I will go," Hamish offered. "I can leave directly after breaking my fast and be back by noon. Susan, you can stay with Rutledge and make sure he behaves like a proper invalid. Yes, and question those who might come to the house in answer to the enquiries we made yesterday."

In the end, after a lot of discussion, Susan agreed. Before Gil would rest, he insisted on making a list of people to contact, and with Hamish away to Dunbar and Gil finally closing his eyes, Susan sat at the small desk in his bed chamber and wrote a covering letter to her father to go with Pendragon's torn page, another letter to Edinburgh Castle asking for an interview with the Governor and with the officer in charge of the battalion quartered there, one to her brother's friend David Wakefield who was an enquiry agent who occasionally worked for the Home Office, and one to the household at Gorburn House in Dirleton, in case Amy escaped and went home.

With those all on their way, she sat and watched Gil in his restless sleep. In twenty years, she had refused to think of him; had put on an armour of thorns whenever in his presence; had pretended indifference, even dislike. Now all that was swept away, and she could no longer refuse to acknowledge, at least to herself, that he was the man dearest to her in the world. But did he feel the same way? And if not, what on earth was she to do about it?

10

"I am sorry to disoblige, Mademoiselle," Mrs Geddes said, when Mam'selle's Cambridge friend Griffin turned up to visit, "but I canna reconcile it with my conscience to allow gentleman callers."

"A most proper sentiment," said Mr Grffin, with a fulsome bow.

Mam'selle standing in the street in front of the house with Pat, enjoying the morning sun while they watched Mam'selle and Mr Griffin.

"I do not trust him," Amy whispered to Pat, under cover of Mr Griffen instructing his sullen groom to walk the horses to somewhere they could be watered, but to keep them harnessed.

Pat agreed with Amy. "I don't, either. He smiles, but it doesn't reach his eyes."

"What do you think he is up to?" Amy wondered, but this time Mam'selle noticed.

"Young ladies, it is not polite to whisper. If you have something to say, speak loudly enough for us all to hear."

Amy blushed at the reprimand. "I beg your pardon, Mademoiselle, Mr Griffin."

Mr Griffin gave another of his crocodile grins. "Not at all, Miss Cunningham. Young ladies will have their chatter. Now, Mademoiselle Cornillac, shall we repair to the doctor's to see what he has arranged?"

"No need," Pat said. "Here he comes."

Sure enough, Dr McAllister was striding up the street, beaming a welcome. "Mademoiselle Cornillac, I have permission for you to accompany me to the prison infirmary today, and to see your brother."

"What good news," Griffin declared, and the doctor stared at him and waited for an introduction, which an excited Mam'selle rushed through. "I must just get my pelisse and my reticule," she said to the doctor. "You will excuse me, Mr Griffin?" Her gaze fell on Amy and Pat, waiting by the house door, and she said to Dr McAllister, "And the young ladies?"

"The pass is just for you, Mademoiselle."

Mam'selle's brow furrowed. "I will need to make arrangements for the young ladies."

"I will take care of them for you, Mademoiselle Cornillac," Mr Griffin said, before Amy could offer to stay inside under the supervision of Mrs Geddes.

Thankfully, Mam'selle refused, though smiling. "Thank you, Mr Griffin. That is most kind of you. But it would not be proper. They are English young ladies and cannot be left in the care of a gentleman." Especially, Amy thought, one like Mr Griffin. He may have Mam'selle fooled, but not her and Pat. She felt Pat reach for her hand, and she gave a squeeze in return.

"I can assure you, dear Mademoiselle..." Mr Griffin argued, but Mam'selle stood firm. "No. I must one day face Miss Amy's mother and Miss Pat's aunt, and assure them I have cared for the girls' reputation and their safety at all times. It is not that I do not trust you, Monsieur. But I have my duty." She bobbed a curtsey to the doctor. "Dr McAllister, I will be with you in a minute. Mr Griffin, can I ask you, perhaps, to walk a way with us? That would be most kind. Young ladies, up to your room, if you please. I will ask Mrs Geddes to keep an eye on you. Go to her for anything you want while I am away."

Very good. Amy and Pat sent Mam'selle off with their best wishes.

"We hope you find your brother well, Mam'selle," Pat told her. "You need not worry about us. We will just sit here and read until you get back."

But half an hour later, Mrs Geddes knocked on the door to let them know she had received a note and had to go out. "I will just lock yer door, young ladies, an' ye will be safe as houses until I return."

Amy protested. "Mrs Geddes, there is no need to lock us in. We will stay here and wait for you to come back."

"It is for your safety, Miss Amy," Mrs Geddes assured her. "I promised Mademoiselle Cornillac I would look after ye, and I dinna mean to leave th' house open to anyone that passes. I don't even ken how long I might be. But if th' door to the house is locked, an' the door to th' bedroom is locked, nay body will be able to reach ye."

Pat liked the idea no more than Amy. "But what if the house burns down while you are gone?"

Mrs Geddes frowned as she thought about that, then her face cleared. "Then you must climb from th' winda, but I will have yer word that ye willna try that except in dire need."

"We have already given our word to Mam'selle that we will stay here, Mrs Geddes," Amy reminded her. With that the landlady was content. The key turned in the door, and a few minutes later they heard her locking the front door before she bustled off down the street.

Amy returned to the discussion Mrs Geddes had interrupted. "We have to let our relatives know we are unhurt, Pat. They will be beside themselves with worry."

"Not my aunt," Pat argued. "She always said I would come to a bad end. And how can we do it without betraying Mam'selle? They will arrest her. You know they will."

"Grandfather will help her if we explain." At least, Amy hoped so. He was the most indulgent of grandfathers, but he was a general with the Horse Guard, and had all sorts of important meetings with other people from the army, the navy and the government.

Pat knew her well. "You don't know that, Amy Cunningham. I

have an idea. We could ask Mam'selle to send a letter, and then it would be her choice."

Amy nodded. That might work. "And it would count in her favour if she writes her own letter, with one from each of us enclosed so they know we are on her side."

Pat lifted her head, listening. "Is that Mrs Geddes back already?"

Amy concentrated, but couldn't hear anything. "I don't think so." Her denial was interrupted by the unmistakable sound of the squeaky tread on the stair, followed shortly after by scratches and scrapes at the door.

Amy and Pat moved closer together. "I don't think that is Mrs Geddes," Pat whispered.

After a few more metallic clicks and scrapes, the door opened, and Mr Griffin followed a gun into the room, his unpleasant groom at his shoulder, grinning broadly.

"Mam'selle said you shouldn't come in," Pat told Mr Griffin, and he laughed.

"Our pretty little French bird is not here, is she?" The crocodile smile was back, but this time with a glint in his eyes that made Amy shiver. "Now we can do this the pleasant way or the unpleasant way, young ladies. You choose."

Amy would not give him the satisfaction of appearing scared. She lifted her chin and glared at him. "What do you want?"

He glared back. "I want the paper you stole from my book."

"We don't have it. We left it in Newcastle, just as we told you."

Mr Griffin gestured impatiently with the hand that held the gun, making her flinch.

"Amelia, isn't it? Your relatives have got it, and I'm going to trade for it. Whatever happens, remember this is all your doing."

"My relatives?" They had been close enough behind to get to Newcastle before Mr Griffin? Where were they now? "My uncles? Or my grandfather?"

"It doesn't matter. I shot one of them. I'll shoot you, too, if you don't do what you are told."

"Oh, Amy," Patrice hugged Amy's waist. "Do what he says."

Mr Griffin sneered. "Good advice, Amy. Do what I say. Now. Patrice. Sit in the chair."

Patrice reluctantly let go of Amy and sat as instructed, and the villainous groom approached with a coil of rope.

"Make it tight, Finlay," Mr Griffin instructed. "We don't want her getting loose until we're well away."

Amy stamped her foot. "You will not get away with this. My family will find me, and you will be in so much trouble."

Mr Griffin snapped, "I don't need your chatter. Button it."

Amy ignored him. "Pat, do not worry. Mam'selle will be back soon, and she will untie you."

"Yes, Pat, do not worry," Mr Griffin mimicked, then dropped his voice to a growl. "Unless your friend is not able to get my paper back, in which case I will give you much to worry about."

"There." Finlay straightened. "She'll not get free of that without help."

Mr Griffin grabbed Amy by the wrist and started to drag her to the door, but she pulled back, shouting to Pat, "Be brave, Pat. He won't hurt me. He just wants his paper."

At another tug on her wrist, she fell into place behind him, waiting until they were outside to wrench it out of his grip and march along beside him.

He caught her looking wildly around, hoping to see one of the women she had met the day before. "If you say anything, I will just tell them that you have a wild imagination. People will believe me because I am an adult, and you are a child. Then I will take you out into the countryside and beat you. But behave, and I won't hurt you. I'll take you back to your mother and you'll be able to forget all about this."

Amy looked over her shoulder at Finlay, following close behind, and he leered at her. "Just be good, little girl," he advised. Amy shuddered, but with two strong men closing her in and no one she knew within sight, she couldn't see a way to escape. Perhaps later?

11

———

Gil slept fitfully and for no more than an hour, then was fretting to get up. By the middle of the morning, he had argued his stubborn nurturing Goddess to a standstill. The arm hurt, yes, but he was perfectly well when he didn't use it and itching to be out looking for Amy. When Hamish arrived home not long after noon, they were down in the parlour of the main house with maps spread over the table, discussing where to look next.

"Hamish!" Susan said. "Any news?"

"They went to Penicuik," Hamish reported. "The boy said he left them in Musselburgh, and when we asked at the livery stables there, they told us that the French lady hired transport to Penicuik, where the French prisoners-of-war are."

Gil was greeting Moffat, his servant, who had met Hamish in Dundas and come home with him, but that caught his attention. "Prisoners of war? Ah yes. I had heard about the new camp. Is her brother there, I wonder?"

"If there is a brother," Hamish said. "I need to let the Transport Board know. Surely it must be some kind of a plot? Perhaps an escape is planned?"

At last. Something useful to do. "Susan and I will go to Penicuik. It is not far, I believe."

"An hour perhaps?" Hamish guessed. "Are you fit to travel, Rutledge?"

Gil spoke over the protest he was sure Susan was about to make. "I am not fit to sit here doing nothing. You go to the castle, Cunningham. We will report back or will send a message if we have to go further on. Moffat, can you manage another couple of hours travel?"

Susan shook her head but said nothing. In a surprisingly short time a carriage large enough for the three of them had been retrieved from a nearby livery stable and they were on their way, with Moffat driving.

"Do you think we will find them there," Susan asked, and then, before he could reply, "…how silly of me to ask. You know no more than I. It is pretty country, is it not, Rutledge?"

She would call him Rutledge while Moffat was present, Gil supposed. Just as well. Given his feverish memories of their kiss and the gentler but even more compelling pleasures of her nursing, he needed a distance between them. The twinge in his arm as they went over the occasional rut in the otherwise easy roads was a good reminder that she barely liked him, and the liberties she had permitted had undoubtedly been prompted by her fear for her daughter and the intimacies of the journey.

At Penicuik, they enquired after a French woman and two young English ladies, and the second person they asked directed her to the house where the trio had been staying.

The landlady answered the door and paled then flushed when she saw Susan.

"You must be her mammy. Th' eyes. Ye're poor wee Amy's mammy. I am so sorry, ma dearie. It is all my fault." And she burst into tears, burying her face in her apron.

Looking around at the interested crowd who had followed them to the house, Gil gave Moffat the nod to return to the horses. "May we come in, madam?" he asked.

Gil managed to usher the landlady into the house, one worried eye on Susan, who had lost all colour in her face and remained upright only by force of her considerable will. In the parlour, he carefully extracted the story. Mrs Geddes had come home from an errand to find one of the girls left in her charge missing, and the other tied to a chair. "It was that Mr Griffin. I never liked him. I wouldna let him into th' house, but he must have broken in after I went out."

"Griffin? Not Pendragon?" Gil asked, but Mrs Geddes just looked at him, bewildered.

"Then Mademoiselle Cornillac cam back from visitin' her brither, and she was that upset! She said she was to blame, an' she must put it right. She hired a carriage, and she and Miss Pat left together."

Gil noted in passing that there was a brother, which hardly mattered at the moment. "What did Pat say had happened to Amy?" he asked.

"That devil took her. That Mr Griffin." Mrs Geddes suddenly surged out of the chair into which she had subsided and grabbed both of Susan's hands. "You musna be frighted, Mrs Cunningham. He wasna gonna hurt her, Miss Pat said. She told Mademoiselle. He promised nae to hurt her if she just went with him."

The promises of a ruffian who would kidnap children did not comfort Gil, but if Susan's mind was eased he wouldn't say what he was thinking.

"Did they say where they were going?" he asked. But Mrs Geddes had not heard a direction.

They examined the rooms where Mademoiselle and the girls had been staying, finding signs of hasty packing, but otherwise no clues about who had been there, why or where they went.

"Where next?" Susan whispered as they retreated back down the stairs.

"Perhaps other people noticed the direction in which the two parties left. We should ask. I'd also like to know for certain why Mademoiselle Cornillac was here." And whether she and this Mr Griffin were on the same side or had parted ways.

As they left the house, he received the answer to the second of his questions. Once again, Amy's resemblance to her mother was her identification, or so said the man who stopped them. "You must be young Miss Amy's mother. I've just heard she was kidnapped and came to tell you what I know. I am Dr McAllister."

Susan agreed immediately. "She was, Doctor. From Cambridge. We have pursued them all this way. This is my friend, Rutledge."

Gil found himself being examined by calm green eyes. "Lord Rutledge, I take it? I know nothing about Cambridge, but this morning I met the reprobate who carried the young lassie off while Miss Cornillac was out."

"Griffin," Gil agreed. "Or possibly Pendragon, which is the name he used in Dundas. I am assuming we are dealing with the same man."

"Nondescript. Neither tall nor short, fat nor thin. Long face, hair a bit over his shoulders, slight stoop. Accent with a touch of Liverpool, I thought. Perhaps even Irish, but if so he tries not to let it sound."

Gil raised both brows and nodded. "You are an acute observer, sir. Yes. That is the man."

"I should perhaps explain," said McAllister, "that I took Miss Cornillac to see her brother, who is a prisoner here, and in the infirmary recovering from a fever. The girls stayed with Mrs Geddes. I must say, sir, that Miss Cornillac was very concerned to keep the girls and their reputation safe. When I said that the commander here would allow only Miss Cornillac entry, the man I described said he would stay to protect the girls, but Miss Cornillac thought that improper and sent him away."

That seemed clear. Gil asked a couple of questions about what had happened at the house, but after her visit to her brother, the doctor had parted from Miss Cornillac just outside the gates to the prison. He had no answers for them.

"I have just this hour heard about the kidnapping and your arrival, and came straight away."

They were about to start seeking witnesses to the departures when a horse galloped up the street and pulled to a showy stop in front of them. The footman who dismounted saluted Gil with a whip to his hat, and handed him a note.

"*My dear Rutledge*," Gil read:

"*If I may make so bold as to impose upon our acquaintance to address you as such. I have this day received surprising visitors. None other than the missing French music mistress and the young lady, Patrice Grahame. Not, alas, our little Amelia.*

I am sorry to advise that the other party in the affair, a man known to Mlle. Cornillac as Roderick Griffin, has taken Amy and is holding her as a hostage to receiving the paper that we examined this morning. Mlle Cornillac has explained all that she knows, and I am satisfied she is innocent in this matter.

Please return to Edinburgh in all haste to listen to her yourself, and to await the note from the kidnapper.

Your sincere and obedient servant. Hamish Cunningham."

In all haste it was. With a few words of explanation to McAllister, they joined Moffat and the buggy and headed back on the road to Edinburgh.

12

"I could not think what else to do, Madame," Mademoiselle Cornillac said, for perhaps the fifth time. Susan's sympathy was fraying under the strain of the music teacher's repeated refrain. Yes, she could concede, the young woman reasons for her actions. She had no way of sending the girls back, and Susan could understand—if not agree with—her choice to keep going instead of turning back. Yes, she had made her choices under difficult circumstances that the girls themselves had precipitated, but Amy was still missing, and self-recrimination and excuses just wasted time.

"Think, Mademoiselle," she said with what patience she could muster. "Did this Griffin person say anything that might give us a clue about which direction to start looking?"

"Only that his employer had sent him to Edinburgh, as I told you. He is a clerk in a mill. Will that help, do you think?"

"We know they must have been coming back to Edinburgh." Gil leaned forward and began to count points off on his fingers. "He said he would exchange Amy for the page from his book. Edinburgh is where the exchange has to take place. We are here. He thinks the note is here. This is where he will come for it. Whether Edinburgh plays a part in his larger plot, or what that plot is, we can't know at the moment."

Pat spoke up from her position by the hearth, where she was patting Hamish's little terrier. "But you will give him the note, will you not? Getting Amy back is more important than any silly note."

Hamish was quick to reassure her. "Yes, of course, Miss Grahame. Isn't that right, cousin Susan."

Susan pressed her lips between her teeth and worried at them, frowning, and Gil answered for her. "We do not have it, Cunningham. Susan posted it this morning. It is on its way to London, to her father."

Gloom settled on the room and no one spoke for some moments.

Pat was the first to recover. "He will contact you, will he not? We just have to wait for his message. Perhaps whoever brings the message will lead you to Amy. That's what they do in the horrid novels."

Susan looked up, a path suddenly clear in her mind. "We must set watchers who can follow whoever brings the message." Action at last! Waiting was always the hardest.

Gil stood, and waved Cunningham to his side. "Moffat will be one. No one sees him if he wants to remain hidden. And that office boy of yours, Cunningham. We'll need a pair at each end of the block; a third could cover that alley across from the house. And a pair posted to your chambers, in case the message goes there. We need at least another six; people who can be trusted to follow without losing the message bearer, and without being seen."

Susan suggested one of the footmen, and Hamish, his manservant. Both were country born and town bred, and knew how to make use of cover when stalking a prey. Patrice offered to help and was turned down. Moffat, summoned to receive his instructions, nominated the boot boy. "Sharp enough to cut himself, that laddie," he said.

Soon the first two pairs of watchers had taken up station outside, and the office boy was on his way to Hamish's chambers to press the senior clerk into service on Hamish's authority.

"The adjutant they sent down from the castle said to call on them at need," Hamish pointed out. "Should I ask them for a couple of soldiers?"

Gil didn't think so. "Soldiers? They're trained to stand out, not to blend in."

"You and I?" Hamish suggested next, but Gil was concerned that whoever Griffin sent would know their faces. "Though he is likely to send an accomplice," he conceded. "We know from Miss Grahame that he has at least one."

They were interrupted by the sound of yelling and scuffling. McMurdo flung open the door, pushing before him a street urchin, who was complaining vociferously in a Scots accent so impenetrable that Susan couldn't follow a word, though she guessed it was largely obscenities from the distaste on McMurdo's usually impassive face.

The butler shook the boy by the neck of his grubby coat and commanded him to show some respect for the ladies and gentleman.

Gil stood, straightening to his full height and suddenly seemed to fill the room with the force of his will. "Let the lad go, McMurdo. Moffat!" The command to his servant was unnecessary, Moffat having moved swiftly to block the door even as the released boy made a dive for it.

He turned at bay, his teeth bared in his thin face, shifting from foot to foot, his eyes darting around the room before they settled on Gil. "Whit ye doin', mon? Ah hae ye a paper. A come ance errant." His own words calmed him, and he stilled his shifting, puffing out his chest as if in challenge.

Gil didn't take his eyes off the wretch but lifted an eyebrow in a request for a translation, which Susan did her best to supply. "He wants to know what you're doing. He has a paper—a message—for you." The next bit eluded her, but Hamish said, "He came on purpose to give it to you."

Gil held out his hand, but the boy shrank back. "He said ye'd glack me mittens."

"Whoever sent him said you would pay for the message," Susan translated.

"I'll need to see the paper first," Gil told the messenger, who reluctantly drew a folded page from inside his coat and handed it over. Susan crossed to Gil's elbow as he opened it. He held it so they could both read it at the same time.

"Is it from..." Pat began, but stopped when Gil caught her eye and shook his head. Susan took the note from his hand and read it again, then passed it to Hamish. She would take Gil's lead in not saying anything in front of this intruder, but she hoped he evicted the boy soon so they could decide what to do next.

Gil seemed in no hurry, though. He leaned back against the table and frowned at the boy. "What is this about?"

But the boy denied any knowledge; claimed not to be able to read; said he'd just been given it in the street along with a coin to deliver it and the promise that he'd be given more by those at the house. He said he did not know the person who paid him, but when Gil handed him a sixpence for his delivery and held up two more, he suddenly produced a detailed description, which Pat recognised after Hamish translated the more unusual expressions into standard English.

"That sounds like the groom, Lord Rutledge. The one who helped kidnap Amy."

The word 'kidnap' spooked the boy, who began edging to the door as he declared he wanted no part of such a crime.

But Gil stopped him with a raised hand. "Lad, the young lady who is missing is the daughter of this lady and has similar eyes and colouring. She is only sixteen and we fear for her. If you see her or hear of her, come and tell us. There'll be a crown for information that helps us to find her, and a sovereign if the information lets us bring her safely home."

The urchin's eyes gleamed. "A nòy? Yoo're oan. Ah'm your mon."

A few minutes later, McMurdo let him out into the street. From the window above, Susan and Gil watched him wander casually in the direction of Old Town, followed discreetly by Moffat and his partner.

"Do we meet the man?" Hamish asked. "We cannot give him

what he asks." Susan hastily explained to Mademoiselle Cornillac and Pat that the message appointed a meeting place and demanded the note in exchange for Amy's safe return.

"What else can we do?" she asked Hamish, responding to his question.

"Tell the Castle and let them arrest him?" Hamish did not sound as if he thought that a good idea, and Susan's protest was immediate. "We cannot. He said his men would kill Amy if we tell anyone about the meeting!"

"We meet him and we tell no one," Gil decreed. "I don't see what else we can do."

As soon as they were through the city walls, Mr Griffin—*no, I will not dignify him with the honorific*—that louse Griffin covered Amy's head with a cloth bag. She struggled, but stilled when Finlay came to his master's aid, grabbing her hands and holding them ruthlessly behind her back while rubbing his horrid body against her.

"This is for your own good, girl," Griffin told her, as he tied the bag around her neck. "Best you can't tell other people what you've seen."

She would listen then, she decided. She had hearing, touch, and smell to guide her, and she'd continue to use them to collect clues she could give her mother when she saw her. She already knew what they were after from listening to Griffin and Finlay arguing on the way from Penicuik. Finlay blamed Griffin for giving what he called the code book to his French piece, and Griffin said it was just as well he had. He'd received word his rooms were to be searched, and he had passed the book to the little teacher just in time. And how was he to know the stupid woman would take off out of Cambridge before he could retrieve it?

Amy also learned her mother was in Edinburgh; and had pursued her from Cambridge with a male relative, whom Griffin had shot that morning. Hamish? No, because Hamish did not fit the description "nasty big gombeen", whatever a gombeen was. Hamish was tall but slender. One of her uncles? She hoped not. She hoped Griffin had missed, though if he'd failed to shoot one of her uncles, she couldn't imagine them allowing him to escape.

She asked no questions, just stretched her remaining senses to catalogue the sounds of Edinburgh changing around her as they moved into narrower streets where more and more people spoke the Leith accent, some of them swearing at the gig as it scraped by.

After several minutes, Finlay stopped the horses, and Griffin told Amy to get down, tugging her hands and lifting her from the seat onto cobblestones. Finlay, recognisable by his onion-laden breath, put an arm around her shoulders and shoved her in the direction of Griffin's retreating footfalls. Down a couple of steps and through a doorway, into an indoor space redolent with the smells of stale alcohol and rancid bodies. Somewhere beyond a wall, voices were engaged in conversation and laughter. Finlay let Amy go. "I'll just fetch us a brew and send ye th' landlord." He left what she thought must be quite a small room. She could hear a burst of louder noise as he opened a door and closed it behind him. She stood still, trying to find another clue, and a moment later the door opened and shut once more.

"Here," a new voice demanded. "What's goin' on, Phoenix? What are ye bringin' quality heer for? You'll have the Castle doon on us."

Griffin gave no quarter. "I need a safe place to stow her for a few hours. I'm giving her back to her people in exchange for something of mine. Don't fret, Will. She doesn't know where she is and she can't lead anyone here."

Will grumbled some more, but half-heartedly, and in the end said, "Here's th' key to th' cellar. Ye ken where t'is. I hope ye ken what you're doin', Phoenix."

Griffin yanked her hand, dragged her stumbling down some uneven stairs and left her at the bottom. The loss of his rough hand left her unmoored in the dark. She could hear the key shifting pieces of a lock, door hinges groaning. Then he was back to seize her arm and push her ahead of him. She preferred his rough indifference to Finlay's lascivious touches.

Even when he pulled her back against his body to untie the band around her neck, she didn't sense the same disgusting physical interest that the other man displayed.

But when Griffin pulled off the bag, she found Finlay had followed them down, and was leaning against the doorway balancing a tray with bread and cheese in one hand and holding two tankards in the other.

The room was small and mostly bare, but for a litter of broken furniture in one corner and some straw that might once have been a pallet in another. No windows. No exit besides the door that Finlay blocked.

"Did you think to offer her food and drink?" Griffin asked. "Here, let me do it."

Offered was the wrong word. He taunted her with them, insisting that she beg, and mocking her when she refused.

"She'll be properly grateful for something by the time we get back, Finlay, won't she?" he said to the horrible man, who stopped laughing at his companion's antics for long enough to leer at her. "I could think of several ways th' wee whore could make it worth our while to feed her."

Griffin slid a cold gaze from her toes to the tip of her hair and back again, and his lip curled. "You'd have to kill her after. Her family would turn this place inside out and flay you alive."

"Proper folks, are they?" Finlay reached out a hand to stroke Amy's cheek and she turned away, eyes narrowed. She held herself rigid, refusing to let her revulsion and fear rule her reactions.

Griffin struck the man's hand down. "Generals and lords and such. Fit only to manure the land with their blood, and so they will when the revolution comes. In the meantime, leave the girl alone. I need her for the exchange. Maybe later."

"Just a taste," Finlay suggested. "I havena ever had a lady-born."

"After the revolution, they'll be selling themselves in the street, same as any whore. We have more important things to do."

Finlay reluctantly backed out of the cellar, taking one of the candles, and Griffin took another. "You have one candle, lady-born. Make it last, because I won't be back for some time."

She wanted to say something defiant, but her throat was so tight she could only croak, and he laughed as he left, shutting the huge heavy door behind him.

Amy lifted her hand from where she had hidden it in her skirt, keen to examine the papers she had stolen from Griffin's pocket. Letters—from what she could see, quite innocuous. But she'd heard too many stories of codes to believe it, and perhaps these would help stop whatever Mr Griffin had in mind. "Next month," he had told Finlay, more than once.

She smirked, just a little. Picking pockets was clearly not a skill the villain expected from a lady-born. The game had been inspired by stories from her not-quite-uncle David Wakefield, the items she carefully lifted returned to the household members from whom she had purloined them. This time, it was in earnest. Perhaps in these letters she had a clue to what the man was waiting for.

By the time she had searched every bit of the room except the pile of straw, which she feared might contain rats or even spiders, Amy was beginning to wish she had not refused the bread and cheese. And she should certainly have accepted something to drink. She could feel the beginnings of a headache as she was parched from the inside out.

The candle was a quarter shorter than when she started. She should blow it out to save it, but she had no way of lighting it again, and the rustling in the straw reinforced her antipathy to being alone in the dark.

She could not afford to stand here frozen. She had to move the straw, rustling or not. If there was a way out other than the door, that was the only place it could be. *Amelia Cunningham, do you want to wait until that horrid man comes back?*

The thought galvanised her into action. From the tangle of broken furniture, she picked out the ladder-back of a chair and a long broom handle—tools to move the straw, and weapons to protect herself, if she could find no way out.

But she was hopeful. If she was right about her general location, under this tavern cellar would be another cellar or even another house. Perhaps even a whole street. Parts of Old Town Edinburgh had been built upon the town of the past, each new incarnation rising over the still living bones of earlier dwellings, where whole communities continued to live and do business deep beneath the bustling upper world.

And the rats must come from somewhere.

Testing her theory, she bashed at the straw with her makeshift tools, flinching away when a particularly panicked rodent scrambled straight for her. But it got itself turned around and burrowed back into the straw, disappearing in seconds.

The straw was still and silent. Tentatively, carefully, she pulled chunks of straw from the pile, growing bolder as no ratty inhabitants appeared to dispute ownership with her. It took several minutes to spread the heap far enough to uncover the trapdoor that lay beneath, one corner rotted away. That's where the rats were getting in. That's where she needed to go.

13

Moffat had lost the urchin within twenty minutes, he explained sheepishly. The boy had been cheeky enough to flip Moffat and the footman a salute before dropping into the vaults under South Bridge, one of Edinburgh's underground warrens. In the dark, surrounded by the denizens of those deeps, Moffat and the footman had no chance of finding out which way their quarry had gone.

Moffat arrived back in time to skulk along behind Hamish and Gil who were going to the meeting with the kidnapper, leaving Susan to keep watch over Pat and Mademoiselle Cornillac.

The long summer day was drawing to a close when the men left, and the women settled in the drawing room to wait for news.

Mademoiselle suggested that Pat should be in bed, but Pat protested. "I could not bear it, Mrs Cunningham. I need to be here when they come back. I won't sleep until I know, and it would be horrid to be awake and on my own."

Since Susan felt the same way, she couldn't argue. She ordered a tea trolley, and made a valiant attempt at conversation, but her mind was out in the city with Gil and her daughter, and the other two were just as preoccupied.

"Perhaps Miss Grahame would play for us," Mademoiselle suggested.

"I haven't practiced for a week," Pat protested, but settled on her knees beside the piano stool to look through the music stored there.

With Pat preoccupied, Mademoiselle Cornillac took Susan by the arm and led her to the furthest side of the room. "I am so sorry, Mrs Cunningham. This is all my fault."

Susan sighed. This guilt was becoming tedious, but Susan had to admit that it seemed sincere. "You are not the first to be taken in by a villain, Mlle Cornillac."

Mademoiselle would not be absolved. "If I had not trusted that man; if I had taken the girls into my confidence…"

Two could play at the self-blame game. "If I had never sent Amy away to school. If I had left earlier and arrived in Cambridge on Friday, as had been my intention. We could go on finding reasons to blame ourselves or one another for hours." Susan shrugged. "But to what purpose? I trust Lord Rutledge and Mr Cunningham to bring Amy home. And then she and Patrice will need to explain what on earth they thought they were about. I am sorry, Mlle Cornillac. I fear that this fantasy of my daughter's has cost you your position."

It was Mademoiselle Cornillac's turn to raise her shoulders and let them drop in an entirely Gallic gesture of negation. "It is of no moment. Until Armand is well again, I must stay, and perhaps I might take a position here in Scotland so I can at least see him from a distance, from time to time. He is all I have, Mrs Cunningham." She smiled as she thought about her brother, but the smile quickly faded. "Though who will employ me to teach their children when I have been dismissed without a character, I do not know."

Susan could at least help with that. "Let me see what I can do. Much of this was not your fault, Mademoiselle Cornillac. You lied about how far you were travelling, but otherwise were truthful. Once you knew the girls were following, you had a dilemma."

Mademoiselle agreed. "I could not desert them. Two gently-born maidens on the Great North Road? I shudder at the thought."

And she did, very prettily Susan noted. "I should, I know, have turned back. But Armand… The letter said he was dying, Mrs Cunningham."

"Yes, I understand. I, too, have brothers. I will speak with Mrs Fellowes and explain that the girls' escapade was not your idea, and that you have gone to some lengths to protect them. She will still, I think, demand your resignation. She was most indignant about your friendship with Mr Griffin. But if we can persuade her to write you a reference, all will yet be well."

"You would do that for me? I am grateful, Madame. More grateful than I can say."

Pat began to pick out the melody of the music she had selected, and Mademoiselle went to sit beside her, and correct her technique. Soon, the pair of them were playing a duet, and Susan was left to sit by the window, watching for Gil's return, hoping he would bring Amy with him.

The appointed place for the meeting was in the vaults under South Bridge, at a little tavern called The Thistle. Moffat had been shadowing Gil and Cunningham, but when they hesitated at the doorway, he slipped past them without acknowledging an acquaintance, pushed aside the rug that hung in the doorway, ducked his head to miss the door jamb, and disappeared into the smelly gloom of the interior.

When Gil led the way in a few minutes later, and cast a glance around the room, Moffat had already been served with a tankard of something, which he was nursing at a corner table, his eyes hooded as if half asleep. Gil was not fooled. The man would miss nothing.

In his scruffiest clothes, Moffat faded into the general ambience, set apart only by his lack of the Edinburgh accent that dominated the room. He was saying nothing and had become near invisible.

Not so Gil and Cunningham. Cunningham probably didn't have a single garment in his wardrobe that wasn't neat, clean, and far too well-tailored for this hovel. Gil could have pulled out the bundle of what his henchman called 'the colonel's adventuring clothes', which he'd ordered packed at the last minute.

But if Cunningham was going to look as he was, a prosperous lawyer out of place in a seedy dive, then Gil might as well match him. Tidy and prosperous it was.

Cunningham was looking around too, and moving uneasily in response to the hostile stares of some of the denizens. One man spat, missing Gil's boot by inches. Gil used the military trick of straightening his back and setting his shoulders to widen his stance, his elbows bent at the ready and his feet placed wide enough apart to give him stability. Gil's friend Rede called it the rutting stag move, and Gil had to acknowledge the analogy.

The best stags seldom fought, using intimidation to chase off their rivals. The trick with his stance made him appear not only larger but more aggressive. Given he was already bigger than most, it usually made the opposition think again, as in this case, where the little weed avoided his eyes and turned away to hunch over his drink, muttering to his friends. Gil was gratified when the friends looked at Gil and then shifted a slight distance to separate themselves from the spitter.

Cunningham ignored the whole interaction. "Is he here, Rutledge?"

Not that Gil had seen. "He could be several of these men, or none. Remember I saw him up close only by candle-light. He will approach me, the note said, so let's sit where he said, and wait."

Cunningham nodded. "Over there."

The table had been well chosen—in a shadowed corner, some distance from the fire, which in any case was not lit on this mild summer evening. More important, it was set apart from the crowded part of the room. The serving girls didn't have to pass it on the way to other clients. Furthermore, there was a gap between the table to which they had been directed, and the couple of tables that divided this corner off from the main crowd.

A group of students sat eating, drinking, and arguing about an exam they had sat that day, the punishment a friend had suffered for his part in the New Year riots, a girl two of them were courting, and the likelihood of crop failure if the weather did not soon improve.

"Drinks?" The bar maid said, with no light quip or welcoming smile, but ready enough to take their money."

"Ale." Gil put a couple of coins on the table and she scooped them up and hurried away. He returned to his eavesdropping to pass the time. The students had moved on to discussion of a woman of easy virtue, who had supplied her services to several of them but showed a marked predilection for one of their number. Her preference won him a discount with the light-heeled lady, her avowals of affection, and the teasing of his friends.

Gil hid a smile at the boy's protestations, feeling some respect for the way he refused to denigrate the woman. "She has been kind to me," he told his tormenters.

The barmaid dumped a tankard in front of him, and another before Cunningham. Gil ignored the manner of delivery and thanked her, which featured him a sharp look and a reluctant half smile.

"Ye be out of place here, English," she told him, not unkindly.

Gil shrugged. He had been in a hundred worse drinking holes in a dozen countries, which was not the point. "We have been directed here to meet someone. A man who is holding my niece captive."

The woman's eyes startled wider, and she shook her head in quick negation. "No business o' mine. I dinna hold with such."

"I did not think for a minute that you would," Gil reassured her. "We will just sit here and drink our ale and wait for him to come in. But perhaps you know him?" He repeated the names Griffin and Pendragon, and described the man as best he could, but without much hope the villain had chosen a tavern where he would be known. Sure enough, the maid shook her head, but with compassion in her eyes.

"How old be the maidie?" she asked.

"Just sixteen, and a fair bonnie lass," Cunningham offered, entering the conversation for the first time. "He chose well, for we would do anything to win her safely home."

The woman shook her head again, in sorrow this time. "I dinna hold with such," she repeated. "No more does my man. Sit and drink yer ale, m'lords, and I'll make sure none bother ye."

The ale was better than expected for such a rundown place. Gil and Cunningham sat in silence, nursing their tankards and sipping from time to time. Since entering the tavern, Gil had felt a prickling at the back of his neck. Imminent physical danger. The warning had stood him in good stead since he was a small child avoiding his older brother, and had seen him and his men safe out of more than one tricky situation around the globe.

No difficulty interpreting the origins this time; their presence was more than resented. Slowly, though, the other patrons returned to their own affairs and forgot about the two strangers, and Gil's prickling subsided. He was almost relaxed, half way through his ale, and thinking about his Goddess, when the door curtain shifted again and Griffin ducked his head to step into the room.

Their eyes met across the heads of the other patrons, and Griffin was starting towards Gil and Cunningham, weaving between the chairs and tables, when another man pushed into the room and grabbed his arm, whispering urgently into Griffin's ear.

Something was wrong. The hair on Gil's neck was at full alert, and he rose, the need to hurl himself across the room at Griffin surging through him.

Griffin had turned to his accoster and was arguing with him. Cunningham started to get up. "What is it, what is happening?"

"Something's wrong." Gil stepped over the bench he'd been occupying and began to round the end of the table. Griffin looked over his companion's shoulder, saw Gil coming, and turned to flee.

After that, the sequence of events became confused. Someone stepped into Gil's way, and someone else flung out a foot to trip him. He barged his way through, using his height, weight, and fighting skills to remove those who tried to stop him, heedless of anything but the need to catch Griffin before he escaped.

But when he found himself out in the street, Cunningham in a groaning heap beside him, Griffin was nowhere to be seen.

Amy kept close to the walls of the houses, making her way down the underground street, trying to remain inconspicuous, helped by the plentiful shadows. It could have been high noon or midnight.

Was it just this morning she had been abducted from Penicuik? The only light came from lanterns hung on house walls, or carried by the people hurrying on their mysterious ways or standing talking in doorways or on corners of the narrow street.

She had heard of the other world beneath Edinburgh—streets buried when newer building used them as a foundation. It was both stranger and more ordinary than she expected.

On both sides, the houses rose until they touched the under structure of the buildings overhead. Behind her, the road sloped upwards until the far vaulted ceiling was almost within touching distance. That had been her preferred direction, but she had turned and fled the other way when a trio of young men had spread across the road and demanded a kiss for toll before they would let her pass.

Sounds echoed, but were also somehow muffled, as if the rock decided what to absorb and what to bounce so wildly it was impossible to tell whether this burst of sudden laughter or that angry shout came from behind her or to the side.

A woman with a matronly figure and a broad smile beckoned to Amy, who hesitated and then crossed the street to stand before her. "Please, ma'am, can you give me directions to the surface?"

The answer was pleasant enough. "Aye, and that I can, lassie. I'll take ye there, besides. But first, just ye step inside while I get me bonnet."

But something in the woman's leer, and the gleam in her eyes, made Amy wary. She backed off a couple of steps. "I will just wait here, ma'am, I thank you."

The woman lunged forward, grabbing for Amy's arm, and shouting for someone called Callum to come and help her catch a ripe one, but Amy evaded the grab and took off down the street again, dodging between people until she felt far enough ahead to look behind her.

Over the shoulders and between the heads of the people who screened her from view, she could see the matronly woman, chivvying two burly men before her. Their battle-worn faces and sour scowls made Amy shudder, and dive into a tiny alley between two buildings.

It was narrow and smelly, and the houses to either side seemed to lean together over the top, but it was blessedly dark, and crowded with boxes and lumber and other rubbish she could hide behind until the woman and her bullies gave up.

She found a spot behind some haphazardly stacked boxes with chinks and gaps between them that gave her a view into the better-lit street. She adjusted an old shawl or blanket that had been thrown on the heap, shifting folds until she had a good view but was concealed in the shadows behind the debris.

Now that she was out of the noise of the street, she could hear scuffling and squeaking in the clutter around her, and she struggled to slow her breathing so it didn't give her away. She stifled a yelp when something shifted not inches from her hand, then scurried out of the heap of boxes and escaped further back into the tunnel behind her. She hoped it was a cat, but she feared it was a rat.

The two men passed the mouth of the alley, the woman waddling behind them, then stopping to berate someone who had obviously objected to her passage.

Amy held her breath and waited, but needed to take another breath and another before the woman moved on.

Still Amy waited. Above her, the buildings seemed to slump even closer, the whole weight of Edinburgh pressing down into the darkness. If Amy could only get safely home to Mama, she would never go adventuring again.

14

───────

The officer sent from the castle was a pompous idiot. "Mademoiselle Cornillac is not a suspect in my daughter's kidnapping, nor is she a spy for the French," Susan told him, for perhaps the fifth time. "I understand you must question her, but she is under my protection and you will not do so except in my presence."

She was walking a fine line, wielding an air of authority while not treading on his tender male dignity. So far, it had worked, the captain being unwilling to offend someone with her connections: daughter of a general, related to a dozen peers, and prominent in both Edinburgh and London Society.

"I will answer any question you have for me, Captain Bowen." Mademoiselle sat composed, the picture of dainty femininity, her embroidery frame in one hand and a needle in the other. From beside her, Pat glared at the captain, though Susan could not give odds on whether she was more affronted by his assertion that Mademoiselle was a criminal or by his patronising dismissal of Pat's evidence to the contrary as schoolgirl storytelling.

Captain Bowen shifted uncomfortably, making the dainty china cup she had given him rattle in the saucer, and he moved a large hand to still it. The delicate tea service had been a master stroke in Susan's efforts to turn what he intended as an inquisition into almost a social visit. Susan gestured to the maid on duty at the tea trolley. "Another sandwich, Captain?"

The captain refused the diversion. "I must insist that Mademoiselle Cornillac accompany me to the castle."

"I must insist she does not. I cannot leave this house until my cousin and Lord Rutledge return with my daughter, and I will not permit her to go without me."

They were at a stalemate. He had the power to simply arrest the poor girl but was reluctant to use it. And Susan had no power at all except her own personality and her willingness to trade on her connections.

Sounds of an arrival in the front hall had her rising to her feet, bringing the captain politely to his.

"You will excuse me?" Susan asked. "That may be them." Surely it must, this late in the day. Who else would be calling? But wouldn't her daughter have come straight to her?

Her heart lodged in her throat, Susan opened the door, but the man talking to Munro was a stranger—a neatly-dressed gentleman she had never before met.

He and the butler turned at her arrival, and the stranger bowed.

"Ma'am, this gentleman is Mr Simeon Grahame, a relative of Miss Patrice. I was just explaining that you are not currently home to visitors."

Susan needed a moment to control her disappointment and paste on a pleasant smile, and in that time Mr Grahame advanced towards her, managing to bow and smile, while still maintaining a grave air of concern.

"Mrs Cunningham. I apologise for bursting in on you like this, but I received your note saying you had my niece staying with you. Following, as it did, a letter from the child's aunt making some disquieting claims—well, I could not wait until tomorrow to find out what has happened, and how little Patrice fares."

"You shall see for yourself," Susan told him, gesturing for him to follow her into the drawing room. Another distraction for the captain. Also, perhaps, the solution for Pat that Susan hoped for when she sent to Mr Grahame to let him know Pat was with her and safe.

Susan performed the introductions, presenting Mr Grahame to Mademoiselle Cornillac, Mr Grahame and Captain Bowen to one another.

"And your niece, of course, you know." Grahame had been darting glances at Pat while making his courtesies to the adults, and at this he advanced on her with both hands out.

Pat, standing, backed against the sofa. She stopped nervously pleating her skirt with one hand and bobbed a hasty curtsy.

Grahame won Susan's cautious approval by noticing the girl's reaction and putting both hands behind his back, stopping more than an arm's length from where she stood. "But my dear Patrice, I would have walked past you in the street without remark. You were —what? Eight years old when your father brought you to see me? Do you remember? And here you are a young lady! And with your father's eyes. Yes. I see the resemblance now. Your mother's colouring, I think?"

He paused for Pat's nod but was interrupted by Captain Bowen.

"Mrs Cunningham, I do not wish to be impolite, but I have my duty, and I do not have time for family reunions."

Susan's sharp ears caught another looming interruption, and this time, surely, it would be Gil and Hamish with Amy, for the front door opened before she heard Munro's tread in the hall, and the butler's greetings were both respectful and familiar.

Sure enough, Gil stepped into the drawing room a moment later, but alone. No Hamish. No Amy. And when his eyes fixed on Susan's from across the room, his were grave.

"You look tired, Rutledge. Come in and let me fix you a drink." Panic threatened. Where was Amy? And why did Gil look so white and so unhappy? She wouldn't ask in front of Captain Bowen but looking after Gil would help keep the void at bay.

As she opened the decanter and poured a couple of fingers of brandy into a glass, she said, "Rutledge, we are visited this evening by Captain Bowen, who is aide to Major Rose at the Castle, and Mr Grahame, Patrice's uncle."

"Gentlemen." Gil bowed slightly in acknowledgement, before lowering himself wearily into a chair, and accepting the glass she brought him. Close up and in the light, she could see the signs of rough treatment: bruises that had not been on his chin before, a button missing from his coat, a slight swelling around the eye.

"Is Hamish with you?" she asked.

Gil nodded. "He has gone upstairs to his rooms to change. He—er—his coat got torn, and wet, when he fell into a… puddle."

The captain waved off this irrelevancy. "I am here to take this wo—" Captain Bowen caught Susan's eye and changed what he had been going to say. "…this lady to the castle to answer questions about her relationship with the French prisoners and her intentions while she is in the vicinity."

Gil addressed the officer, his voice firm. "Captain Bowen, I had intended to repair to the castle myself, to seek help searching the Old Town near the Tron. I'm sorry, Mrs Cunningham. Griffin showed for the meeting, but something went wrong. A man spoke to him and he ran. By the time we got through the crowd who tried to hamper our leaving, he was nowhere in sight, and not one person—man, woman, or child—knew which direction."

Susan sank onto the chair opposite Gil's, suddenly boneless. "Amy?"

He shook his head. "He did not have her with him. I'm sorry."

Patrice slipped past her uncle and dropped to the floor next to Susan's chair, taking Susan's hand. "Do not worry, Mrs Cunning-ham. Amy is smart and brave. I am sure she is unharmed and will back with us soon."

Susan had no such confidence, but Pat's words were enough to stiffen her faltering resolve. She gave Patrice's hand a firm press. "Thank you, dear. We shall hope, shall we?"

Mr Grahame shifted restlessly from one foot to another. "I have come at a bad time, but it seems the letter I received from Miss Fellowes was not entirely hysterical imaginings. I could not believe it: French spies, and the two girls running away from school, and my brother's little girl dressing as a boy. I will not ask for the whole story now, when your need is so much more urgent, Mrs Cunningham, but please let me put myself and my resources at your service. How might I help?"

Gil answered. "As soon as Hamish is changed, we mean to go back. Do you know the Tron area? Because we need a local who will support us. I have men out asking questions—someone must have seen the villain—but they won't talk to us."

Grahame thinned his lips. "They would not, no. It is a rough area, and decent people who lodge there would not want to attract attention by talking to a stranger. I might be able—I employ people from that part of Edinburgh. I will see what I can find out. Time is of the essence, of course, so I shall call on my foreman now, if you will excuse me, Mrs Cunningham. Patrice, my dear, I look forward to hearing all about your adventures."

The next few minutes were spent convincing Captain Bowen to leave Mademoiselle Cornillac in Susan's custody until the morning, and to return to the castle to enquire after soldiers who knew that part of town. After he left, Susan sent Pat off to bed.

"But Mrs Cunningham, I could not sleep while Amy is still missing," Pat complained.

Susan was firm. "You shall go to bed, nevertheless, Pat. You may take a lamp and read, if you wish. Mademoiselle, would you go up with Pat and supervise to make sure all is safe?"

Mademoiselle murmured an agreement. Pat looked ready to argue, but caught a raised eyebrow and subsided, allowing Mademoiselle to usher her out of the room.

With only Gil in the room, Susan's assumption of calm drained out of her like whey through a sieve, and she sank into the nearest chair, fighting back the fear that wanted to erupt in wrenching sobs. Gil dropped on his knees before her and took her face in his hands. "Tears, Susan?" He wiped them away with gentle sweeps of his thumbs, then cupped her head and pulled it to rest on his shoulder, patting her back with his other hand.

"Weep away, my dear. But do not despair. We will get her back."

For a moment, she let her head relax, taking comfort in his

strength and his gentleness. "My little baby, Gil. Lost in that dreadful place. It is all my fault."

"No, no. We will find her, Susan. We've put out word of a reward, and of retribution if she is harmed in any way."

"If only I'd arrived earlier in Cambridge! I dallied for a bonnet. Can you believe it? My darling child is lost because I did not want to leave Gorburn without my new bonnet." And half-a-dozen household matters, and an unsatisfactory meeting with Michael's factor who shared Hamish's opinion about women interfering in the running of the estate, and other trivial things that seemed important at the time.

"You left her where you had every right to think she was safe." Gil drew his head back so that he could look into her eyes. "In battle, we make the choices we can with the information we have, Goddess. And we never know enough. We never can. Don't blame yourself for not being God."

Susan managed a chuckle, though it sounded dismal even to her. "I do not even lay claim to being a Goddess," she reminded him.

Sounds of another arrival had Gil releasing her and rising to his feet. He was on the other side of the room by the time the door opened, to disclose Moffat and the urchin who had brought the message the day before.

"Moffat," Gill exclaimed. "What news?"

"Young lad here can lead us to where that villain was staying, m'lord."

Cunningham—washed, bandaged, and in clean clothes—arrived in time to hear Moffat's brief tale, summarised so they could leave with all haste. "I followed that Griffin when he left the tavern. I thought I'd lost him in a cellar under the Exchange, but then Lowper here found me, told me where the bast… the man is roosting. Lowper's left someone to watch Griffin, and we came straight here to get you, m'lord."

Gil nodded. "You've won your reward, boy. And if we find our young lady safe and sound, you'll have double."

"Best hurry, then, laird," Lowper told him.

"You, me, and Moffat," Gil asked Cunningham, who nodded his agreement and called for his hat.

Gil stopped on the way to fetch his. Susan, faced with other eyes than his, had donned her calm composure, but he had been privileged to see what a facade it was. He took both of her hands in his own.

"We will find her, Susan."

She clung to his hands, her own trembling with her urgency. "I want to come, Gil."

The thought of Susan in that sewer made him shudder. "You have made a promise to the captain to keep watch on Mademoiselle, and what if Amy finds her own way home? I know it will be hard for you to wait here, but you will be working as much as I."

"And you fear my presence will be a distraction to you and the others. Very well, Gil. But you do not know what you are asking of me." She withdrew her hands and returned to her seat, picking up her embroidery. "Go with God and bring yourself and my daughter home safe," she instructed him, before hiding her eyes by turning them down to her needlework, her lips pressed tightly together.

Gil hesitated in the doorway, desperate to comfort her.

Cunningham recalled him to his duty, saying impatiently, "Rutledge? We must go."

With the addition of Munro and two of the Cunningham footmen, they made a band of seven, six of them strong sturdy men. Gil hoped Amy's freedom could be bought for gold, but six should be enough to wrest her from her abductors if the locals stayed out of any fight. Munro thought they'd be reluctant to become involved if Gil made it clear he was returning the child to her mother.

It was a fifteen-minute walk, and on the way Lowper and Moffat filled in the detail in the story they had told. Griffin was staying in a drinking hole so low it had no name, on a narrow alley in the heart of the stews. He'd arrived with a Leith man who vouched for him, or a foreigner like Griffin would not have been accepted. To the people of the slums of the Old Town, anyone not from their streets was a foreigner, and an Irishman like Griffin might as well have come from the other side of the moon.

"Irish," Gil asked? "What makes you think he is Irish?"

Lowper's superior sniff was positively ducal. "That's whit 'e tauld th' landlord, didn't 'e. Landlord said 'e didn't hauld wi' th' English, an' Phoenix tauld heem 'e was Irish."

"Here!" Moffat complained. "Who's this Phoenix. We're after a Griffin."

"Our quarry was Pendragon at Dundas," Gil reminded him. "He has a penchant for mythical beasts. A habit of using their names, young Lowper."

They wound further into the tangle of narrow lanes, each less well-lit than the one before. Despite the gloom, the residents were out and about on their business, the shadows buzzing with activity and conversation that stilled when their group drew near and began more furiously than ever when they had passed.

"T'is here," Lowper told them as they approached a building indistinguishable from any of the others. Another boy, this one even younger, lifted himself from the wall he had been draped against and loped towards Lowper.

"He's gone. Jack went after him. So are these th' English? Did they give ye th' bunsens?"

At a glance from Lowper, Gil produced a sixpence, which Lowper handed over with the instruction not to spend it all at once.

Gil managed to contain himself until the money had changed hands, then snapped, "Did he take the girl?"

"No, mister. No lassie. Just him on his own, and th' other gent legged it th' other way. On his own, too."

"She went in with them, right enough," Lowper confirmed. "Lots o' folks seen 'er. But she hasn't come out. Not that anyone kens, anyway."

Cunningham's shoulders dropped as the tension went out of them with his sigh of relief. "Then she's here, and we'll have her free in a moment."

Gil met Moffat's eyes and shook his head minutely. Their experience suggested other, far more terrible scenarios, but no point in upsetting Cunningham unnecessarily. "The landlord will answer some questions," he stated, firmly.

The landlord was in no mind to do so, attempting to flee out a back door when Gil announced their errand. "Wasna to do wi' me," he insisted, when Gil let a hand off his throat to allow him to speak. "I told Phoenix I didna want trouble."

Gil firmed the hand until the landlord was gasping. "Trouble is here and will get worse if you don't take us to the girl."

The landlord's eyes slid to a door off to one side of the room. "She's gone, mister. I promise ye."

"She didna leave, mister," the urchin repeated.

Gil fixed the landlord with a glare and raised his eyebrows in question.

"She's gone, I tell ye. Out by th' trapdoor in th' cellar. Phoenix went off somewhere; left his man Finlay in charge. Finlay went to see to the lassie, an' she wasna there. He was spittin' mad. Had plans for her." The landlord choked to a stop when Gil's grip convulsed and could not speak for coughing when Gil let him go.

"Show us this cellar," he commanded. "Moffat, take someone with you and search the rest of the building, in case either of those two scum are hiding somewhere."

Down a precipitous flight of stairs, they came to a near new door with a large bolt on the outside. It was hanging open, and through the doorway they could see a dank hole littered with rubbish.

Gil led the way, his candle flickering in a breeze that came from one corner.

"She got out of here?" Cunningham asked.

"Yes. See here behind these boxes?"

"A trapdoor. Dear God, little Amy, down in the tunnels? How are we to tell her mother?"

"We don't," Gil decided. "We go after her. I am not returning to Susan until I have good news. Lowper, do you know the underground streets?"

"Nane better," Lowper claimed. "I'll help ye fin' th' lassie, maister. Ne'er ye fash yerse'."

"Here!" Cunningham interrupted, his voice sharp. "Where has the landlord gone?"

"Let him go," Gil said. "We can always come back for him."

"They're gone, all right," Moffat confirmed leading the way into the little cellar room. "No sign of Griffin or this Finlay. Room could do with a turn out and the bed has been slept in, but no luggage and no sign of where they might have gone."

"We're going down there," Gil told him, pointing to the trapdoor. "Anyone who wants to go home, leave now. The rest of us are going to save Miss Amelia."

15

Even here in the endless twilight, the denizens kept some observance of night and day. Concealed in her alley, Amy put her head on her arm and slept fitfully, jerking awake at every loud noise or closer rustle, until the first edge was off her exhaustion. Sitting propped up against the boxes that sheltered her, she listened carefully. Surely the sounds from the street had diminished?

She stood and cautiously rounded her sheltering haven to venture almost to the mouth of the alley. The business of earlier in the evening had slackened, with far fewer people in the streets and most houses unlit. Even those still out and about mostly seemed to be hurrying to a destination rather than lingering to talk to friends. Heading home?

Home. How she longed for her home and her mother. Perhaps she could now make her way to the surface?

She needed a disguise. Something to conceal all the ways she did not fit in this place and with these people. She returned to fetch the fabric she had hidden behind. In the better light near the street, she could confirm it was an old shawl: torn, dirty, and probably riddled with vermin.

Needs must when the devil rides, her old nurse would have said.

Somehow, she had retained her bonnet; the one that Mademoiselle had purchased in Newcastle, but it would have to be left. She hung it carefully on a nail that protruded from one wall, half thinking that at least the rats wouldn't be able to reach it, and wrapped the shawl around her shoulders and head.

At least her skirts were now soiled and rumpled enough to pass in the darkness for the sort of garments a woman of this place might wear.

She ventured from the alley and headed up the street, keeping to the shadows. With luck, no one would look at her twice.

No more than one hundred yards up the slope, just at the foot of some cobbled steps, her luck ran out.

They came out through a lighted door just as Amy passed it, two men, calling farewells to those behind them. Amy dodged to avoid a collision, but one of them shot out a hand and caught her by the wrist.

"What 'ave we here?"

His companion grabbed her shawl and pulled it back, exposing her face. "Bonnie. What's yer price, my bonnie?"

Amy's tongue refused to come unglued in her mouth. She shook her head, and shook it harder when the two men laughed.

"I ken a place," the first one said, and began pulling her back down the way she had come.

Amy struggled, and shouted, hoping someone would come to her aid. "No! Leave me alone! Let me go." Her assailants dragged her past a couple who averted their eyes and hastened their steps. "My mother..." Amy shouted, before the second man clapped a hand over her mouth and pinched her nostrils to stop her cries.

"Be a good lassie, and I'll give ye a florin," he said, his mouth so close to her ear she could feel the wet warmth of his breath.

Don't panic. That's what Aunt Ella said. Aunt Ella had insisted on her uncles teaching her a few tricks of self-protection, and had added a few choice moves herself. "I grew up as ignorant as a girl can be whose family follows the drum, and it is a dangerous state for a girl," she told Amy. "You need to know what you have to fear, how to avoid trouble, and how to face it."

Don't panic. Amy took a deep breath through her mouth and let it out through her nose. Then another.

But what could she do against two of them, and them so much stronger than her? Now that she had stopped struggling, they no longer held her so tightly. When the man removed his hand, hovering it ready in case she called out again, she remained silent. Let them think she was compliant, while she waited for her chance.

Sure enough, he let his hand drop and moved back enough to grab her other wrist. "She likes th' sound of a florin, Col," he said to her companion.

The other was scornful. "Have ye even got a florin?" He continued dragging Amy downhill, his grip on her wrist like iron.

"Between the two of us we'll make it. Ye'd not deny a working lassie her coin."

"Please, sirs, let me go. I'm a maid, an' me mither expects me home." On instinct, fearful of their response if they heard her educated English, she mimicked the speech of the maids at Gorburn Hall.

"Do ye think…" the second man stopped, and his friend perforce stopped too, Amy stretched between them.

"No, dinna believe her." The first man tugged, and they moved off again. "Out in this place at this time o' night? She's just tryin' to drive up th' price."

"Truly," Amy tried again, but was interrupted.

"Stop!" The speaker, a burly man with a red angry face, stood in the way of their little procession. "Who have ye got there? Is that th' lassie Phoenix wants? Th' English spy?"

Phoenix? The landlord back at that hovel with the cellar had called Griffin that. Amy froze again, fighting to keep her breathing steady. Thank goodness she had disguised her accent.

First assailant was shoving at the burly man's chest, to move him front the way. "English? What would an English be doin' here? This be a good Scots harlot, an' ye're holdin' us up in our pleasures."

Burly man refused to budge, but deigned to explain, examining Amy with his eyes as he spoke. "We captured an English spy, lady-born, disguised as a schoolgirl. She has swiped some papers an'

Phoenix wants them back." His gaze on Amy turned avid, as if he was removing her clothing, and she turned her head so she did not have to look at him face on. "She's a bonnie body."

On the other side of the street, a group of young men had stopped and were watching the interaction. They were younger than the men who had captured her, and far better dressed, in pantaloons and stockings, with cutaway coats, embroidered waistcoats and cravats in the English fashion. A higher quality fabric and cut than she expected in such a place, but she had heard that sons of the gentry found gambling and less reputable activities in the slums. After her sojourn in Cambridge she thought she recognised the type: university students with pretensions to dandyism.

The burly man was negotiating with the first two assailants for what he called a piece of the action, and all three had relaxed their vigilance for the moment, the second man even dropping his grip on Amy's arm the better to demonstrate with both hands what he intended to do during his turn with Amy's flesh.

The thought fed strength into the tug with which she freed her other hand, the force with which she fuelled her first wild leap towards the student. "Alec!" she shouted. "Alec, I'm here. I came to meet ye. Save me!"

The three men were after her in a moment, but one of the students had stepped towards her at her first shout, and the other five followed, placing themselves—arm's linked—as a barrier between Amy and her pursuers.

The student who had led the way said, "Leave her alone. She's with us, are you not, Mary?"

Fully into her part, Amy grabbed his arm and clung to it. "I told them, Alec. No, I said. Let me go, I begged. But they wouldna listen."

Assailant one exchanged glances with assailant two, and then squared his shoulders and clenched his fists. "She's ours. We saw her first."

The silence that followed was broken by the sound of guns being cocked. Two of them, small pocket pistols that would nonetheless make a nasty hole in each of the assailants. The burly man was already edging away. "None of my business. It's an English spy I was sent to find, not a Scots harlot."

The second assailant thumped the first, none too gently. "Give it up, Col. Flora at th' King's Ship has a kind nature. This body is too much trouble."

The students and Amy watched them walk away, continuing down into the depths.

Amy watched them disappear in the gloom then turned to see the leader examining her, his head tipped to one side. "Not Mary, then, I assume."

Now Amy would find out if her nanny's adage about firepans and fires was going to continue to prove true. With this audience, being a lady might weigh in her favour. She dipped a creditable curtsey and made her own introduction. "Miss Amelia Cunningham of Gorburn Hall. Thank you for your rescue, sir. May I know the name of my saviours?"

The young man took a step back. "Good Lord."

"She is English, right enough," one of the others commented.

"And educated. Our own sort," said another.

The fourth narrowed his eyes. "But is she a spy?"

The fifth shook his head. "Don't look like one," he opined.

"She's just a little girl, no older than my sisters," the sixth said, moving up beside her. "Don't be frightened, Miss Cunningham. We shall see you safely home."

"Of course we will," the leader agreed. "Where is Gorburn Hall, Miss Cunningham? Oh. I beg your pardon. I am Alistair McCormack, at your service, and these are my friends."

Amy offered her hand to the students in turn as Mr McCormack named them, thanking each one. "I have never been more scared in my life," she told them, "and I am very grateful. My mother will be, too. If you would be kind enough to take me to my brother's town house on Cumberland Street, you will compound my family's debt."

They bowed and declared themselves delighted. Alistair offered his arm, as did another student introduced as Colin, and she retraced the path up the street with a tall guard on either side, and the other four spread out behind.

The closer they approached the undercroft of the topside buildings, the lighter her heart. When she was home, she was going to hug her mother and never let her go.

They were about to turn onto steps that Alistair said would take them out into the upper world, when a rush of bootsteps and a shout alerted them to another attack: the burly man with reinforcements, at least seven others, all armed with clubs and shouting that the English spy was theirs.

"Step away from th' lassie and we willna hurt ye."

"I, on the other hand," replied Alistair, "make no such promises."

"It's only a pack of wee jimmies," burly man shouted. "Rush them, lads."

Alistair set her against the wall. "Stay there, Miss Cunningham. We'll just deal with the nuisance."

He dived into the melee, with a joyful shout echoed by his fellows, except the one who moved into place in front of her, his small gun ready. "Don't worry, Miss Cunningham," he told her. "We like fighting."

Amy edged to one side of Euan Murdoch, her guard, so she could watch as the other five took on the eight slum dwellers. Her students had science and training on their side. The attackers boasted superior numbers, greater weight, and the willingness to fight dirty. The students were valiant but were soon being driven back, step by hard-fought step, from the safety of the stairs that led to the upper world. The gap between the fight and the spot where she and Euan waited widened by the second.

One of the attackers dropped back from the fight, and turned toward them, grinning at Euan. "What you gonna do with that wee gun, boyo? Think one bullet'll take me?"

"There! By the steps." The shout came from a shadowed arch close under the under croft, and in a moment more men rushed down to join the struggle, two bypassing the knot of fighting men. In moments, the man who faced Amy and Euan was groaning on the ground, felled by a single blow from one of the new arrivals, who stood over him threatening further retribution if he stirred.

The other brandished a gun at Euan. "Get away from her."

Amy peered over Euan's shoulder. "Cousin Hamish, Euan is my friend. He is protecting me."

She threw herself into her cousin's arms, and he wrapped them around her. "There now, lassie, you're safe."

By the time she emerged from Hamish's hug, the fight was over, with most of the attackers fled, and a few left scattered across the cobbles. Amy's students and the new arrivals were congratulating one another, excitedly reliving moments of the battle, and clapping one another on the back. Amy recognised several footmen from her brother's townhouse, and—was that Uncle Alex's friend, Colonel— no, Lord Rutledge, giving quiet orders for securing the remaining fallen?

Alistair limped up. "Is this your father, Miss Cunningham?"

"Cousin Hamish, allow me to make you acquainted with Mr Alistair McCormack. Mr McCormack, my cousin, Mr Hamish Cunningham. Mr McCormack and his friends rescued me, cousin, and were taking me home when we were attacked."

Hamish held out his hand, realising as he extended it that it still held his gun, which he shifted to his other hand so he could shake Alistair's. "Our family owes you a considerable debt, Mr McCor- mack. Thank you."

Alistair reddened, and shifted uncomfortably. "Not at all, sir. It is the least we could do. Lady in distress." His eyes slid sideways to Amy, and he smiled.

"Had you not been there, Mr McCormack, I would have been..." A sudden vivid image of her likely fate hit Amy, and she shuddered convulsively, sucking in a huge sobbing breath, so that Hamish moved closer and put a comforting arm around her shoulder.

Amy leant her head into Hamish's chest. "I cannot bear to think of it." She blinked back tears and returned Alistair's smile. "You saved me."

"Well done. I'm Rutledge, by the way." Lord Rutledge had

joined them, and was extracting the gun from Hamish's other hand, while offering his own to Alistair.

Alistair introduced his friends to Lord Rutledge and Cousin Hamish, while Amy took the time to calm her breathing. She would be home soon enough. She was safe now, with her six brave knights errant, half the servants from the townhouse, Cousin Hamish, and Lord Rutledge all to protect her. Lord Rutledge was instructing a man called Moffat to "clean up the trash", and giving a handful of coins to a skinny little urchin with a cheeky grin. "You did well, Lowper."

"He did," Hamish agreed. "Rutledge, we should get this dear girl home. Her Mama will be anxious."

"Is Mama very angry with me?" Amy wondered.

Lord Rutledge's grin in response still bore some fierce warrior's delight in battle, as well as the triumph of victory. "Your Mama will undoubtedly growl, Miss Cunningham, but never doubt that she is proud of you. You did excellent work leaving the notes for us to follow, you stuck to your task, you got away from Griffin. And if the whole mission was a mistake, you will learn from it and be wiser next time."

Amy blushed, looking down at her toes. She had made a mess of things from start to finish. It had been Pat who suggested hunting for spies among the teachers and servants at the Academy, but Amy had agreed. And following Mam'selle had been entirely her idea. Lord Rutledge was being too kind. She peeped up at him. He was nice, if a little gruff and aloof. She didn't know him well, but she knew he admired Mama, and he had always shown a courteous interest when they had met.

Lord Rutledge's examination of her had turned anxious. "Have you taken any hurt, Miss Cunningham?"

"Yes, Amy," Hamish added, patting her shoulder, "are you injured in any way?"

Only in my pride. And my confidence. "No. I have taken no hurt. Thanks to Mr McCormack and his friends. And to you, arriving when you did." If she lay wakeful in the night imagining the hurts that might have been, it was no more than she deserved. She would not complain.

"We have Rutledge to thank," Hamish explained. "Him and his man Moffat. Their military training came in handy!"

Yes, she had seen that in the fight. But what was Lord Rutledge doing in Edinburgh?

"Lord Rutledge, did Grandfather send you?"

"I met your Mama by chance in Cambridge, on the day she found you were missing. Let's get you back to her. There will be time enough to hear about our adventures and yours. Cumberland Street, troops."

"Cumberland St, it is," Alistair agreed, offering Amy his arm with a cheeky twinkle in his eye as he scooped her from under Hamish's watchful eye. Hamish followed close on their heels up the steps, with the other five students close behind and Lord Rutledge bringing up the rear.

16

Susan paced the floor, composed herself to sit, took up her embroidery and made a few desolutory stitches, hurried to the window at a noise in the street. When it proved to be a carter making late deliveries, or a group of noisy men, or a neighbour arriving home, she began pacing again, and repeated the cycle.

Mademoiselle returned downstairs to report that Pat had surrendered to sleep. Thankfully she didn't try to talk; just settled herself at the piano and began playing—the sound a musical accompaniment to Susan's worrying.

At last the front door opened, and in moments Susan was in the hall, her arms around her daughter, her nose buried in Amy's hair and the tears she had been holding in for days streaming down her face.

"I am sorry, Mama. I am so sorry. I was so frightened, Mama."

"Hush, my love. Mama has you. You are safe." She managed to draw back enough to examine her child, a hand either side of the beloved face. "Are you hurt?"

Amy reassured her with a quick shake of the head. "Just dirty and tired. They came in time, Cousin Hamish and Colonel Rutledge—Lord Rutledge, I mean." She turned her head to smile shyly at the two men. "And the students, of course." The last sentence was drowned in an enormous yawn.

Susan spared a moment to give Gil her warmest smile. It was him, of course. Hamish was not a man of action, and Gil was a warrior; in this mission, her warrior. Another yawn called her full attention back to her daughter.

"You shall tell me all about it tomorrow, dearest. Hamish, will you order a bath to my room? Gentlemen, if you will excuse us, Amy is going to bed."

She wrapped her arm around Amy's waist, unwilling to be separated even by a few inches while they walked up the stairs, and Amy put her own arm around Susan. Frequent pauses for hugs slowed the bath and then the preparations for bed. Susan allowed the maid to hover, but waited on her daughter herself, with many kisses to the forehead. Amy happily submitted to being undressed, washed, and dressed again in a nightrail before being gently tucked into Susan's bed like a child barely out of the nursery instead of the competent young woman she had proved herself to be.

Amy was asleep almost before her head reached the pillow, oblivious to the noise of the maids emptying the bath water. Susan sat and watched, until she was called back to awareness by the sound of the door shutting behind the last of the maids. Heavens! She had barely thanked Gil and Hamish, and she owed them everything.

The men were still in the drawing room, sitting one either side of the hearth, nursing a brandy each and conversing quietly. They stood when Susan entered, reporting as she came, "Amy is asleep."

"Would you care for something to drink?" Gil asked, crossing to the brandy decanter, but Susan shook her head. "I am nearly asleep myself, and I wish to return to Amy. I just wanted to thank you again. And the servants, and the young men Amy met. I am so grateful to you all. She has been frightened, but not hurt. It could have been so much worse."

They were silent for a moment, all three of them with enough experience to visualise how much worse it nearly was.

"Frightened is good," Gil offered. "Frightened means she will take more thought before another such start."

Susan managed a smile at the reassurance, and if the amusement was no more than a ghost, this morning she had thought she might never smile again. "We can hope," she responded. "Gil, I had another reason to come downstairs. My daughter has acquired an unexpected talent, and I wished to show you the fruit of it." She held out the package of letters and other papers that Amy had handed her a few minutes ago.

"Amy had these from Griffin. She picked his pocket, apparently."

The men reacted predictably; Hamish shocked and Gil amused.

"Where on earth did she learn to pick pockets?" Hamish expostulated.

"Clever girl. But no wonder he sent his bullies after her," Gil commented, holding his hand out for the papers. He glanced through them quickly, as Susan had, and drew the same conclusion as her. "We'll need to show these to the Castle, but I think there'll be no reading them without the key, and that means both the code we sent to Lord Henry and the poetry book. The same edition as Griffin has."

Hamish left off shaking his head over his young cousin's scandalous hobby to look over Gil's shoulder. "Mademoiselle Cornillac is familiar with the book. I wonder if she would recognise the edition if we could find a copy in Edinburgh's book shops?"

"It is certainly worth trying." Gil downed the last of his brandy and put the glass down. "But let us consider that in the morning. Susan, you are nearly asleep on your feet, and I am in no better condition. I will bid you goodnight. Hamish, do you think we could use the internal door one more time, to save the steps?"

Susan frowned. Gil was pale, his eyes weary above blue bruises. She had forgotten that less than twenty-four hours ago he had been shot, and since then he'd been for a long drive, chased Griffin through the slums of Edinburgh, and finished the day with a fight.

She narrowed her eyes. "How is your wound," she asked.

He shrugged. "I hardly notice it. Moffat will redress the wound before I sleep." He must have seen that she was not satisfied, because he smiled, reassuringly. "Nothing that a good rest will not heal, Susan. And with Amy and Patrice safe, we can leave chasing after Griffin to the Castle and your father."

With that, she had to be satisfied, bidding the men goodnight as they took the shortcut through the house to Gil's apartments. But she would certainly insist on him being seen once more by the doctor.

17

They slept into the early afternoon, and Gil woke with a fever. Moffat ventured the opinion that 'my lord' would do better to stay in bed, and then called in heavy reinforcements when Gil refused. Susan's intervention had him grumbling but obedient, and silently grateful that his lady's command gave him an excuse to ignore his pride and give in to his physical weakness.

"But Captain Bowen will wish to talk to me," he insisted. Captain Bowen, according to Moffat, had called three times today, and been turned away twice because the principals in last night's drama were still asleep.

"A short visit," Susan decreed, "and he shall come to you, Gil." As she spoke, she was tidying up the paraphernalia that had collected on his bedside table. "Sit forward?" One by one, she removed the pillows he had been leaning against and shook them vigorously, before punching into the middle from each end. She restored them in a new configuration that moulded to his body as he lay back against them. "There. Is that more comfortable?" She put a hand to his forehead, and her brow creased. "You will need something soothing to drink. I shall see what cordials cook has. And perhaps some willow bark for the fever."

Being fussed over was pleasant. Gil had seen other men on the receiving end of such feminine nurturing and had wondered why they tamely submitted to domestic tyranny. At the hands of The Goddess, it felt like loving concern rather than a household rebellion. "I am at your command, general," he teased, which won him a smile.

"Moffat," Susan said to the hovering servant, "come down with me to the kitchen to fetch a light breakfast for your master. A coddled egg, Gil. Nothing that will add to the heat. And I shall bring the captain up to you once you have eaten."

"Traitor," he said to Moffat, when the servant returned with the promised egg, the willow bark tea flavoured with lemon and sweetened with honey, and some finely sliced white bread spread with butter. "Remember who pays your wages."

"Rolled up by a superior force, colonel," Moffat replied. "There you are. Just see how much of that you can manage."

Not much, was the answer, and Gil wanted to sleep right after, but Bowen had to be endured. Thankfully, Cunningham came up with him, answered most of Bowen's questions, and cut the interview short after twenty minutes. "Leave the rest of your questions until tomorrow, Captain, and let Rutledge rest, or we'll both have my cousin after us. We have plenty to go on with. These papers of Griffin's, for a start. We should get your people looking at those. I'll come up to the castle with Mademoiselle Cornillac, as we agreed, and we'll see what comes of the sketches that the young ladies are making of this Griffin fellow."

When Gil awoke, Susan was sitting beside the bed, her head bowed over some needlework. The maid she needed for propriety was almost invisible in the corner, likewise absorbed in whatever her needle was creating.

The domesticity of the scene wrenched at his heart. If only he could go back in time and be the boy who had once dreamed of deserving her. He ruthlessly crushed the tendril of hope that tried to sprout. It was too late for him; too late for them, had been too late before it even started. Even if he could persuade Susan to take on a broken warrior with a mortgaged estate and a ruined family name, he couldn't expect her to bring her family, two of them innocent girls, into his own poisoned home.

She looked up to find his eyes on her. "Good afternoon, Rutledge."

So, they were back on a formal footing, were they? It was for the best. "Any word of Cunningham and Mademoiselle Cornillac?" he asked.

"A message to say they are scouring bookshops and will be home for dinner. Which is yet some hours away, Rutledge, and you must be hungry."

He was, now that she mentioned it. "Yes, a little."

Susan rose so she could reach the bell pull. "I shall order food fetched."

Gil's body, once consulted, had other needs to be addressed. "If you would be so kind, Susan, would you order Moffat fetched? I have—that is…"

"Of course." Susan took his mumbling in her stride. "You wish to freshen up. If you will excuse me, I will send him to you."

He watched her leave the room, the maid emerging from her corner and scurrying behind her. Fool that he was, he immediately wished her back. Not just in his room, but in his bed and in his life. The dream he denied refused to die, but it must. Yearning after the impossible would only bring him misery.

Gil obeyed Susan's dictate that he stay in bed and rest, and that worried her more than the temperature that rose towards evening. It forced her to cut short Hamish's report on his visit to the castle, and the bookshops he and Mademoiselle Cornillac would visit tomorrow, as today's expedition had been unsuccessful.

"His lordship will bounce back, ma'am," Moffat assured her. "I've seen him in much worse states than this, and up and back into battle in a week.

Moffat, Hamish's man, and one of the footmen had arranged to share the night watch by the injured man, and Susan went reluctantly to bed after exacting a promise that she would be woken, no matter the time, if Gil took a turn for the worse.

The temptation to throw propriety to the wind and take her warrior's care on herself had been almost overwhelming all day, tempered only by her need to constantly check that her daughter was really back in her care, and really safe. She had stretched boundaries almost to breaking by making herself at home in his bedchamber during the day with a maid in the same room. To be alone with him at night was impossible, especially with her daughter under the same roof and Hamish watching for evidence she was an unfit guardian for Michael.

She had a restless night, but one undisturbed by any summons to Gil's bedside, and Moffat proved to be a true prophet when she checked on the patient. He was already up, dressed in his pantaloons and shirt with a magnificently gaudy banyan wrapped over the top, sitting by his fireside and tucking into a tray of meats, pastries, and other food she would never have permitted an invalid.

He correctly interpreted her silence. "I am well, Susan, truly, and will be all the better for some fuel to heal on. Just let me get this lot into me, and I'll be ready to do my part in hunting Griffin and discovering his plans."

Sure enough, the fever was gone, his eyes were clear, and the wound—when she checked it—showed no signs of swelling or heat. Susan alleviated her mix of relief and exasperation by setting some rules. "You are still recovering, Gil. Come downstairs if you must, but no further. Let others run errands for you."

And so, the drawing room became command central, with Gil as general and the rest of them his aides and foot soldiers. Not just Susan, Hamish, the two girls, and Mademoiselle Cornillac, but also Captain Bowen, Pat's uncle Simeon Grahame, and Alistair McCormack and his friends. Gil marshalled more support from below stairs: Moffat, Munro, and various other servants. Lowper arrived at odd points during the day, usually ushering some denizen of Edinburgh's underbelly who had agreed to talk to 'the English mi'lord'.

Mademoiselle and Hamish found another copy of the poetry book on the second day of their search, by which time Susan had written to her father telling him about Amy's purloined papers and asking him to send them a copy of the key to the code.

Armed with sketches that Pat and Amy had made of Griffin and his accomplice, the others fanned out through Edinburgh trying to find the men.

"Griffin is one of the aliases of a radical agitator," Grahame reported, when the investigators gathered to share information at the end of the third evening. Amy and Patrice had gone reluctantly to bed, and Hamish had produced decanters and served brandy or whisky or port to those who remained.

Grahame accepted the glass he was offered and held it up in an ironic toast. "One of those 'the French had it right' lot. Kill the aristos and enter a new world of brotherhood and hope."

Hamish's huff was an eloquent dismissal of such aspirations.

"He has left Edinburgh," McCormack said. "No one has seen him since he ran from you and Mr Cunningham, Lord Rutledge. They say he has gone back south, but that might be a guess, since he comes from the south."

"Do we have any idea where in the south?" Gil asked. He was in effortless command of the room though it was Susan's son's house, Hamish's home, and Bowen's investigation. "Cambridge?"

"Cambridge is not his home," Mademoiselle Cornillac offered. "Or, at least, so I understood. He told me that he travelled much with his work as a clerk for the owner of mills. He inspected his employer's manufactories, he said. He mentioned Edinburgh, but also Manchester, Liverpool, Birmingham." Lisette Cornillac was either an innocent French refugee, as she claimed, or an extremely clever actor. Susan inclined to the former, but continued to watch for the later, though most of the men—even Captain Bowen—had moved from regarding her as the enemy to considering her part of the team.

Captain Bowen was nodding, wisely. "A good story. It would explain all his travelling. He is known to our friends at the Home Office, under the name Griffin. Also Phoenix and Pendragon and, we think, probably Unicorn and Manticore. He is a popular speaker at radical rallies and meetings. Goes from town to town around

Britain telling people how badly the government is oppressing them."

He gave a heady sigh. "Our people up at the Castle are somewhat upset they have not been kept informed. Particularly in the light of the other sketch your young ladies gave us."

Gil raised a brow. "Finlay?"

"One of ours, I'm afraid. Or so they thought until they recognised him from the sketch. A paid informer, and as elusive as Griffin. Gone. No message, no forwarding address, and the man who commissioned him says he was due a payment several days ago and has not turned up to collect it."

"On the run?" McCormack asked, and then dropped his voice and added, with ghoulish emphasis, "or has Griffin cut off the loose ends?"

Susan, having heard from Amy of the man's threats and intentions, rather hoped it was the later.

Gil took in a deep breath and released it in a sigh. "At our end, we seem to have nothing but loose ends. No trail to Griffin. Finlay gone. The code key and papers may yet help someone somewhere, but we do not have them and can't use them." Lord Henry had replied to the Castle's request for a copy of the key code with a peremptory command that the papers and the book Hamish and Lisette had found be sent to the Horse Guard by fastest messenger, to be shared with the shadowy 'friends in the Home Office' to whom Captain Bowen had referred,

"Is there more we can do?" Grahame asked. "I am willing, but it seems futile, and I need to settle with my wards' great-aunt and their school, which means a trip to Cambridge. I thought my sister-in-law's maiden aunt had done a fair job of raising her and was better suited to raising her children than a bachelor uncle. But by the letters she has written me this past week, the old lady is half crazed. I'll not leave the girls there."

Susan also needed to bring this interlude to an end, though she would miss Gil. In fact, she needed to end it because she would miss Gil. "I see no reason for Amy and me to remain in Edinburgh. I must go home to my other children, and I, too, need to speak with the school. Can we leave Edinburgh, Captain Bowen?"

Captain Bowen steepled his fingers in front of his mouth as he thought. "Mademoiselle Cornillac must remain under our supervision, but I see no reason why the rest of you should stay. I shall speak with my superiors, but I imagine they will not wish to put any barriers in your way."

Susan rather thought they would not. A viscount, a prominent Edinburgh business man, and the daughter of a brigadier-general with the Horse Guard? No, their path would be made smooth, but an anonymous émigré had no such protections. She opened her mouth to demand fair treatment for Lisette, but Hamish spoke before she could.

"Mademoiselle will stay here, of course. I have my own rooms, ye ken. It would not be improper, Mademoiselle." He challenged the rest of the room with an obstinate glare. "I am confident she is not a risk to the Realm, but I am well qualified to watch her, and also to see that she is not bullied or otherwise disadvantaged." His face gentled as he turned back to Lisette. "And from here, it is but an hour's drive to visit your brother, and you shall be able to send letters back and forth."

Captain Bowen made no objection.

"We shall plan to leave the day after tomorrow," Gil decided, and Susan's heart lifted at his assumption they would go as a party.

"As long as you are well enough to travel, Rutledge" she admonished.

"I am recovering well enough," he assured her. "I am certainly capable of assisting Grahame here to provide you with an escort on the road and wouldn't dream of letting you travel without one."

Susan disguised her delight in a scold. "And I would not dream of letting you travel without me there to supervise the care of your wound, for you do not look after yourself, Rutledge."

The night before they left Edinburgh, Gil went to bed early, as he had since Susan had first allowed him to leave his room. Tonight, sleep did not come easily. After lying there for an age regretting that his time with his Goddess was coming to an end and going over and over all the reasons why a marriage between them was impossible, he at last decided to light the lamp and read.

His book was not on his bedside table. That's right. He'd taken it downstairs so he'd have something to occupy his time in the gap between visitors. Probably the internal door was unlocked, as it had been since his illness. He could try.

And yes. He let himself from Cunningham's apartment into the main house, and descended the stairs, keeping his footfalls light so that he did not disturb the sleeping house.

But clearly, he was not the only sleepless inhabitant, for light shone from the drawing room through the partly open door, and he could hear voices.

He had his hand on the door to push it wider when he caught his name.

"…Rutledge admires you, I know. And he would be a good stepfather for Michael."

Gil froze. Listening was dishonourable, but he could no more resist than he could turn himself invisible and observe the conversation close up.

"Hamish, I will not discuss Rutledge with you," The Goddess said. "As for marrying again, you know my views on that."

"I know my cousin was not the most attentive of husbands, but surely he was not so bad as to give you a distaste for the institution forever?" Cunningham sounded puzzled.

Susan sighed. "You are a man, Hamish. You cannot possibly understand what it is like to be a wife, and therefore to have no legal existence. As a widow with my own property, I am free to make my own decisions. I can choose what to buy and where and how I live. I answer to no one. Why would I wish to change that state?"

Until this moment, Gil believed he had given up all hope of a future with his Goddess. He had been wrong. Her words strangled the remnants of his pipe dream. He leant back against the wall to the side of the door, his eyes shut, grieving, as Susan continued to speak. "You are concerned about Michael, but I assure you that I am very conscious of my responsibilities, and I have the help of my father and brothers—and of you—to raise him to be a good man."

"Well," Cunningham, the Scots strong in his voice, was not surrendering, "I still think ye could do worse than Rutledge."

"Rutledge is a good man," Susan agreed, "but I do not need a husband, cousin."

Never mind the book. Gil made his way back upstairs. He did not want to hear any more.

They travelled by easy stages, taking twice as long on the return journey as they'd spent on the mad dash to Scotland. The servants, too, made life more comfortable. Susan had borrowed two maids from the townhouse to attend to her and the girls, with a promise of a tour of London before they were put back on a coach to return to Edinburgh. Moffat and Grahame's man McGuinness treated the pair with a mix of avuncular tolerance and respectful flirting, and their mobile servants' hall soon turned each stop into a home away from home.

The trips between stops were more comfortable, too, even with seven adults and the two school girls, since they had not only Susan's stylish cabriolet-phaeton, but also an old-fashioned travelling coach from Gorburn Hall that could seat them all inside if the weather was really unpleasant.

It mainly continued fine, however, and Susan, Grahame, and Gil took it in turns to drive Susan's vehicle, giving everyone the opportunity to enjoy the ride on the more modern springs and with a better view of the countryside than from the coach.

Susan still hovered over Amy, watching her at all times and constantly touching her with a pat, a kiss or a hug as if she needed the physical reminder her child was safe. Amy had nestled into the nurturing at first, but after they left Edinburgh and the safety of their own home, Susan's heightened awareness began to grate. Gil saw the signs of incipient rebellion, and was not surprised when the storm broke in Newcastle.

"May we go to the market if we take the maids, Mama?" Amy asked. "I got such a pretty bonnet when I was here last time. Pat's uncle says he will give permission if you do."

Susan, her travelling desk set up before her with the paper and pen already prepared for her evening task, was already considering the first paragraph she intended to write, and barely glanced at her daughter. "I cannot tonight, Amy. I must write to your aunts and your grandfather."

Amy jutted her chin. "We will be safe with the maids, Mama."

The pettish tone fetched a sharp response. "Young ladies do not walk around strange towns with only their maids. You will need to wait until I can accompany you, Amy."

"That is so unfair! What about when you rode to Longford all on your own to buy your brother cake from the baker's after you pushed him from a tree and he broke his arm? There were lots of times, were there not, Lord Rutledge?"

Gil raised both hands in self defence. "I beg you to leave me out of this, Miss Amy." He then compounded the sin of trying to remain uninvolved by saying to Susan, "I can send Moffatt with them, or go myself, if you prefer."

Susan glared, then softened. "You will stay with Lord Rutledge at all times and obey him in every particular."

"Yes, Mama." Amy's submissive tone warred with her dancing eyes.

"And remember you brought this on yourself, Rutledge," Susan warned. But after Newcastle, she hovered less.

At inn after inn, the proprietor and servants Susan and Gil had met on their way to Edinburgh greeted them with delight. Mr Withers, at the White Rose in York, summed up the general mood. "Young ladies, I am so pleased to meet you again, and devoutly thankful you have been delivered." The girls were embarrassed by the attention, and Gil rather wished they had chosen a different route home, for the happy outcome to the escapade would put the seal upon the story being spread the length and breadth of Britain.

At least they were back in their schoolgirl blues, Amy having had several spare sets in her chambers at Gorburn Hall. Their hair in plaits, they looked far too young and too innocent for any salacious inference to be made, and Gil and Grahame followed Susan's lead in carefully emphasising their youth and their constant chaperonage by Mademoiselle, who (as it had transpired) was an anxious sister, and not a French spy.

It was the best they could do and should suffice to protect the girls' reputation. With good fortune, the tales of the girls' venture on behalf of their king and country would eclipse any tales that Susan had been alone with her escort for days while she pursued them.

Driving Pat and Amy in the cabriolet-phaeton one day, Gil found himself the subject of a polite and subtle, but inexorable, inquisition on his character, his estate, his prospects, and his views and intentions on marriage.

Not that he realised their intent for some time. Gil had spent his entire adult life in the army. Schoolgirls were foreign terrain, and gently-born females an alien species. He knew young men, and he had met and admired many women who followed the drum with bravery and a devotion to their menfolk he could only admire.

But these two girls were nothing like the brash youths he had commanded or the camp followers who had welcomed their man's officer to their fires. Nor were they like his sisters, the two timid girls he remembered from his own schoolboy days.

If asked, he would have conceded that Pat and Amy had shown courage, initiative, and intelligence on their adventure—and a level of foolhardiness he would have expected from a boy of their age but did not associate with females who, he would have said, were altogether daintier in their interests and more cautious in their ventures. Girls, especially girls of their class, were decorative shallow creatures who bored him witless within a quarter of a dance set, with his Goddess always the one shining exception.

He was rapidly extending the exception category. Amy gave him the benefit of an oration on the stupidities of primogeniture, and Pat was trenchant in her support for women controlling their own inheritances and even running businesses, should they choose.

Appealed to for his view, he diffidently suggested that many women seemed to prefer having the leadership and protection of a man.

Amy's response was a rude snort. "Of course. Because that's what they've been taught. And because the law defends men and not women, so having one you can trust on your side is only sensible."

"But how can you know who to trust?" Pat asked. "People pretend all the time. Look at Anna Blakelock. Even we thought Lieutenant Miller genuinely loved her and wanted to marry her, but when Mr Blakelock offered him money instead, he took it."

Amy explained. "Anna was at our school last term, Lord Rutledge, but was discovered sneaking out after dark to meet an officer of the local regiment. Her father took her home after she was discovered, and she is rusticating."

Not the first impoverished officer to attempt to use charm and the attraction of the uniform to improve his financial position.

"If the young lady's father put pressure on the lieutenant's commander, the young man may have had no choice," Gil suggested, wondering how far the dalliance had gone, and whether the rustication was to hide consequences that would ruin the poor girl more surely than an unwise interest in a scarlet coat.

Pat clearly wondered, too. "Such a hard choice. Would it be better to be married to someone who doesn't really love you? Or to be alone, perhaps with a baby that must be given away or hidden?"

"It depends what you expect, I suppose," Amy declared. "If you think you have married for love, and you find out the other person only wants your money or your family connections, it would be rather horrid. People do marry for love, though, and stay in love. My uncles Rick and Alex both did, and they and my aunts are very happy. But there are other reasons to marry, and they might be less disappointing in the long run." She didn't mention her Uncle Jules, who had married to save his wife's reputation and left England immediately after the wedding. Come to think of it, Mia Redepenning had been younger than Amy at the time.

"Yes, a woman might want children. She should marry for that," Pat agreed.

"Or marrying to join estates or businesses might be sensible, if the two people don't mind one another," Amy suggested.

That was an even more jaundiced view of marriage than his own. "Will you hold out for love," he asked, "or will you marry for a sensible reason?"

Amy and Pat exchanged a long glance.

"I would like love," Amy replied, decidedly. "I think it unlikely, however. My teachers say I will have to temper my opinions if I am to attract a man, but I think that any man who is attracted to someone I am pretending to be will not love the real me, so I would be wasting my time with him. I expect I will marry one day, for I should like to have a home of my own, and children. The girls at school, and even the teachers, propose that we act like insipid ninnies until we have someone's ring on our finger." She waved her left hand in the air as if showing a wedding ring. "That seems silly to me. Imagine my husband's shock when he realised I had ideas of my own! And I could certainly not put on a false face for a lifetime."

"Precisely," Pat agreed. "And who would want to spend a lifetime with a man who prefers an insipid ninny?"

Gil smothered a grin. These girls were refreshing, and he would not want them to think he was laughing at them. "I suspect many men would prefer wives who can be partners in the marriage, and friends. I know I would."

Both girls stilled, and Gil's war-honed instincts caught the lack of movement and the sudden alertness. "You are a viscount, of course," Amy acknowledged, her voice carefully bland, "so you must secure the succession."

"And you are not a young man," said Pat, adding over Amy's instant protest, "I am not saying he is old, so you needn't poke me, Amelia Cunningham. I just meant that a girl fresh from the schoolroom would not suit you, Lord Rutledge."

"A mature woman," Amy agreed. "Not too old to have more children, mind. If she already had children, that is."

After one sharp glance at their profiles, both studiously turned to the road ahead, Gil kept his own eyes forward. "I have an heir," he disclosed. "A distant cousin. He seems a nice enough person."

"But…" Pat began, and stopped abruptly. From the movement Gil had caught with his peripheral vision, Amy had poked her again. Both girls were silent for a moment, then Amy responded. "That is good. You have the freedom to marry as you please then. Someone you already know well, perhaps. An old friend. Still, you would make a good father, I think, Lord Rutledge."

For a long moment he was seduced by the vision she offered: Susan at his side, perhaps carrying his child. He had dreamed of it many times, updating the mental images as they both aged, but this trip had brought the fantasy into sharp focus, and added this clever young woman and her brother and sister as part of his personal Eden. Which could never happen. He would not bring any child into his mother's orbit. Not Susan's; not his own. Time for diversionary tactics.

"Young McCormack did not appear to mind your intelligence or your opinions," he ventured.

He felt rather than saw her assessing gaze, but Amy accepted the change of subject. "He was indulging a child. I amused him. Mostly he kept visiting because he admired you, Lord Rutledge."

Gil disagreed. The boy was fascinated by the investigation, but more so by the daughter of the house, though he was too well bred for more than the occasional longing glance when he thought it unnoticed, and instant attention when Amy joined the conversation.

"Mama says I have years before I will be ready to consider courtship and marriage. And Alist—Mr McCormack is only at the start of his university training. But an Edinburgh-trained doctor would not be an unsuitable match for a Cunningham of Gorburn Hall." She paused, and then added, "If I cared about such things. Mama says that one should take pride in one's own accomplishments and responsibility for one's own mistakes, and not those of other people, however closely related."

A Cunningham of Gorburn Hall. That was a turn of phrase he had heard repeatedly from Hamish Cunningham, who had also been anxious to bend his ear on the topic of marriage to Susan.

Surely the older man had not enlisted the child in that cause? No, he could not imagine it. Amy was advocating on her own behalf, and Gil was both flattered and tempted. But his relatives, especially the dead ones, were a millstone around his neck.

He kept the conversation focused. "I am confident you will have many choices, when you make your debut. Yes, and you too, Miss Grahame."

Pat was diverted. "I expect I shall debut in Edinburgh, since I am to live with my uncle. Amy will have London, of course, with her family connections, and I do not expect to move in the highest circles, as she can. But Amy, I hope your Mama will spend at least part of the summer in Edinburgh, so we can attend entertainments together."

Amy took her friend's hands and vowed that the Cunninghams would surely continue to summer in Scotland, and that she and Pat would weather the gauntlet of gormless young men and silly young ladies together, even if only by letter.

"And I expect we are pretty enough and wealthy enough to garner at least some partners," she consoled, "even if we do refuse to hide that we have opinions of our own."

"Your mother has always been a strong and capable woman," Gil argued, "and had a score of admirers—yes, and several proposals—when she was a debutante." It was a tactical error, for Amy countered with, "not only as a debutante." And she proceeded to thoroughly revenge herself on Gil for refusing her overtures by describing several recent suitors and sharing her opinions of their suitability as candidates for Susan's hand.

Gil was only slightly relieved to find that Amy approved of none of them, and thought her mother shared his opinion.

18

———

They spent the final night out of Cambridge at Stamford, at the inn where Susan's groom had been taken ill, and where a note waited from Susan's father, Lord Henry. The note mentioned Lyons and continued, "The children and I are looking forward to hearing your adventures, and will be waiting for you in Cambridge, Susan."

Susan felt suddenly lighter. She was seldom apart from Michael and Chrissie for more than a single night here or there, and tomorrow she would hold them again. "Your grandfather will be waiting for us in Cambridge with your brother and sister," she told Amy, who briefly interrupted a low-voiced conversation with her friend to agree politely that seeing her family would be nice.

Susan suppressed a smile at their different reactions, and went to find Gil, who would at least be pleased that she was happy.

He was talking to the innkeeper but turned at her approach. "I was just asking after your man, Lyons. Apparently, he is recovering nicely, and your father arranged to move him home to London."

"Yes, I have a note from Father. He and the children will be meeting us in Cambridge."

His smile was broad and unfeigned. "You will be glad to have them under your wing again, Susan."

"More than delighted," she agreed, though it would also mean the end of her time with Gil. Soon, perhaps even tomorrow, they would go their separate ways, and she did not want them to part. But what could a woman do? Since that one kiss, he had shown no further romantic interest, behaving exactly as if the brotherly role he claimed was his by blood.

Cousin Hamish had taken her aside to advise her to marry the man, as if she would hesitate for a moment. Had he also spoken to Gil? If so, he had blundered, for Gil had his affable walls up, a mile thick and impregnable.

On the spur of the moment, she said, "I would like to visit the woman who cared for Lyon, Rutledge. May I have your escort?"

"Of course."

He offered his arm, and they told Grahame and the servants where they were going and stepped out into the late afternoon streets.

The woman who had nursed Lyons gave a good report of his recovery. After a slight hesitation, she made to return the guinea bonus Susan offered her, explaining that the lord who came up from London had already paid her in full and given her some extra. "You deserve it, and must keep this as well," Susan said. "We are grateful for your care of Lyons. He is dear to me and my children."

Gil was preoccupied on the walk back. Silly to suppose he was preparing himself mentally to flee from her as he had done so many times. Silly to think of his departures as fleeing—she had no hold, no rights, no expectations.

But for the first time since they were children, she and he had been easy together, and if she could not have the prize she desired, she wanted that friendship back again. "A penny for your thoughts, Rutledge."

He glanced down at her, a quick and fleeting smile warming his face. "Over-valued at a penny. I was thinking of my next errand."

"To the Selby estate in Essex, to see your brother's widow."

He sobered again. "Yes. Do you know, I have never met her? Or my nieces? They had left Thornbury Hall before I returned to England."

"Fled." The story had travelled the neighbourhood with the speed of wildfire. The dowager had confined the widow and her two daughters for days after the death of the previous viscount, while the older woman raved and grieved. No one was allowed to see the younger Lady Rutledge, not even Miss Cleghorn, her older sister. She came immediately on hearing that Gideon Rutledge was dead and was turned away at the door.

Two days later, the widow, Miss Cleghorn, and the two little girls arrived on foot at Longford Court in the early hours of the morning, asking for the Countess of Chirbury. The public story stopped there, except for awed accounts of the confrontation between Gil's mother and Anne, the Countess of Chirbury. But Anne was Susan's cousin and her friend; Susan knew that Anne had offered Chloe refuge at her own estate.

"Fled," Gil repeated. "Fled my mother, for her husband was already dead. And me, I imagine, for God alone knows what stories she has heard about me."

"Good ones from Anne, you can be sure. You are Rede's friend, after all."

Another of those fleeting smiles. "Thank you. I hope so. It is my duty to see her, and to make sure she has all that she needs, but I do not want to frighten her. Or my little nieces. Have you met her, Goddess? What is she like?"

"Several times. Your mother kept her close, but Anne is the most powerful peeress in the district and was determined to befriend her." *And took me in her wake when I was at Longford.* The dowager Lady Rutledge could not deny every visit from a determined countess backed by the power of the Redepennings, though she blocked as many as she could, and sat vigilantly at watch when her denials were unavailing. Still, Anne had clearly found ways to see the younger Lady Rutledge alone, or at least to convey support strongly enough that the little group of females had risked turning to Anne in their need. "Poor child."

"She is young, isn't she," Gil agreed, his voice taunt with control.

"I was shocked when I looked in the family bible. Not that I should have been, but she has been married six years, has two daughters and is not yet twenty. My brother was a monster, Goddess. What was Cleghorn thinking, putting his innocent sister into Gideon's power?"

"He was one of your brother's cronies and no better: one of the group of young men Lord Carrington gathered around him. Rumour has it that Lady Rutledge and Miss Cleghorn tried to run away before the wedding."

"And who can blame them?"

"Not I, certainly." Susan shrugged. Rumour was often exaggerated, but this rang true, with the supporting detail. "It would explain why Miss Cleghorn was absent that day. She was confined to bed for some weeks, so they say. And Lady Rutledge remained veiled when in public for over a week."

Gil shuddered. "I cannot imagine what her life has been. My mother says she belongs at home with us, but I think it must be a place of horror for her. Of course, my mother takes Gideon's side, as she always has. No wonder Chloe ran as soon as she could. Anne Chirbury wouldn't breach the poor girl's confidence, but she said enough to make it clear that Chloe was as frightened of Mother as she was of Gideon. Which I hate to think about, Goddess. Who wants to believe their mother a monster? And to a defenceless woman and her own two little granddaughters?"

Susan could believe it. The dowager Lady Rutledge was one of the nastiest women Susan had ever met—totally oblivious to anyone's needs but her own and those of her despicable eldest son.

"It happens. I have seen it before—women in the power of a ruthless bully who choose to help him victimise others in order to save themselves."

"A ruthless bully. Yes, that was my father and my brother, and my mother too." He stopped in his tracks and pulled her to face him, ignoring the passers-by, his face twisted. "What if the taint is in me, Goddess? I have done things... You cannot know what war is like, and I hope you never do. But blood will out, or so they say."

How could he think such nonsense? Gil? The most honourable

man of her acquaintance? "Did you take joy in the things you had to do as a soldier, Gil?"

He struggled to suppress his anguish so he could give his answer considered thought. "Joy? Satisfaction, perhaps. At the time. Exhilaration, sometimes. There can be a fierce pleasure in violence, Goddess."

She nodded and probed a bit more. "You enjoyed degrading and subduing women and children?"

That prompted pure shock. "No! Never. How could…"

"Exactly." She drove home the lesson. "Then you are nothing like your father and brother. You did what you needed to, and you cannot tell me that you gloated over it afterwards, for I won't believe you. You are the kind of man who does his duty, grieves over any suffering he causes, then goes out to do his duty the next day. So I will not have you comparing yourself with those monsters, who relished fear and lived to hurt others. You are nothing like them, and I thank God for it."

Gil was still thinking about that conversation when they arrived in Cambridge just after noon the next the day to find that Lord Henry Redepenning had taken over an entire wing of the hotel and ordered it to his convenience. When the carriage pulled into the coachyard, they heard an excited shout from one of the galleried verandas. There, up on the third floor, Michael Cunningham was jumping up and down, held back from leaping bodily down the steps by a harried looking nurse. "Grandpapa, it is Mama! Mama, I'm up here!"

In moments, Lord Henry and Susan's middle child, Christina, had joined the pair from one of the hotel's suites, and the four were hurrying down into the courtyard, where Susan and Amy barely waited for the horses to draw to a halt before tumbling from the carriage and racing to meet their family, their skirts kicking up behind them, propriety cast to the winds in their delight at the reunion.

Gil watched from his position by the carriage, half an ear on their servants who were unloading the luggage and arranging its transport into the inn, or haggling with the grooms, or—in Moffat's case—seeking a messenger to send for Gil's horse and his own, who were on grass just outside of Cambridge.

The Goddess enveloped both children in a hug, Amy joining in from one side and Lord Henry from the other, then Chrissie and Amy broke off into their own huddle, holding hands and both talking at once. The Goddess dropped to a crouch to look up at her son, and Gil did not need to be close enough to see the shine in her eyes, the glow that lit her face. Michael's grin was in plain view though, as he told his mother some story that had his whole body moving in a mime to reinforce his points.

Lord Henry watched over them with a benign smile, until Grahame and Pat descended from the cabriolet-phaeton and approached tentatively. Then the older man came to meet those two, his hand held out as he clearly introduced himself to Grahame. He was in turn introduced to Pat, and bowed with courtly grace, to which she responded with a curtsey.

Lord Henry looked up then, over Pat's head, and caught Gil's eye, smiled, and mouthed, "Thank you," easing a knot of concern of which Gil had not been aware. Logically, he knew he could not have stopped Susan from pursuing Amy; could not have reached Scotland any more quickly. Deep down, he felt he should have been able to save both of them without putting their reputations at risk. But if the general was grateful, perhaps Gil could ignore his feelings.

While he had been preoccupied, the servants had moved off into the hotel, all but Moffat whose voice he could hear in the stable, giving orders to a groom.

His job was done; Amy retrieved and both she and Susan returned safely to the loving arms of the head of their family. Perhaps he and Moffat should ride on tonight.

He turned to give the order, but Susan was calling him over, enticing him to leave his cold duty for just a few more hours to bask in the spilled over warmth of the love that surrounded her.

"Gil, Papa has ordered a cold collation in the garden, and after that Mr Grahame is going to call on Miss Foster, and Papa will be taking the children to see the places of his greatest triumph as a cricketer."

"Grandpapa made his century against Magdalen," Michael informed Gil. "Grandpapa was at King's, which is the best college."

Gil met Lord Henry's smile with one of his own, as Lord Henry spread his hands in demurral. "A long time ago."

"Gil, can I trouble you to escort me to the Academy?" Susan continued, and Gil had agreed before he thought about how it might look. He quelled his doubts, but they returned fourfold when he descended from washing in his room just behind two gossipmongers who were quacking about a notorious widow and her escapades on the Great North Road. "She travelled all that way with a Rutledge, dear. Need I say more?"

The other protested. "But not the Vile Viscount, Millie. This is the younger brother. One of Wellington's war heroes, and a family friend of the Redepennings. It is only natural he would offer his help to the sister of his friend."

Gil should make his presence known, but a perverse need to hear the worst consumed him, and he stopped just above a turn in the stairs to listen.

"A war hero he may be. I say nothing to that. But a man may be brave, and still be a killer and a villain. They say the Vile Viscount killed his first wife, and perhaps his second—though..." the speaker paused, clearly determined if reluctant to be fair... "she may have died in childbed, I suppose. Certainly, his third must be glad he is dead, poor little thing."

If Gil had been his unknown sister-in-law, he would have danced on Gideon's grave out of sheer relief, though running away as she did was a practical step, he supposed.

The second woman was still fighting his corner. "The new Lord Rutledge is accepted everywhere, Millie. You know perfectly well that his brother was barred from all but the lowest of places."

Millie was not impressed by the argument, her harrumph expressing both scorn and disbelief. "The influence of his friends. And look at what friends, Lettie! The Redepennings!

Rakes to a man and a woman. Why Countess Chirbury is a Selby, and they are as bad as the Rutledges. And Renshaw married a madwoman, who killed her first husband. I had it from the man's own sister! The apple does not fall far from the tree, Lettie. Susan Cunningham may walk very high in the instep, but she is no better than a trollop, travelling alone with a Rutledge."

"Enough," Gil said, quietly, making them both jump.

Millie was the first to recover, drawing herself up to her full height, still a full head shorter than Gil, even after he rounded her to stand one stair below, blocking her way to the inn's next floor. He fixed her with his best Colonel Rock Ledge glare.

"Do I know you, sir?" she demanded, haughtily.

"No, madam, you do not. Nor do you know my friends, although you do appear to have a passing acquaintance with my brother."

"Then you are interrupting a private conversation," she informed him, and flapped both hands at him as if he were an importunate chicken that could be scared into a scurried retreat. "Go away. I do not speak with men to whom I have not been introduced."

"Your name, madam?" He asked the second lady, a hint of command infusing the words so that she had introduced herself as 'Mrs Robert Fenhaven, and this is my friend, Miss Stenhouse."

Gil ignored Miss Stenhouse's hissed protest to her friend and bowed. "I am Rutledge, Mrs Fenhaven, and I have a particular interest in a conversation about myself, in which I and my friends are made the subject of scurrilous and evil lies."

Mrs Fenhaven paled, and Miss Stenhouse coloured but rallied. "Those who eavesdrop seldom hear good of themselves."

"Those who spread lies about prominent members of Society seldom prosper," he countered. "I do not know you, Miss Stenhouse, and I do not care to further the acquaintance. I very much doubt that you are personally known to any of the people whose names you freely malign in an open stairway of a public inn. However, I am confident that Mrs Cunningham and the other ladies of her family can find out all about you, your family, your connections, and any skeletons in your family tree."

"Are you threatening me?" The stance was still belligerent, but the slight quaver in the voice suggested uncertainty, and Mrs Fenhaven was gabbling apologies as fast as her tongue could wag.

Gil nodded, gravely. "Not a threat, precisely, madam. Consider it, instead, a promise. I have spent my entire adult life defending my country, as Mrs Fenhaven has pointed out. I will defend my friends from any attack, including those by ignorant muckrakers spreading false rumours. I promise you, Miss Stenhouse, you would be wise to keep your ill-informed opinions to yourself."

Mrs Fenhaven was whispering urgently to Miss Stenhouse, who had deflated like the silly hen she was, her eyes glancing everywhere except at Gil, as if seeking a way to leave the battlefield with dignity.

Gil took pity on the poor friend, and stepped to one side, allowing them to pass, Mrs Fenhaven curtseying slightly and saying, in a harried tone, "So nice to meet you, my lord, at least it would have been… oh dear, oh Millie, how could you."

In the private parlour Lord Henry had ordered for their meal, the rest of his party was already gathered, but after they had eaten and the nursemaid had taken the children upstairs to get their coats for their outing, he told Lord Henry and Susan about the encounter. Susan was scornful. "I've never heard of the woman, and I doubt she knows anyone who matters, Rutledge. She cannot harm me or mine. Though I would have paid pounds for a ringside seat on her dressing down. I am sure she must have been shaking in her shoes."

Gil was less inclined to be amused. "Unfortunately, I doubt I've spiked her guns, and she is only one, besides. We can't deny that we did travel together, and alone, and though you and I know it was in all innocence, people will believe what they will."

He cast an anxious glance at Lord Henry. "I am sorry, general."

"No apology required, my boy. Susan has told me how you looked after her; yes, and found and rescued Amy, too."

Susan made a small delicate noise of disgust. "Apologies, indeed. Are you sorry you came with me, Rutledge? I was going anyway, as you full well know, and while I am fully conscious of what I owe you, I do not appreciate the suggestion that either you or my father controls my behaviour."

Gil had to smile at that, a wry twist of the lips. No one controlled his Goddess. She was a force of nature. Nonetheless, he could not be as blithe about the rumours as her. "Perhaps I should take the children to see the playing fields, and the General should come with you to the school, Susan. My presence will only add fuel to the fire of the rumours."

Susan shook her head. "Your absence, when you are known to be in Cambridge, will look like guilt, Gil. Be damned to the rumour-mongers. I would appreciate your escort."

Gil glanced at Lord Henry, who said, "Susan is right. The only way to deal with rumours is to act as if you have done nothing at all of which to be ashamed."

Susan gave a deep sigh. "There. You have the agreement of the male head of my family. Satisfied, Rutledge?"

Even Gil, who had lived in an almost entirely male world since he was a schoolboy, knew better than to give an honest answer to that. "It shall be as you wish, Susan."

At the school, they were ushered into the head mistress's private parlour and invited to take a seat while a maid fetched Mrs Fellowes.

She lost no time in arriving, greeting them with frosty courtesy. "Mrs Cunningham. So, you have returned. And this would be Lord Rutledge, I assume."

Susan returned the ice seven-fold, inclining her head in a display of aristocratic hauteur that had the beldam shrinking a little and tempted Gil to check his nose for icicles.

"Mrs Fellowes."

The foolish woman went straight to attack without first checking the accuracy of her cannon or the disposition of her troops. "We have heard the rumours about the girls' behaviour, Mrs Cunning-ham. And your own."

Susan raised both eyebrows, and smiled, just a little. "I sincerely trust, Mrs Fellowes, that you do not teach the girls in your charge to accept baseless rumours as fact. I had assumed that this foolish start by my daughter and her friend arose from imagination and youthful patriotism, but if rumour and hearsay pass for truth in your school, perhaps I should hold you accountable for their mistaken belief that your music teacher was a French spy."

A devastating fusillade, by George. The Fellowes would have difficulty coming back from that.

Yes. Her response was a weak, "Well, I never!"

Susan showed her generosity to a fallen foe. "Come. We both, I take it, want the best thing for the school and for the two girls. Let us work together."

Mrs Fellowes stiffened, scenting in compromise the possibility of stealing the battle. "I do not know what I can do for you, Mrs Cunningham. I must think of the Academy and its reputation. The rumours are false, you say, and I believe you, for I take you for a gentlewoman." Take her for a gentlewoman? Oh my. Gil sat back to enjoy Susan's response, but the headmistress had not yet finished. "However, I must consider how to advise parents who come to me with concerns. Or, worse still, how to respond to those who take their daughters from the school without explanation."

Susan examined the tips of her gloves and said nothing.

Gil decided that was his cue. "Without support and evidence—" he looked up, a sharp glance that pinned the headmistress in silence, "and there is no support, Mrs Fellowes, I assure you—the rumours will die."

Oops. His cannonade was mistimed. Susan was shaking her head, and the headmistress was looking smug again. "Ah. You are correct, Lord Rutledge. However, while I wait for them to die, the school will be losing patrons." She turned back to Susan. "I cannot think it just that my school should suffer and fail because of the actions of your daughter and her friend, no matter how innocently they meant them."

Gil opened his mouth, but Susan stopped him, the amusement in her voice warning him that she still had a troop or two in reserve.

"No, Rutledge, let Mrs Fellowes finish. I suspect she has a solution in mind."

The old besom moved fussily in her seat, settling her gown around her. "Two possible solutions, Mrs Cunningham. First, I expel the girls from the school, thus separating myself and my other pupils from any possible contamination."

"Potentially an unwise move, given my family connections," Susan observed to Rutledge. Mrs Fellowes coloured, but did not acknowledge the remark.

"Second, I ignore the whole matter and deny the rumours, which I am willing to do for such an esteemed family, with some compensation for my probable losses, of course." She waited for Susan to comment, then broke the silence herself, satisfaction colouring her voice. "Shall we say five hundred pounds?"

Susan smiled, benignly. Uh oh. Goddess attack on the flank. "Mrs Fellowes, you are much mistaken if you think those are the only two options. I see a third, and one furthermore to which I incline. I take my daughter from your school. She will be happier, I think, at an academy in London, where she can attend as a day pupil. I understand Mr Grahame, the uncle and guardian of the Misses Grahame, intends the same solution for his nieces, but in Edinburgh."

Mrs Fellowes, her eye undoubtedly on her disappearing five hundred pounds, said stiffly, "I cannot see how that will be received by my patrons any differently than my first solution, Mrs Cunningham."

"Can you not?" Susan asked, sweetly? "And yet they will go to their new academies with a letter from you giving them a good character, which I am sure you will be happy to write, as it will be true. Lively and intelligent? Those would be appropriate words, I am sure." Susan let the silence drag while Mrs Fellowes' mind worked furiously behind shifting eyes. Not an unintelligent woman, Gil thought, but unimaginative, and definitely outclassed in this conflict. She opened her mouth and Susan cut in before she could speak. "Oh, and a character for Mademoiselle Cornillac, who will be seeking employment in Scotland so she can be close to her brother."

Mrs Fellowes sniffed. "It grieves me to displease you, Mrs Cunningham, but I do not see my way to being able to write such letters."

Susan's voice dropped still lower, as she presented the fusillade that ended the battle, except for mopping up the survivors and treating the wounded. "It grieves me to use such tactics, Mrs Fellowes, but should you be unable to write as I require, I do see my way to discussing with all my friends and relatives the lax supervision, poor judgement, and harsh treatment that sent two girl-children into danger on the busiest highway in Great Britain."

For the mercifully short rest of the interview, Gil avoided Susan's eyes, certain he would call disgrace on himself by giving way to the humour of the encounter. Soon, though, the requested letters were safely tucked into Susan's reticule and the school servants had been ordered to pack Amy's effects for sending to London. "Mr Grahame," Susan told Mrs Fellowes, "will undoubtedly make his own arrangements. He shall be calling on you himself, and I trust you will be of every assistance to him."

Mrs Fellowes, thoroughly routed, nodded her agreement, and Gil managed to contain his reaction until he and Susan had walked two streets away from the Academy. Unable to hold it in any longer, and passing a handy alley where they would be somewhat sheltered from curious eyes, Gil darted into the narrow space and succumbed. Susan took one look at him whooping with amusement and joined in, until they were both leaning weakly against a wall, gasping for breath, each meeting of the eyes prompting another gale of laughter.

"You were magnificent, Goddess," Gil told her, once he could speak again, and then, in a false falsetto, "It grieves me to displease you, Mrs Cunningham..." which set them both off again.

"Which will be a lesson to me, Gil," Susan said, at last, "for Mrs Fellowes came highly recommended by several very dear friends, and it is only now that I realise that they are all quite the silliest of women, and their daughters are made in their mould. A bright girl like Amy needs company that will challenge her and a preceptress she can admire."

The Grahames were back to the hotel before them, and Lord Henry and his grandchildren returned soon after. Miss Foster, Grahame confided to Susan, had refused to allow Pat to even step foot inside of the house, and had been delighted to wash her hands of Clementine, as well. "I am a Christian woman, Mr Grahame, but I cannot be asked to tolerate impudence and impurity. The younger girl will not take correction and the older was seen in boys' clothes the length of the North Road. And with that widow and her fancy man. You cannot expect it of me."

Grahame had agreed, with considerable alacrity, and had brought Clementine away with him immediately. "Would you lend me a maid, Mrs Cunningham, to pack for the girls? I would not know how to start, and I fear if I leave it to Miss Foster, she will have their things in the road or disposed of in the rubbish."

"Of course," Susan agreed. "I will give the orders now." She sent both of the maids from Scotland, with Grahame's man to ensure no miscommunication. Gil had disappeared by the time she returned to the small parlour they had taken over. Lord Henry, who was playing spillikins on the rug with the children, said he had gone to write letters.

Susan seated herself behind the tea trolley that had been delivered, and poured her father's preferred Oolong, black, with a slice of lemon.

"Tea, Mr Grahame?"

He sat in a nearby chair, watching the hilarity on the hearth rug.

"Thank you, Mrs Cunningham. Milk and one sugar, if you will."

Susan poured the tea and added the milk and sugar. "We could help one another, Mr Grahame, if you will consent to break your journey in London, before returning to Edinburgh. You need a maid to attend the girls on their way home with you, and I need to return two maids to my son's establishments in Scotland. I have, however, promised them a visit to London."

"I am certain my nieces would not forgive me should they miss the pleasures of a London tour, Mrs Cunningham. I accept your commission with pleasure and count myself the beneficiary of your kindness.

Susan smiled her satisfaction as the door opened and she looked up to see Gil in the doorway. "Rutledge," she said. "Mr Grahame has routed his own dragon and will be returning to London with us."

Gil crossed the room to join them and accepted the proffered cup of tea, listening with sober interest to Grahame's story but leaving it to Susan to tell their own. Something was on his mind, for he'd lost the light-hearted joy of the early afternoon. His sister-in-law, probably. Poor Gil. He carried the weight of his family on his shoulders, and none of it was his fault.

19

Gil brooded through the rest of the afternoon and into dinner. Grahame seemed on very good terms with The Goddess. Well, he was a fine and handsome man, and if he was in trade, businessmen such as he were highly respected in Scotland. Why should he not look so high? Especially now he had girls to raise. Gil could console himself that Susan had her mind set against marriage, but he was not reassured.

He managed, just, not to glare at the interloper across the table, and scolded himself for sour grapes. He would not, could not, court Susan himself. Did he expect her to live alone then? If he couldn't have her, nobody could? He would not be such a bear.

The three younger children had been given a nursery tea upstairs, and were in bed, but Amy and Pat had been permitted to dress in gowns that Mademoiselle Cornillac had selected and join the four adults for an early dinner. After a false start, when they were sent back upstairs to take their hair down as befitted the schoolgirls they were, they were partway through the first remove when a knock at the door was followed by the entry of David Wakefield, an old school friend of Gil's and a celebrated enquiry agent.

Lord Henry greeted him without surprise. "Ah. Wakefield. I'm glad you made it. Some dinner?" Without waiting for an answer, he ordered another place set, and in moments, Wakefield was helping himself from the various dishes on the table.

They kept the conversation bland while the servants were in the room, though Gil could sense that Susan burned with the same curiosity he had. That Lord Henry and Wakefield had planned this meeting seemed obvious. Something to do with Griffin's notes? Probably, though whether the secretive agent, or the genial but discreet Horse Guard general, intended to share their findings with the civilians of the party, was another matter entirely.

However, Gil was to be pleasantly surprised when the last of the meal was cleared away and Susan began to make noises about sending Amy and Pat up to the room they would share for the night.

Lord Henry put out a hand to ask her to wait and spoke to the enquiry agent. "If it is not a Crown secret, Wakefield, I think Amy and Pat deserve to know what the plot they have uncovered is about. May they stay?"

The girls, arrested in the act of getting up, exchanged wide-eyed glances, and Wakefield smiled at them. "Very well. But it is a secret, young ladies. Can I trust you to keep it one? That means not telling anyone else, not even your sisters or your dearest friends."

The girls spoke over one another in their eagerness to give the required promises, losing any pretence at adult poise when they crossed their hearts and hoped to die, with nursery earnestness. Wakefield accepted their commitment with the same grave decorum he showed in taking a glass of port poured by Lord Henry and passed by Gil.

"Mr Grahame?" Wakefield asked. "I mean no offence, but it is my duty to request the same commitment from you, sir."

This clearly thrilled the girls even more, as they bounced in their seats, and a glass each of much watered port set the seal on their evening. Hints of the women they would become settled over them once more as they drew themselves straight in their chairs and lifted their glasses, checking with Susan to see if they were holding them correctly.

Wakefield began with a quick summary of the story they all

knew, and then moved on to the new part of the story: what happened when the Horse Guard and the Home Office joined forces to decipher the materials that Gil and Susan had sent south. Wakefield became involved because one of his agents had a gift for cracking codes. 'Not, that the task was much of a challenge for a woman of her skills', Wakefield said.

A woman who broke codes? The thought set the girls bouncing again, until they remembered their adult dignity.

"The poetry book and its key allowed us to read the notes that Amy took from Griffin," Wakefield explained, with a nod to Amy. "He is definitely working with the French, but on behalf, we think, of radical elements in England and in Ireland."

Amy could contain herself no longer, "And Scotland, Mr Wakefield? Because of the men in Edinburgh?"

Another grave nod. "We think so, and the papers you found will help us to track them down and make sure they can't work against the King."

The girls glowed, and Susan spoke the warning that Gil was thinking. "You have done the Crown a service, young ladies, but I would remind you it was largely by accident, and that the outcome might have been very different had Lord Rutledge and I not been close enough to rescue you at need."

Pat's frown deepened to something more genuine and Amy shuddered. "Do not worry, Mama. I have never been more frightened in my life, and I know well what I owe Lord Rutledge and Cousin Hamish. And Mr McCormack. I will not be chasing spies again." She muttered quietly to Pat, and Gil leaned sideways to hear her. "Not without a gun, more target practice and a good plan, anyway."

From the pursed lips, Susan caught that aside as well. Amy would find herself well supervised, beyond a doubt. To cover his smile, Gil asked Wakefield what Griffin and his co-plotters were up to.

Wakefield shook his head. "They are planning something big, but we have no idea what. Only that Birmingham, Liverpool, Manchester, and Leeds have been mentioned. And also the Essex and Suffolk coast, though how that ties to the rest, I do not know."

"Luddite riots to cover an invasion?" Amy suggested. "The coast sounds like an invasion,"

"Unlikely, we think, Amy." Wakefield answered. "Near to impossible, with Napoleon's navy still in ruins and his armies engaged in Russia and in Spain. And I'd have said not the Luddites in the Midlands and the North, either. The unrest appears to have been well and truly quelled. Still, we cannot be sure, so I am travelling on to Nottingham to meet with someone who might know."

"The frame breakers are no keener on a French invasion than we are," Lord Henry argued. "I cannot see them rising at the word of a French spy."

"They might not realise," Wakefield said, rather sadly. "They have been easy enough for the government informers to infiltrate, heaven knows. Why not a French spy? Although they may have learned caution after all the arrests."

They continued to explore possibilities until they began repeating themselves, at which point Susan excused herself and escorted the girls upstairs. "There won't really be an invasion, will there?" Pat asked Susan.

"I trust my father and Mr Wakefield, Pat. If they say Napoleon cannot invade, then they have reason to know, and neither of them would tell us comfortable lies."

The girls had been sobered by the conversation and went quietly off to bed, and Susan was soon free to return to the parlour, just in time to see Gil stepping into the hall and closing the door. He saw Susan on the stairs and stopped to wait for her.

"Susan" he said, "I will say goodnight now in case I don't catch you in the morning."

Susan had expected this; had watched him carefully detaching himself over the past few days, but still his declaration was a shock. She kept her voice calm and even.

"Why? Are you leaving?"

"Yes, there's no point in delaying." He was not meeting her eyes. "I can be of no use to you or to Wakefield's spy hunt, so I am taking up my own duties. I sent a message to my sister-in-law this afternoon asking if she would receive me, just so she is not taken by surprise, but I don't plan to wait on an answer."

"So, you ride in the morning." Suddenly, she could not bear it. "Gil, may I come with you?" Part of her screamed at the thought of further separation from her children, panic rising again in her throat as it had a hundred times since she first lost Amy. But the truth was Amy would be relieved to be spared her anxious attention, and Chrissie and Michael were perfectly happy in her father's care. She could be of use to Gil, and the alternative was to let him go alone, and to lose him again. She was not ready.

He had been about to turn away, but her request brought him back, his full attention suddenly focused on her face. "But you are going back to London."

It was the right thing to do. She owed Gil her support, and she could at least store a few more memories to keep her warm in the long years ahead. "Father will take the children, and I suppose we will not be long separated." Susan put her hand on Gil's arm, looking up into his eyes; she was sure he must be able to see her feelings for him written plain on her face, though she would not embarrass them both by putting them into words. "Gil, I do not like to think of my friend going alone into who knows what emotional mess. Please. Let me come. I promise not to interfere, but you deserve to have someone who is unreservedly on your side."

"Are you?" Gil sounded more mystified than disbelieving. "You are too good to me, Goddess. I do not deserve such support."

Silly man. He persisted in thinking of himself as a villain, when everyone around him knew him to be a hero. "You deserve much more than you give yourself credit for. I may come then?"

A tension of which she had not been aware eased from Gil's shoulders and his voice warmed. "Yes. Yes, please, if your father is content to take your little tribe home with him. I will not keep you from them long." He laughed then, and added, "And I will not hold you to your promise not to interfere, either, you martinet, for if you see something that needs fixing you will not be able to help yourself, and you certainly get good results when you go into battle."

It should have been a day's drive, but they made a late start from Cambridge with many hugs and last-minute instructions. Then they were dogged by rain, poor roads, and a sign some trickster had turned about, so they went ten miles out of their way before discovering the mistake.

Moffat had taken Gil's horses on to London, and would meet them at the Selby estate, so they were crowded three into Susan's cabriolet-phaeton, Susan, Gil, and Susan's maid Banner, who effaced herself politely at each stop. Susan relished the time on the road, ranging over the issues of the day—the election, the war, the situation with the United States—and sharing news of people they both knew. Nothing private, in the presence of the maid, but there was an intimacy in the shared conversation of old friendship that eased her heart.

They were fifteen miles from the Selby estate when the wheel jammed in a rut and then broke.

"It's gone," Gil reported from his position inspecting the wheel in the fading light. He insisted on the women staying in the relative dry of the cabriolet-phaeton, but his hair was slicked to his head and rain ran down his face as he looked up. "This carriage is going nowhere."

"We go back to the previous village?" Susan asked.

Gil nodded. They had passed through a small village perhaps ten minutes earlier, and it had a pretty inn. "We'll ride, if you feel up to it, Goddess."

Susan grinned. Two carriage horses not broken to saddle? Of course she was up to it.

The horses were bewildered but tired and compliant. Gil took a nervous Banner up behind him, and they headed into the wind, tracing their steps back to the village, which they reached without incident but wet, cold, and ready for a hot fire and a substantial dinner.

Susan lay awake, listening to her maid snore from the trundle bed on the floor, and waiting for the sounds of the waking inn to trail off into silence.

She did not have to go through with it. Unsure of her welcome, unsure even what she hoped her plan would achieve, she told herself she could stay here in the warm bed and no one would be the wiser. Certainly not Gil, who had been oblivious to inviting glances and semi-accidental touches alike.

He had wanted her when they kissed. She had been a faithful wife and a chaste widow, but she was not so naive as to miss the shape of an aroused male. She shifted at the thought of that never-to-be forgotten kiss, burning and melting with a sharp longing that called her into the inn's halls.

He had withdrawn since they left Scotland. Beyond a doubt, Hamish had bent his ear on the subject of marriage. Was his reaction not message enough? He did not want a permanent relationship; said he would never take a wife. She could not accept less. Would not. This one man was everything she dreamed of: confident enough to allow her to be herself, passionate, kind, and a dear friend since they were children, though they had lost one another for a time.

She risked losing that friendship, but what if she cast her hand and won! What if they could be friends, lovers, and partners for a lifetime?

What if he rejected her? What if he went back to the cold distance with which he had armoured himself before this trip together broke the ice?

Banner gave another loud snore, and rolled to her side, snuffling into silence.

There could not be a better opportunity. Banner would sleep through the second coming, and Moffat was in the grooms' quarters near the horses. Even if some of the inn's servants were still about, what of it? To avoid feeding the rumour mill still further, they had booked adjoining rooms as brother and sister, under a false name. Anyone seeing her enter Gil's room—or, perhaps, being turned away from Gil's room—would have no identity to attach to whatever scandalous story they could imagine.

Oh, she hoped there would be a scandalous story.

But there would not be if her courage failed. She slid out from under the blankets and went to find the robe she had put ready, and a shawl to cover her hair and conceal her face. She was going to do this. She was going to try. Humiliation? Triumph? Even if all she gained was one night of love; one memory to keep her warm after Gil was gone; it would be better than dwindling into old age never having been treasured by the man who called her his Goddess and meant it.

Susan shivered, and almost turned back, but she took a deep breath, straightened her back, and glided to the door.

20

———

Gil was not in bed. The evening with Susan had been torture, with no one else present to distract him from his constant longing. He thought he had managed well enough to disguise his absorption with controlling his unruly body, but some of his responses had been so erratic she must have noticed. Though she was preoccupied with something herself: had made several odd remarks that went nowhere, and was unusually clumsy, reaching for things at the same time as him so that their hands touched, and twice—when moving around the room—coming so close to him that her hip and later her arm brushed his, and only the most powerful discipline stopped him from hauling her into his arms for another kiss like the one that haunted his nights.

Why had he ever agreed to her joining this trip?

Because he was addicted to her; could not bear to end the sweet torment of having her near, just out of reach, for as long as he could keep her.

Once again, the dreams danced across his brain: fantasies of exiling his mother to a remote estate, marrying Susan out of hand, and settling in the Gloucestershire countryside to raise babies. He'd have to buy a remote estate with money he didn't have, change The

Goddess's mind about the whole institution of marriage against all her experience, and risk bringing another generation of Rutledge monsters into the world.

Gil Rock Ledge; the man to lead a forlorn hope. But that was in the army, where he belonged. Not in the world of silk, scandal, and infamy Gideon had bequeathed to him.

Gil paced across the floor for the thousandth time. Staying awake all night was better than facing his sister-in-law tomorrow with a hangover. There. Thoughts of his brother and his brother's widow had finally subdued Gil's raging erection.

The knock on the door was so quiet, even in the silence of the night, that he had to stop and listen for it again to be sure he had not imagined it.

He stood, stunned, in the doorway. The Goddess could not be here. Almost in his room. Mere feet from his bed. Looking up at him from expectant blue eyes.

He couldn't find words to ask what she needed. One part of his anatomy had drained the blood from his brain to leap to joyous attention, anxious to take from her what he needed.

Susan's smile faltered. "Well? Are you planning to let me in?"

He moved silently to one side, letting her pass, then looked out into the hall. No one was watching.

With the door closed against the outside world, he managed to make his tongue move. "Is something wrong, Susan? Can I help you?"

She blushed, but didn't answer, avoiding his eyes and crossing quickly to the fireplace, to drop her shawl on a chair by the hearth. The glow from the fire shone through her nightgown, outlining the body within, and he had to swallow before he could speak. "You shouldn't be here, Susan. What if someone saw you?"

She looked straight at him then, provoked—as always—to respond to a direct challenge. "I am a widow. Such things are nodded at, if the woman is discreet."

With dawning hope, he began to wonder if his cock had the right of it. "Not by Hamish," he warned.

"No, so I have been very discreet. Banner would sleep through an earthquake, and no-one else is on this floor." She smiled, quirking an eyebrow at him. "Your reputation is safe, my dear Gil."

His reputation? He had no reputation, whereas she... "You know perfectly well, woman—"

"Yes, I know." In another sudden movement she took two quick strides and put her hands on his waist, lifting her face to his. "Kiss me, Gil."

He drew his head out of reach. Kiss her? As if he could stop at kissing her! "Goddess, don't—you don't know—if we—"

She reached one hand, and tangled it into his hair, dragging his mouth lower. "Sshh. Don't fret. Just enjoy."

Gil made one last attempt. "If you don't want me to toss you on that bed and take my pleasure, Goddess, you had better leave right now."

She grinned, a glow of pure delight. "Why on earth do you suppose I came, you Rock Ledge you? Though I hope we shall both take pleasure."

He surrendered. To her. To himself. He hardly knew, conscious only of growling, "you can be sure of that," as he lowered his mouth to plunder hers, only the barest thread of sanity keeping his hands gentle as she plastered herself against him and plundered back.

The incandescent moment left Susan limp and speechless. Gil had reached for his release as she cried out in hers, and now his weight pressed her to the mattress. So real. So far beyond anything she had imagined. She turned her head slightly to press a kiss to the hollow of at the base of his neck, and he shifted, lifting himself onto his forearms, then sliding them under her and rolling so she ended up on top of him, still joined, but slipping as he softened.

"I was crushing you," he explained.

"I liked it," Susan grumbled.

He was kissing her forehead near her hairline, and she felt his lips stretch into a smile. "I need you to be able to breath, my Goddess, for when I recover a little. I didn't hurt you?"

"You are big, but I liked it," she repeated. In truth, it had been more than three years since she had last been bedded, and she would be sore tomorrow. But it was worth it.

"Slower, next time," Gil commanded.

And it was. She would never again have to suppress a burst of irritation when she heard the name that had plagued her childhood. Instead, whenever he slipped and called her 'Goddess', she would remember this night of—yes—worship. With eyes, hands, and his beautifully carved and mobile lips and tongue, he paid devout and prayerful attention to every inch of her anatomy, until she was one screaming flame. She would not forget how he held her after her peak, and then drove her back into the heights again.

"See?" she said, when he was gently tracing the silver striations on her abdomen that bore witness to her childbearing, "I am no celestial being."

"Not from the Christian heaven," he agreed, and bent to replace the explorations of his finger with his tongue. In short bursts between licks, kisses, and nips, he said, "A pagan Goddess: strong, magnificent," his eyes laughed up at her for a moment before he turned back to his task, "lusty."

"Flawed," she insisted.

"Bearing the honourable scars of service given to others," he countered, his kisses tending down into her curls, following the fingers that had already dived into the waiting warmth, so that she whimpered his name.

He had his own scars, and in the quiet moments as they recovered between bouts, she asked about some of them, shuddering to think how often he had been close to death. And she returned him his own argument when he claimed they made him ugly. "Honourable scars of service given to others."

He buried his face in her hair, hugging her with a fierce strength that still he tempered so he did not crush her. "The ones on my soul are worse, Goddess, but for tonight I will not care, if you do not."

Susan had not survived seventeen years of careless affection and neglect without scars of her own, but tonight began the healing of wounds she had not known she had. To be the sole focus of such a man's adoration! She had had no idea. And to think, if she could just persuade him, they could have this for the rest of their lives!

She pressed a kiss to Gil's chest, and he lifted her chin so he could connect his mouth with hers. They did not speak again for some time.

Somewhere on the far side of heaven, when he had been brooding alone in his bed chamber, Gil had known he would not sleep this night. As the dawn began to lighten the sky outside, he watched Susan sleeping in his arms.

He had been right, but oh how different a night it was than the one he had expected. This was a treasure to keep him warm into old age, a memory to lift out when his life was at its bleakest. The night his Goddess had granted his lifelong wish and given him the precious gift of herself. He didn't understand why he had been so favoured, but he was grateful beyond measure, and he wished he could do something for her, in return.

On impulse, he said what he was thinking. "Ah, Goddess. If you knew how long I have dreamed of this."

She was not asleep after all, cracking one lid open and shifting her head back to see his face. "And did it live up to your expectations?"

He kissed her forehead. "More. Far more."

"For me, too. I tried not to wonder. But I could never have imagined…" She trailed off, and he could not help a smug warmth at the awe in her voice.

But she was pulling back, looking over him towards the window. "I must go. Banner will be awake soon, and the inn's maids will be about."

He reluctantly released her and followed her out of bed to hand her a cloth to wash in the cold water on the wash stand, and then her night rail and her shawl.

"Thank you," she said, as she settled the shawl around her shoulders and unlocked the door.

Gil opened it for her, then pulled her to him for another kiss.

"Thank you, Goddess. I feel I should be apologising, but this night has been a rare treasure. I will always hold it in my heart."

She looked up at him, her brow creased as if his words displeased her, but footsteps on the stairs sent her hurrying down the hall to let herself into the next room, and he was alone. Alone, but deeply at peace, with a heart full of rejoicing. Perhaps, after all, he could manage an hour's sleep.

Susan had not realised how hard it would be to behave as if nothing had changed. When she and Gil met over breakfast, she kept her eyes turned down, afraid that the bustling servants would see something different in the way she looked at him. Even so, she could feel her body leaning towards his as he spoke, that deep voice vibrating in places that ached pleasantly from the night's activity.

It was a relief to walk with him to the wheelwright's, propriety allowing her hand to rest lightly on his arm, the bonnet sheltering her expression even from him. They talked of commonplaces; the day's journey, the weather, which was still a little sullen but looked to clear during the day. Never voluble, today Gil was more laconic than ever, but his eyes softened with an intense heat whenever she could no longer resist looking at him.

Heavens. If Banner caught that look, her secret would be a secret no longer! Surely now he would see they were meant to be together? But she had used her entire store of daring. He would have to make the next move.

Gil returned her to the inn before riding out with the wheelwright, and she took some sewing down into the private parlour they had hired, hoping the man would make short work of the repairs. They needed to reach Lady Rutledge's refuge, where the presence of others would dilute the effects of the night.

Susan was uncomfortable that morning. Did she regret the most glorious night of Gil's entire life? He hoped not, but she wouldn't look at him, and she kept the conversation firmly on general matters of little interest or importance.

What did that mean for their future? This morning, he would have asked her to marry him, had he not been interrupted by the waking inn and her determination to return unseen to her room.

"Courage, Rutledge," he told himself. "Susan, I need to meet with my sister-in-law, but after that…" *After I've found the money to give her an allowance, and reworked my finances yet again, perhaps I can afford a wife.* It was hopeless, but wasn't he known for winning against hopeless odds? And he had never yearned so earnestly after victory.

She filled the space left by his silence. "I daresay I shall leave you once the first meeting is over, Gil. I must return to my own life."

That was it, then. She was not thinking of a future with him at all. He listened as best he could while she chattered about the people she would see in London, and the holiday she planned with her brothers and their families. To his ears, attuned to her every mood, she sounded nervous.

To set her better at ease, he left her at the inn with her maid and took the wheelwright out to the abandoned carriage.

Fortunately, the repairs proved simple, and by mid-morning they were on their way again, approaching the Selby estate not long before noon. Gil sent Moffat on ahead to warn Lady Rutledge of their imminent arrival, and they were immediately ushered through to warm parlour by a stern but courteous butler.

"Mrs Cunningham and Lord Rutledge, my lady," the butler announced, and Gil caught Lady Rutledge's flinch at the second name.

He knew straight away that the sitting woman was his sister-in-law. The other, who stood behind her, glaring at him, would not have suited Gideon at all. She was the epitome of an English countrywoman: sturdily built, square shouldered, with a strong jaw and a challenging frown. The kind of woman the generous described as handsome, her chief beauties the dark hair neatly piled into an intricate folded knot on her head and fine dark eyes that flashed irritation at Gil, as if resenting his existence.

Which she no doubt did.

The sitting woman was another type altogether. She had the ethereal beauty that Gideon admired: the pale hair, the blue eyes, the frail bones that looked as if they would snap at a cross word. She was little too, under five feet tall, which helped to make her look much younger than her nineteen years, like a schoolgirl dressed in her mother's clothes, pretending to be an adult and afraid of being caught. She was valiantly hiding her fear behind a rictus of a welcoming smile, while holding the hand her protective sister rested on her shoulder with a grip that turned her knuckles white.

Susan broke the silence. "Lady Rutledge, I do not know if you remember me, but I met you several times when I accompanied my cousin, Lady Chirbury, into Chipping Niddwick."

"I do remember," Lady Rutledge acknowledged, in a high girlish voice. "Mrs Cunningham, may I make known to you my sister, Miss Cleghorn."

Susan inclined her head, as did the sister.

After a moment, when no one said anything further, Susan completed the introductions. "And this, of course, is Gil, the new Lord Rutledge. He has come to see how you go on and to find if he can be of any assistance."

Lady Rutledge shot a quick glance at Gil then looked down at the hand in her lap, seemed to realise that it was twitching at her skirts, stilled it, then bit her lip.

Susan opened her mouth, but before she could speak, Miss Cleghorn said, as if dredging her manners from some dark well and dragging them into the light, "Would you like to sit down? I will send for tea."

"Thank you," Susan agreed. "That would be pleasant."

Gil took a chair far enough from his reluctant hostess that he would not spook her with his size. At least now, given permission to sit, he was not looming over the poor little thing.

He cast about for a way to start a conversation, but nothing occurred, and he was grateful when Susan broke the silence. "You were perhaps expecting us yesterday? We stopped over at Little Epping last night. The turn in the weather slowed us, and then a problem with the carriage… I trust you were not inconvenienced?"

Miss Cleghorn turned from giving instructions to the butler, and said, "Lord Rutledge did not tell us what day he was coming."

"Ah. Of course. He was uncertain of his plans."

Miss Cleghorn resumed her place at her sister's shoulder. Susan tried again, this time addressing Lady Rutledge directly. "I trust your daughters are well? You have two, I believe. I am sorry. I do not remember their names."

Miss Cleghorn answered. "Paeony and Rose. They are beautiful. And well cared for, I can assure you."

Those were not the names Gil's mother had told him, and he was startled into comments. "Paeony and Rose? I thought…" Eunice and Gertrude, the dowager had said, each girl bearing one of the dowager's own names.

Susan spoke over his remark. "What pretty names. A tribute to your sister, Lady Rutledge? Your given name is Flora, is it not, Miss Cleghorn?"

Something sparked deep in Lady Rutledge's eyes, a flash of spirit that lightened Gil's heart. She was stronger than she looked, and Gideon had not succeeded in destroying her. "My sister has been a tower of strength," she said. "And they are perfectly proper names."

Gil smiled his warmest smile. "I will lay odds that my mother did not like them. I do, though. Good for you, Lady Rutledge. Paeony and Rose it is."

The tea arrived with a succession of maids, and conversation lapsed again, but Lady Rutledge had given him one startled look at his remark and kept sneaking further peeks as Miss Cleghorn directed the placement of the tea makings.

When the last servant had left the room, Gil could contain himself no longer. "Look, you have nothing to fear from me. I just want to assure myself that you and my nieces have everything you need. And I would like to get to know them a little, if you permit."

Miss Cleghorn paused in the act of pouring a cup of tea for Susan and firmed her jaw. "With what purpose, my lord? My sister and her children have been through enough at the hands of your family."

"Flora!" Lady Rutledge protested.

"Chloe, we cannot trust him," Miss Cleghorn insisted. "He is that man's brother."

Susan shook her head. "He is brother to the late Lord Rutledge and has suffered much at that evil man's hands. No, Gil, let me speak." She reached across from her chair to touch Lady Rutledge lightly on the knee. "Lady Rutledge, I first met Gil when he was a boy of twelve, and I know him as a gentle man of great integrity. I grew up knowing him, since our family became his place of refuge from his own. I realise that trust must be hard for you, and I honour your sister for her caution on your behalf, but please believe that Gil is not your enemy."

Lady Rutledge grabbed Susan's hand in both of hers, and spoke only to her, her words tumbling over one another. "You have daughters, I remember. Mine are all I have; the only good thing to come from my marriage. Mama-in-law said she would make her son take the girls; that I was not fit to raise them. She said I was mad, and that Lord Rutledge would have me committed to an asylum and she would bring my daughters up to be proper gentlewomen. But I will never let my girls go to that woman. I would rather die."

Gil heartily approved of the sentiment, though killing someone else, his mother, for example, would be a more practical form of defence. "So would I," he agreed. "After what she allowed to happen to her own daughters? I would not put a dog I was responsible for into the care of my mother."

The two sisters looked at each other, shaking their heads in doubt, and Miss Cleghorn demanded, "Is that true? You will not obey the dowager in this?"

Susan's response was a not inelegant snort. Thank goodness she was here. "You know his nickname is Rock Ledge? No one shifts Gil from his way. And he is on your side in this, Lady Rutledge."

Gil nodded, doing his best to look harmless and amiable, and the two sisters relaxed back into their seats. Miss Cleghorn finished pouring Susan's cup, and then prepared one for her sister before asking Gil his preference, but the silence was no longer as oppressive as it had been.

Lady Rutledge took several sips, then asked, "Are you staying? That is, have you bespoken rooms in the village, or would you wish to stay here?"

Gil and Susan had discussed this point, agreeing Lady Rutledge would more quickly become comfortable with them if they stayed, and Anne had assured Gil that the manor was well supplied with rooms, bed linen, and servants. "If you would permit, we will stay with you," Gil said, when Susan did not answer.

Again, the sisters exchanged a silent message in a glance, and Miss Cleghorn rose to give Gil his cup, then said, "I will give the instructions. Just sit, Chloe. I can do it."

"May I call you Chloe?" Gil ventured, after Miss Cleghorn had left the room, "And will you call me Gil? We are brother and sister, after all."

Another flash of that hidden spirit, this time with an amused twinkle. "Not Rock Ledge?"

Gil groaned. "How cruel of Susan to tell you. She gave me that name, you know, when I was a boy, and it has dogged my heels ever since. Gil, if you please."

"Gil, then," Chloe agreed.

"In revenge, as you well know, you hound," Susan said, and explained how he had given her a nickname, and how her brothers had taken it up, joined it with their own nickname for her, and turned them into form of torment until she demanded a simpler name and gained her parents' consent to be called Susan.

Gil was horrified. He knew she had objected to the title he bestowed, but he had never realised he had opened her to such teasing. No wonder she hated him! Except last night showed that she didn't, did she? Or not any more.

Miss Cleghorn interrupted his train of thought, and just as well before the physical response to his memories was too powerful to subdue. "There. Your rooms will be ready soon. I have ordered your luggage taken up, and water so that you can freshen after your journey."

Chloe rose gracefully to her feet. "Lord Rut—Gil, would you like to meet the children while you wait? We could go up to the nursery."

Miss Cleghorn opened her mouth, then took a good look at her sister's face and said nothing.

"I would enjoy that." Gil told Chloe. "Susan? Would you care to join us?" If his Goddess could work her magic with the little girls, this visit would be off to a good start.

21

The Rutledge girls were little mice, shrinking into their mother's and their aunt's skirts and watching Gil with wide-eyed caution, as if waiting for him to explode. The nurse hovered watchfully, clearly anxious, but obedient to Miss Cleghorn's unspoken command to remain at a slight distance.

The girls were five years and three years, but much of a size, the older a diminutive sprite in the mould of her mother, and the other enough like childhood portraits of Gideon to make Gil wonder how Chloe coped with the reminder.

Chloe pulled them forward and gently but firmly insisted they curtsey to their Uncle Gil, which Rose did with fairy grace and the younger, Paeony, with considerable reluctance. Gil gravely returned a bow, and then asked for permission to sit on the floor, "For I am afraid that if I remain with my head up here near the ceiling, the young ladies will get sore necks," he explained.

The joke fetched half a smile from Miss Cleghorn, so was not completely wasted. The little girls watched with awe as he lowered himself to the rug, and their eyes opened even wider when Susan joined him. Miss Cleghorn grinned and plopped herself down as well. "Come on, Chloe. The party is down here," she said.

They stayed only a few minutes, sitting on the floor talking about which of the toys belonged in the Selby nursery (most of them), and which were the property of the Rutledge girls (a few books and one rag doll each, made by their mother). Rose had her doll clutched tightly, and Paeony, after seeing the attention that Rose's baby garnered, broke away from her aunt and ran into the little alcove where she had her cot, coming back with the doll held by one arm.

She almost brought it to Gil but veered at the last minute to hold it up before Susan. "Dolly," she said. "My dolly."

"She is very pretty," Susan said. The doll had a delicately painted face, almost life-like in its rendition. Wool curled into rolls and tightly sewn to the head gave it a neat hairstyle, and it was dressed in a pinafore very like the one Paeony wore herself.

After that spurt of confidence, Paeony withdrew back to her aunt's knee, and Susan clearly decided they had made enough of a start, rising gracefully to her feet.

"Thank you for your hospitality, young ladies," she said. "Uncle Gil and I will visit again."

Miss Cleghorn gave Paeony a kiss and handed her to the nurse, and Chloe did the same for Rose. "I shall be back up for our story," Chloe promised.

Gil half expected a protest, but the children merely nodded, meekly, and followed their nurse's instruction to return to a game the adults had interrupted; some activity with blocks laid out on the nursery table.

"Did you paint the dolls' faces?" he asked Chloe. "They are very good."

"They are better than good," Susan said, while Chloe blushed and demurred. "You are a talented artist, Chloe."

Miss Cleghorn was delighted at this praise of her sister, and said so. "She is a very good painter, and I hope she will take it up again. Not just dolls, but real painting."

Gil followed a summoned footman to his appointed room, wondering for the thousandth time what his poor sister-in-law's life had been like in the lair of the monster. It was, of course, Gideon's habit to take from his victims anything that made their life bearable. Gil hoped that Chloe would indeed return to what Miss Cleghorn called 'real painting'.

Susan found her own way back down to the parlour after she had washed and changed, and hesitated outside long enough to be tempted to eavesdrop on the conversation within.

"Do you think he is sincere?" That was Chloe, sounding doubtful.

Flora was not convinced, either. "Time will tell, dearest. I like her more than I expected."

Chloe's voice hinted at agreement. "She is not at all like the women he used to bring home." Susan raised an eyebrow. She should think not. The former Lord Rutledge preferred rabbits. Timid and easy to dominate.

Flora was chuckling. "I put them in separate rooms on different sides of the manor." Clearly, the two women had made up their minds that Susan was Gil's lover. Susan supposed it was a natural assumption. She was surprised by the thought that, after last night, it was a true assumption.

Chloe was worried about Flora's arrangements. "Oh dear. I hope it does not make him angry. I suppose he will make her come to him." He wouldn't try, and she would not go if he did. Perhaps, if their bedrooms had been adjacent, she might have taken the risk of being seen by a servant. But crossing the entire manor? Any nascent plan to repeat the previous night had to be dropped, at least while they stayed.

"She does not seem like the sort of woman one makes," Flora said thoughtfully. "I like her, Chloe."

That was enough. Susan was being rude, listening in on a conversation not intended for her ears. She took a few quick steps away from the door, caught sight of Gil descending the stairs, and waited for him to come up to her. "I have a beautiful view of the park from my window, Gil," she said, pitching her voice just a little louder to warn the sisters of their approach. "Anne is to be congratulated. The manor is lovely."

Now the ice was broken, the little family of women slowly relaxed around their visitors. A dozen times, Gil gave thanks that Susan was there, smoothing over the moments when an abrupt movement from him or a misinterpreted word froze Gideon's victims like a mouse caught in the gaze of a cat.

Gil took his lead from her and opted for complete frankness: about his wish to repair, as well as he could, the damage done by his brother and mother, and about his intention to give Chloe a living allowance from which she could support herself and the little girls in a style suitable to the family of a Viscount. Yes, and her sister too.

The amount he had in mind seemed modest to him but stunned her into silence for a moment.

"But can you afford it," she asked, anxiously, and Gil assured her that the estate could take the charge. Supplemented from his private investments, which he had intended to use to recover the estate. But the viscountess and her daughters took priority, and the repairs and improvements he intended would just have to wait.

His only concern was to ensure she could manage her allowance without falling into debt. He didn't want to insult Chloe when they were reaching their way towards an amiable acquaintance, but he would be damned before he set her up to fail.

Consulted, Susan advised involving Flora in the discussion, and continuing his policy of frankness. "Not me, I think, Gil. This is a family matter," and she went off to have a dolls' party in the nursery with the little girls.

Asked for a private conversation over a cup of tea, both women were apprehensive, so Gil decided to get straight to the point. "I have spoken with Chloe about her allowance, Flora," he said to the older sister, who nodded. "She should have an allowance," she agreed. "She should always have had an allowance instead of asking That Man or his mother for every little thing."

Gil nodded. It was as he thought. Chloe had never been permitted to manage money. And he knew from examining his brother's papers that she had no marriage settlement, no agreed widow's jointure. With Gideon leaving only the entailed estate, and that in debt and disarray, she had been surviving on the charity of the Chirburys. Thank God for Rede and Anne, but both Chloe and Flora agreed that they could not stay at the Selby manor forever. "And I have not been able to imagine where we might go or how we could support ourselves," Flora told him.

"It is only right that Chloe have an allowance to support herself and the children," he agreed. "But Chloe and Flora, I do have one concern, and I hope that together we can work out how to handle it."

It was the right approach. By the end of the discussion, he knew that Flora had been managing her brother's household—yes, and the home farm—since she was seventeen, "And it was not easy, Gil, for I could never be sure when he would arrive home and take the income from the farm, or would win and be amenable to giving me some of his plunder. I needed to always act as if the resources I had were all I would ever have, and to build up stores when I could."

Gil hadn't known Cleghorn except by reputation, which was enough. If Flora had kept her servants paid and fed on what she could glean from the bastard, she could certainly teach her sister the rudiments of managing a simple budget.

He named the amount he had in mind, and both sisters reacted with awed silence, before a burst of excited calculations.

The three of them agreed that Chloe would make the decisions, with Flora to advise her, and would send her accounts to Gil every month for him to review. "Monthly to start with," he said. "Quarterly once you are in the way of things. And Chloe, I will not be questioning how you choose to spend your own money. I will just be checking to make sure you are not being cheated in any way, and that I am giving you enough for your needs."

He handed her the first quarter's allowance, which he had brought with him. "That is for the coming quarter," he said. "When I leave here, I will arrange to send you what you are owed since my brother died." Another seven months, which would mean selling something to raise the money. But it was only fair.

"But it is far too much," Chloe protested.

"Not once you decide on a home of your own," he argued. "Your sister knows the cost of servants, and all the household appointments. Indeed, even if you save what you do not need to spend at the moment, I will expect you to apply to me to help you set up your new household once you have decided where to go."

He left the two sisters discussing new clothes for the little girls and an assistant nursemaid for the girl's nurse, who had been their own when they were children, and who was currently working for love of her former charges. "We will be able to pay Nanna, Flora," Chloe said. "How wonderful!"

His job here was done, Gil told Susan, but she informed him that he needed to stay long enough to get to know the children. "Read to them from their books, Rutledge. Ask them about their dolls. Take them out into the garden and show them how to catch a ball."

He followed her prescription and was rewarded with favourite uncle status when the little girls discovered his ability to make accurate farm animal noises. The women caught him at it, coming into the nursery with fabric and tape measures when he was on the rug with Paeony and Rose, one on each knee. He was imitating the hog pictured in the book of rhymes he had been reading, and Paeony was helpless with laughter. Even Rose was giggling, muffling the noise in the hollow of his neck. And Nanna's stiff caution around him had turned to benign approval, so when his ladies entered he cast dignity to the wind and managed another loud succession of oinks.

They lingered for several more days. Susan was helping the sisters to make clothes for the children and a new gown each in half-mourning instead of the black they had been wearing when he arrived. And Gil was in no hurry to end the idyll. Getting to know Gideon's daughters had been a good idea. They showed no sign of their father's stain. Indeed, they were as sweet-natured as their mother, and nothing like his own. He watched Susan with them. Surely, with her as a mother, any children he might have would be proof against the monstrous cruelty that plagued the Rutledges? But Susan had her mind set against marriage; had shown no sign of wanting even a repeat of their lovemaking in the inn, though Gil lay awake each night fighting his own body to remain in his bed instead of scandalising the household by demanding access to her room.

"Are you taking a ride this morning, Gil?" she asked him over breakfast one morning. "For if so, I have a commission for you." He would take any commission, of course, even buying more ribbon of a particular colour, as she requested, though he hoped the village storekeeper would be better at matching the sample she supplied than he expected to be himself.

He and Moffatt could exercise the horses in that direction as well as any other. He checked with Chloe and Flora to see if they wanted anything and promised his nieces a sweetmeat from the village bakery, though Flora warned him that cook would scold, since the baker was her sister and the two had a fine rivalry over feeding treats to the two little Rutledges.

They were coming out of the shop with bags in hand when Gil stopped, his eyes narrowing. Across the road, just disappearing into the blacksmith's forge leading a limping horse, was a man who looked familiar.

Moffatt frowned. "That looked like that villain Griffin," he said.

"Unlikely. What would he be doing here? But we will check, Moffatt. Put these parcels into the saddle bags and follow me. Quietly now."

He found a vantage point where he could look into the forge without being observed. The man was the right size but turned away from Gil while he complained to the blacksmith about his important commission and his horse's need for immediate attention. The voice was right, too. Gil waited patiently for the man to turn. It seemed too much of a coincidence that Griffin should chance to be here, in the same village as Gil, at the same time.

But he was. He turned to look out of the door, just as Moffatt came up behind Gil, and it was Griffin beyond question. "I need to be back by noon," Griffin fretted.

The smith's voice was deep and soothing. "I'll have thy horse for thee in fifteen minutes, mister, and not a minute more for all thy worrying. Thee'll have time for a pint, if thee will, to wet thy throat before thee head back to the coast."

Gil drew Moffatt with him out of sight and back across to their horses. "Go back to the house, Moffat, and tell Mrs Cunningham that I have seen Griffin and am following him."

"But, my lord, I should come with you——"

Gil shook his head. "One is less likely to be seen than two. Go. Follow your orders." He relented at Moffatt's worried expression. "I'll leave the usual marks. You can follow me once you have passed on your message."

Gil waited behind a hedge just out of the village on the road that led to the coast, hoping he had guessed correctly. Before long, his patience was rewarded as Griffin passed him, holding his horse to a brisk walk. Gil shadowed him on the inward side of the hedge, jumping fences at need, listening carefully for any change in his quarry's pace or direction.

Twice, he had to leave the cover of the fields when Griffin took a turn down another lane, and once he came to a hedge too high to jump and had to circle back to find a way through. But each time, he caught up with Griffin again, and glimpses let him know that Griffin was totally oblivious to the pursuit, looking ahead, his mind clearly focused elsewhere.

In half an hour, Gil pulled to a halt just inside the cover of a small copse. Before him, Griffin rode across cleared ground to a Martello Tower, one in a chain of defensive watchtowers built along the coast in response to the threat of invasion. It loomed squat and solid out of the marshland, a round stone tower with the only access by a ladder to a door well above head height on this inland side.

The guard who watched from the top of the ladder waved at

Griffin as he approached, and Griffin saluted him back. Gil frowned. He was expected, then. More traitors? But they wore British uniforms: Gil recognised the colours and markings of the local Essex militia.

A man came from a tent near the foot of the tower to take Griffin's horse, and Griffin himself swiftly climbed the ladder and disappeared inside.

Gil needed more information. He nudged his horse into a walk and set out across the open land.

22

Susan received Moffatt's message in horror. "Your master is doing what? Is he mad? Chloe, I will need to borrow a horse. And do you have a gun?" Chloe, her eyes wide, shook her head.

"Finch," Susan demanded of the butler, "the keys to the gun room, please. Are you armed, Moffatt? Is Lord Rutledge?" Dear God, what is that foolish man walking into? "Come. There is no time to lose."

Flora protested. "Susan, you are not going after them? But what can you do? You are a woman?"

Susan stopped on her way to the door. "I am a woman whose man is in danger, and I will not sit at home waiting for him to die."

Moffatt took the opportunity to get between her and the door. "The colonel can deal with one man, ma'am," he said, soothingly, "You don't need to worry."

"And if that one man is meeting others?" Susan demanded. "Moffatt, you can help me or stand out of the way."

Chloe leapt to her feet. "Yes. We must send more men. Finch, ask for volunteers among the servants. We must help Lord Rutledge contain this villain."

Susan nodded quickly. "Thank you, Chloe. I will not wait but send them after us. Moffatt, you know where to go?"

"The colonel—that is, my lord will have left a trail, ma'am."

Susan followed the butler down the hall towards the gun room, saying over her shoulder, "Explain what to look for to whomever is leading the relief party, and organise me a horse, please Moffatt."

She looked back a few moments later when she heard running steps behind her. "Lady Rutledge is arranging the horses and organising the rescue party," Moffatt said, before she could ask him why he wasn't following her orders. "My lord would never forgive me if I didn't help you choose the right gun, ma'am."

His jaw was set, and arguing would waste time, so Susan hurried on after the butler and left him to follow. Stubborn men.

It took only a few minutes to select the two guns she could handle, with a horse holster that would fit them both, and everything she needed to load them. Moffatt watched closely, but said nothing, then helped himself to another weapon to go with the one he had fetched from his master's room.

Chloe had fresh horses for them both saddled and ready in the stable-yard, and several of the estate's groundworkers and footmen—old soldiers, by the way they held themselves, waiting for Moffatt's instructions.

"Ten minutes," Chloe told her. "Give us ten minutes to arm them and get them mounted, Susan. You cannot go on your own."

"I cannot wait. Moffatt and I will be careful, I promise, but I am leaving now, Chloe."

Moffatt returned from a low-voiced conversation with the leader of the rescue party. Susan gave her horse the signal to move off at a brisk trot before he had even mounted, but in moments he drew level with her. "We'll cut across the fields to the coast road, ma'am," he said. "Save a bit of time."

Susan fretted about possibly missing the trail until Moffatt, ranging into the fields on the side of the road, triumphantly showed her two whippy branches tied into one at rider height, bent so that they pointed south, in the direction of the coast. Moffatt stopped for long enough to tie his neckerchief in the gap he'd pushed through in the hedge. "Hope those house boys can figure that out," he grumbled.

After that, they stayed in the field, except where another sign— tied branches, chalked arrows, twigs laid in a pattern on the ground —indicated that Gil had changed direction.

The road twisted and forked, but always a sign sent them down the right path, until the smell of salt and pools of standing water in the hollows beside the lane spoke of the approaching coast.

In the flat land, they saw the tower before the sea came into view. It loomed above a copse of trees, solid and uncompromising. But it was the fire on top that had Susan hauling her horse to a stop in order to see better. "One of them invasion towers," Moffatt said.

"A Martello tower, yes, but why the fire?"

"A signal?" Moffatt suggested, and on the thought, they both clapped their heels to their horses and dropped their hands.

As they rounded the copse, some native caution reinserted itself, and Susan hauled her horse to a stop, just as a very young man stepped out from behind a bush to her right, a gun pointed at her chest. He wore what she was certain was a British uniform, and he was at least hesitating about shooting her, though his alarmed look at Moffatt, who was coming up on her left shoulder, suggested he might change his mind at any minute.

Time for a gamble. If he was with Griffin, it was the wrong hand to play. She said a quick prayer that the man was what he seemed to be; a boy drafted from a nearby farm as part of the Tower's complement of staff. "Are you from the Tower," she asked. "Can you tell us what is happening? We have a relief force coming, but Lord Rutledge rode ahead alone to try to stop the traitor."

The boy lowered his weapon, his face relaxing in relief. Heavens. He was right to trust her in this instance, of course, but as a general principle she could not approve. "'is lordship went up inside, Missus. After the shooting started and the bonfire. But the Frenchie shot at us and hit Martin. He's the other groom, Missus. And 'is lordship said to watch out for anyone coming, because he'd sent for help. The Frenchie pulled up the ladder, but he made another one out of a tree. 'E's a right one, 'is lordship." The boy shook his head in admiration.

"Show me the ladder," Susan commanded, her eyes on the wall that surrounded the top of the tower. Silhouetted against the glow of the fire, two men struggled, first one then the other having the advantage.

She chirruped the horse into another walk, keeping it firmly in hand, though it shied at the approach to the tower. Another man sat with his back against a rock, one bloodied leg stretched out in front of him and a gun resting across his knees. Martin, no doubt.

Above them, a shot sounded, and then another, as the two on top of the Tower circled, leapt out of sight, and reappeared to grapple again on the very edge of the wall. "Does Griffin have accomplices in the Tower?" Susan asked, as she dismounted. Gil's ladder was a tree trunk with lopped branches roughly nailed at intervals that suited his legs and would stretch hers. But she would manage. She would have to manage.

"Who's Griffin, Missus?"

Moffatt clouted him, lightly. "The villain, you fool. How many of them up there are working with him?"

The boy ducked, clearly used to such treatment. "Not any, I reckon. Most everyone is asleep. I reckon sommat in the stew? Martin and me, we was about to have ours when the rest of the grooms started dropping where they sat, and his lordship said likely it was the same up in the Tower."

At that moment, there was another shot, and then a scream, high pitched and coming closer, until the sound of impact told the tale. Susan, fighting faintness, moved back until she could see the crumpled body and take a deep breath. It was too small to be Gil. He was still up there.

She turned back to the Tower, stripping off her jacket and her sash and then tying the sash again around her hips so she could kilt her skirts out of her way. "Moffatt, hold the ladder steady for me."

Moffatt was still looking after the body. "Reckon that villain be dead, ma'am, falling from that height."

"Undoubtedly," Susan said impatiently, "but once I can get

inside, Moffatt, you shall check, and stay down here to guard my back."

Moffatt was shaking his head. "I can't let you go up there alone, ma'am. His lordship would kill me. We don't know how many of them there are."

Susan had no time for patience. She tried reason first. "If that man had accomplices, they were not helping in the fight. Nor have we heard them coming to investigate. And I do not want them coming in behind me, Moffatt. I need you out here while I go to attend to Lord Rutledge."

Moffatt wasn't convinced. "I should go up first, ma'am."

Susan pulled hundreds of years of aristocratic heritage into her voice and her glare. "You will do what you are told, Moffatt. I am going to Lord Rutledge, over you, if necessary. Hold the ladder."

He grumbled but could not quite bring himself to physically stop her. Not that he obeyed completely. Once she had made her scrambling and inelegant way to the top, she heard him order the boy to steady the ladder, and it began to shake again as he climbed behind. Susan ignored him, crossing the large room, passing several men asleep with their heads on the table beside plates of stew.

The stair upwards was inside the thick wall. She ran up until she came out onto the top of the tower. The centre was well ablaze, the cannon engulfed in fire. Someone had packed it around with barrels and firewood, and the heat from the conflagration beat against her face. She circled around it, searching for Gil, barely conscious of Moffatt following her onto the roof.

There. On the wall, and far too close to the edge. The top lip of the outer wall sloped down to a gutter, and Gil lay with his head and one arm over the inner edge, one boot swinging free over the void, and the other wedged in the gutter. Susan climbed up to where she could reach his head, putting her hand over his mouth and sighing with relief when she felt his warm breath on his hand.

"He lives," she told Moffatt.

She checked him as well as she could, stretching to run her hands over his torso, flinching when one came away from his side covered in blood. He was wounded again, the annoying man. He stirred at the touch and turned his head to see her. "Goddess?"

"Gil, you have been wounded. We need to move you, but I want to be sure I will not do more damage."

He was sucking in air, trying to talk. "Need—to put—fire out. Signal for—French."

Moffatt met her eyes and left to circle the fire to the other side and look out to sea. He returned, shaking his head.

"No sign of any ships, my lord," he reassured Gil.

"You there—Moffat? Help—lady—put out—fire."

"I will see what I can do, Gil," Susan reassured him. "But first, we have to get you down to safety. Where do you hurt? Here. Let us help you."

Together, she and Moffatt eased Gil as gently as they could down into the relative safety of the roof's interior, ignoring his continued protests.

"Just—creased—me. Leave me—here. Stop—signal for—ships." He knocked Susan's hand away.

"I see no ships, Gil. Stay still, you foolish man. You've been wounded. Oh, very well. Moffat, go and fetch some blankets. If we have enough, we might be able to smother the flame."

"Something—to knock—wood apart," Gil instructed. "Smother one—log at—a time."

Moffatt disappeared behind the fire, and Susan bent to kiss Gil behind its shelter. The iron rammer for the cannon caught her eye, and she began knocking pieces from the fire, being careful to push them away from where Gil lay. Moffatt joined her, dropping a pile of blankets and disappeared again, reappearing a few minutes later with two buckets of water to tip over the blankets, then hurrying downstairs again to come back with a pike.

Hot and dirty, burnt and scratched, they worked side by side, knocking pieces from the beacon and smothering them with the wet blankets, one log or barrel at a time, barely seeming to make headway, but stopping at intervals to see that the beacon was smaller. Susan used the pauses to check on Gil, who kept insisting he was fine, though he lapsed in and out of consciousness.

Noises below had her grabbing for her guns, but the groom from the ground led a company of militia and the party from Selby Manor onto the roof, and their ordeal was over.

It seemed like no time at all before the militia had the rest of the blaze extinguished, and Susan was able to focus on checking Gil's wound, which was worse than Gil had said, a gunshot in the side, and the bullet still within. Yes, and another scrape on the arm that had been injured in Edinburgh, and she didn't know how many bruises and bangs and scratches. She would not cry. She did not have time for such nonsense. She could not leave him here, but moving him was not without risk.

"Organise a horse stretcher," she ordered the militia captain. "We will take Lord Rutledge back to Selby Manor. Moffatt, are you fit to ride?"

"I can ride, ma'am. Should I go for the doctor?"

"Let one of the footmen do that, Moffatt. I will trust you to lead my lord's horses. We will need to be very careful not to jolt him."

Gil could not have said how long the ride home took. He surfaced occasionally to a sea of pain, and each time The Goddess rode beside him, within arm's reach, her eyes fixed anxiously on his.

She was usually glaring at him, which made him smile. "I am so angry with you, Gilbert Rutledge," she told him, perhaps more than once. "How could you put yourself at risk like that? Oh my darling, what am I to do with you?"

His voice slurred as he answered. "Always loved you, Goddess. Remember me when I am gone?"

"You are going to live, you awful man," she commanded. "I will not let you die. Do you hear me? Moffatt, have a care."

The next time he struggled into consciousness, the rocking had ceased and his sister-in-law was within earshot, asking, "Has he been hurt?"

"He has been shot, Chloe," The Goddess answered. "I have sent a footman for the doctor."

Selby Manor then. Gil let the world fade away.

Later, he had a drowsy memory of several more interludes of half consciousness. The doctor, a gruff man with hands as gentle and deft as they could be under the circumstances, swam in and out of focus, asking Susan questions. "Your betrothed," he called Gil. He had asked Susan to marry him? Gil had thought of it so many times, but could not remember putting the question, or hearing her say yes. When the doctor dug for the bullet in his side, he let the puzzle go and sank into the white emptiness of the pain.

It could have been minutes later or hours when the darkness released him again. The doctor was gone, and so was Susan. Chloe and Flora sat beside the bed, holding hands, watching his face anxiously, and Chloe leapt to her feet when he opened his eyes a crack. "Gil. You are awake. Fetch Susan, Flora. Can you take a sip of water, Gil?" He accepted her ministrations, the cool water, flavoured with a hint of lemon, soaking blissfully into the heat of his throat. He tried to remain in the room to wait for The Goddess, but after two more sips he slipped back into the darkness.

After that, she was mostly there when he woke, though they were never in the same place twice. From some distant observation point, Gil knew he had created his surroundings from memories. Somewhere beyond a flickering fire in Jamaica or the confining logs of a Canadian forest fort, the smells and sounds of an English manor continued to exist, but his fever returned him to every sick bed he had occupied in his long military career.

The saried house-girl who sponged his fevered head on a sultry verandah in Calcutta while he recovered from the last vicious swipe of the man-eating tiger he had killed wore his Goddess's face. She was, improbably, the naval surgeon in scruffy uniform who nursed him back from his first bout with swamp fever in the West Indies, plying him with Jesuit Bark until the fever ran its course. She was the sergeant's wife who took him, along with her husband, into her own tent when the hospital beds were full after the Battle of Albuera.

In the real world, others washed him, fed him, changed his dressings. Moffatt, his sister-in-law, faceless hands hidden on the other side of the web of dreams that held him. Only his Goddess came inside, in all her disguises, populating his memories with her glorious eyes and her loving touches.

Then one day the fever was gone, and he woke to a quiet bed chamber.

23

For three days, Gil had tossed and turned in fever. Susan was his chief nurse. She claimed him as her betrothed to give her authority over the doctor and maintained the fiction to justify her place in his bed chamber. Moffatt accepted her without question, deferring to her instructions as if she were Lady Rutledge in truth, and one of them was always with him, though Chloe and several of the maids took turns at assisting.

The local magistrate insisted on interviewing them both and went away satisfied. Anxious to return to Gil, she barely listened to his comments about the continued absence of any French presence —or, indeed, any radical elements who might have been prone to revolution. She wondered later, as she sat beside Gil through yet another restless night. What had Griffin been planning, and why?

He was dead, his neck broken in the fall, and there, it seemed, went their answers. Gil would be displeased if they were denied the full story.

She glanced up from the gown she was making for Paeony's doll from some fabric scraps from the child's own new Sunday best dress, and Gil was looking back at her, a small smile playing around his lips, his colour good and his eyes clear.

"Gil?" She put down her sewing and crossed to the bed so that she could lay her hand on his forehead. No excess heat; no clamminess.

He reached up a tentative finger to touch her cheek. "Real," he pronounced, and she smiled her relief. "Alive," she replied.

"I am not dead," he agreed, "Though I feel as if my bones have turned to aspic. Griffin?"

"He is dead," Susan said, firmly, "and a good thing, too."

He nodded, unsurprised. "The French?"

"No sign of them, Gil. No ships, no troops, nothing." That bought a frown, so she hastened to explain the measures the magistrate had described. "The local militia have been quartering the woods and the swamps, and the constables have been interviewing everyone in every village and farm for miles around. Griffin appears to have been completely on his own. And what he hoped to achieve, I have no idea."

Gil shook his head, a tiny movement that hinted at his weakness. "It makes no sense. What could he hope to accomplish on his own?"

"He did rather well," Susan admitted. "He'd managed somehow to get himself taken onto the tower's crew, as a cook."

"He drugged them?"

Susan nodded. "The beer and the stew. They have all recovered, but the officer is on charges."

"Quite right, too," said the old soldier, his outrage clear.

His voice trailed off, and she changed the subject. "You are tired. Rest, Gil. Do you think you could manage some broth?"

She rang the bell and sent the maid for broth, helped Gil to some water, and blushed as she assisted him to attend to the consequent pressure. Somehow, it had been different when he was unconscious.

To cover her embarrassment, she bustled around the room tidying, and telling him of the doings of his nieces in the past few days. He lay back on the freshly plumped pillows, and by the time the broth arrived he was asleep again.

Gil woke later in the afternoon, ate, and slept some more, then managed almost the whole night in undisturbed rest. By the following morning, he was grumbling about being kept in bed, mostly because he had not seen Susan for several hours. Until he complained to Chloe, who rounded on him, in furious outrage.

"You will not dare get up one moment before Susan says you may. She has been so worried, Gil. I do not think you have any idea how close you came to death, and she has barely left your side, until she was certain you were out of danger. You will not spoil her good work or cast the gift of her loving care in her teeth."

Gil stared back at her, his eyes wide in disbelief that his timid sister-in-law could scold like that. Moffat was taken by a fit of coughing and faced the wall, his shoulders heaving. No support from his man then. "I beg your pardon, Chloe," he said.

She had barely left his side? The dark shadows under her eyes were witness to sleepless nights and his chest clutched with guilt at the thought he'd been keeping her from her sleep. "I hope she is sleeping now," he said, and his sister-in-law rewarded him with beaming smile.

"Yes. When she went to bed in the early hours of this morning, I gave instructions for no one to call her, and for that part of the house to be avoided so she could sleep her fill."

"Good," Gill said, approvingly, and meekly obeyed the orders of his temporary nurses until the early afternoon, when Susan arrived looking much refreshed. But his good mood was thwarted when she was called away almost immediately, and Chloe with her.

Left to the mercies of Moffatt, Gil tried to command a shirt and some trousers, but Moffatt answered, "I am not running afoul of Mrs Cunningham, my lord, and that's a fact." Before Gil could decide whether to be annoyed or relieved, Susan returned to announce that David Wakefield had arrived. "He has a story to tell us, it seems, and I know you would not forgive me, Gil, if I did not bring him up so that you can hear it in person. I thought you would wish Moffatt to help you dress, so you look more the thing while he is here."

Gil overcame the childish urge to stick his tongue out at Moffatt in his triumph, but the two men exchanged glances brimming with amusement until Susan asked for an explanation and laughed at their response. "Quite right, Moffatt, but it will do his body no harm and his pride good if he is able to sit in a chair, dressed like a gentleman, even though he will no doubt want to sleep again after the interview."

Moffatt helped him into fresh smallclothes, a shirt, and his most comfortable pair of trousers, then tied a plain cravat in a simple knot. Susan brought his silk banyan and assisted him to shrug into it. Both helpers supported him across the room and settled him into a chair by the fire, propping pillows around him to make him comfortable, putting slippers on his feet and tucking a blanket over his lap.

He rested his head back for a moment, then straightened when he caught Susan watching with concern. He was tired from just that small excursion, but he wouldn't have her worrying—or sending him back to bed without the treat of the visitor.

Her small smile hinted that she read his thoughts without difficulty. "I will send to let Wakefield know he can come up," she said.

Wakefield must have been waiting on the landing, for moments later Chloe and Flora ushered him in.

"Good to see you up, Gil," he said. "You have had some excitement, I understand. Shot?" He raised a single eyebrow in question.

"Recovering," Gil insisted. The ladies were disposing themselves; Chloe and Flora together on the window seat, and Susan in the chair twin to his own on the other side of the hearth. Gil sent her a smile.

"Wounded while saving England, they tell me, with some help from Susan," Wakefield's smile was for Moffatt, who was standing quietly in the background, "And your man Moffatt."

"Mostly Susan and Moffatt," Gil said. "I was out for much of it."

Wakefield nodded. "After you had followed the villain to the tower, stopped him from murdering the men stationed there, and accosted him as he signalled the French. You are the hero of the hour. You, too, Susan. They admire you enormously. I understand you rode to his rescue and singlehandedly put out the fire, thereby saving Gil and the poisoned men."

Susan was as displeased with the village stories as Gil. "Hardly. I had help putting out the fire, and the tower is of stone and was not in danger."

Wakefield chuckled. "A pity to allow facts to get in the way of a good story." He sobered. "And our French spy is dead."

"Yes," Susan agreed. "If Gil's bullet didn't kill him, the fall from the top of the tower did. He was definitely a French spy?"

"He certainly thought so," Wakefield said, "or at least he thought the French were his chief paymasters, though he was an Anglo-Irish radical with a tragic family history rather than a Bonapartist. Fellow travellers for a while, but no real sympathy."

He surveyed his audience and began his tale. "As Gil and Susan know, I went north to meet with a contact. I will say no more about that, except to tell you that I found out why Griffin's plans were so confusing, and why none of them worked."

Gil had been thinking about that, and could think of only one reason. "He had several plans?"

Wakefield inclined his head in appreciation, and said to Susan, "Amy was right. He planned for—had paid for—uprisings in the north-western manufactories, to distract government attention away from a French invasion here in Essex."

Gil frowned. "You mean we really stopped a French invasion?" *Then where were they?*

But Wakefield was shaking his head. "The French never had any intention of invading"

Either Gil was still sicker than he realised, or Wakefield wasn't making sense. "I don't understand."

But Chloe was ahead of him. "He was tricked."

"Very good, Lady Rutledge," Wakefield told her. "You are right. His spymaster lied to him. Lied about the money that would be sent to the agitators, lied about the ships that would come when he lit his signal fire." Wakefield shrugged, a dismissive lift of the shoulders. "Lied about anything that would push him into attracting the attention of the Crown, so we could dispose of their problem."

Susan asked the question that was on the minds of them all. "But why?"

"He had become dangerously unstable, I was told. It goes back to Ireland. He and his brother and sister blamed the English for the deaths of the rest of their family, including an elderly grandmother and the sister's husband and children. In the past two years, both brother and sister died; the brother in a riot, and the sister in custody. Hatred can be a flame to focus the mind, but his burned out of control and was inclined to explode without warning. His French spymaster tried to cut him loose a year ago, but he wouldn't believe it. Kept coming up with wilder and wilder plans. In the end, they decided to give him the rope to hang himself."

"Poor man," Chloe said.

Susan, whose daughter had nearly paid a terrible price for Griffin's obsession, was less sympathetic. "Poor man who would have seen the whole of Britain subjected to Napoleon because of his need for revenge."

Once the story had devolved into speculation and conjecture, Susan called a halt, one eye on her flagging patient. But after a couple of hours sleep, he was restored; still weak but showing no signs of a relapse, and eager for something more than broth to eat. "A man needs substance to recover on, Goddess," he told Susan, and she laughed and had the cook send up a plain but solid meal, and David Wakefield to share it with him.

When she joined them after her own dinner with Chloe and Flora, Gil had nodded off, and Wakefield was sitting in the chair opposite him, reading a book, which he closed and tucked back into his coat pocket as he stood to acknowledge Susan's arrival.

"He has been asleep for perhaps ten minutes, Susan," he reported, "and made a good showing at his dinner before that. What does the doctor say?"

"That he is on the mend, but needs to remember he is no longer a youth," she said, her voice dry.

Wakefield flashed the briefest of grins. "We all need to remember that. He and I will be forty years on this earth at our next birthdays." He shook his head, disbelieving.

And Susan would turn thirty-eight, which seemed impossible until she looked in the mirror. Her daughter now stood in the wings to be the debutante with the world at her feet, and Susan's day was nearly two decades in the past. How foolish to dream of a future with Gil when she was so old. He needed a young woman to defer to him, to admire him, to bear and raise his children, not an ageing widow with a managing disposition.

Wakefield was politely ignoring her preoccupation, though the man who noticed everything had undoubtedly seen it. "When will Gil be ready to travel, Susan?"

She put aside the squirrel trap of her thoughts to consider the question. "The doctor says not for at least two weeks."

Wakefield nodded thoughtfully. "I can't delay that long. My— the people I report to on this matter want an eyewitness account of what happened at the Martello Tower. Will you come to London with me?"

"To London?" Susan repeated. Of course, to London. Where her children waited for her and must be wondering why the few days she had promised had turned into more than a week.

She examined her beloved's sleeping face. Was he out of danger? The doctor was hopeful, but the fever had broken only yesterday.

Wakefield read her reservations correctly. "I can spare a day if you wish to be sure that Gil is not about to relapse."

Susan laughed, mostly at herself and her own transparency. "You and Moffatt both assure me that he has formidable powers of recuperation, and I saw it myself last time he was shot."

"Ah yes. In Scotland. Don't give me your answer now, Susan, but leave me and Moffatt to see your patient to bed and think about it. You can tell me your decision in the morning."

And who else would go if she didn't? Susan looked up and met Moffatt's eyes. Yes, undoubtedly the government would requisition Gil's servant to meet their information needs. Better her. After all, she had to return to her children. And her life. Reluctantly, she left Gil to the men, and went off to tell Chloe and Flora that she would be leaving for London with David Wakefield.

Now that Gil was conscious and fast improving, Susan's quiet hours of sitting with him were over. The next morning, he demanded his nieces so he could read to them from their animal book. They stayed for about twenty minutes before Gil faded on a particularly loud donkey bray, which brought Nanna's wrath down on him and had him scolded as if he were one of her charges. "We have been here quite long enough. You have been hurt, Lord Rutledge, and very sick. We have been very worried about you. If you will promise not to overdo things, I will bring the young ladies back to see you this afternoon."

"And perhaps this evening, for a kiss before bed?" Gil begged, his eyes dancing as they flicked to catch the amusement in Susan's. Paeony then had to be lifted for a kiss, and Rose after her, before Nanna carried them off.

After a short rest, he played cards with Wakefield for a while, then Chloe and Flora brought their embroidery up and sat with him, while Susan read from a book of essays on wildlife they had discovered at a market stall in Stamford.

"It is far more interesting than I expected," Gil observed. "He observes keenly and has a clever hand with a description. I feel I am on his rambles with him."

"Her," Susan corrected. She lifted the book as proof, showing the title page. "By a country gentlewoman."

"Ah." Gil recovered smoothly. "I rescind my surprise, then. One expects superior observation and writing from the female of the species."

"Wonder of wonders," Wakefield joked. "The Rock Ledge becomes a flatterer."

No one mentioned the trip to London, and Susan waited to broach the subject until she had a few minutes alone with Gil.

Her chance came, but she would not have long. Wakefield had gone to deal with correspondence. Chloe and Flora were busy downstairs considering what could be done to make Gil a day bedroom where he could be part of the house, but still rest or even sleep without having to climb the stairs again.

"Gil, Wakefield wishes me to go to London to describe what I saw at the tower."

Gil sucked his upper lip between his teeth, his face otherwise expressionless. "You will want to get home to your children. You should go."

"I do not wish to leave you." *Ever. I do not want to leave you ever, you stupid man. You wonderful, confusing, stubborn, stupid man.*

"I am in good hands. Chloe and Flora—yes, and Nanna and the girls—are martinets in the sick room, and I shall be back in top form in no time."

He wasn't hearing her deeper messages. She should take her dismissal in good part. Their idyll was over before it had begun, and she had promised herself that whatever he could offer would be enough. "You think I should go, then."

"I wish you could stay, Goddess." For a moment, his eyes flooded with something that spoke to the longing in hers, but then he shuttered them. "But it is best that you go."

The following morning, Susan came to Gil's new quarters to bid him goodbye. The sisters had transformed a sunny room into a comfortable half-bedroom, half-sitting room for an invalid. He was sitting up in a chair set in a flood of sunbeams, and he could see he'd soon be pushing the rug Moffatt had insisted on off his knees.

Damnable weakness. He yearned to be well enough to go with her—to string their time of closeness out by a few more days. Instead, he set himself to make a clean break of it, for her sake as well as his.

"I've come to say goodbye, Gil," she said. "Or farewell, I hope. Goodbye sounds so final."

It did. It sank like iron into his soul, tying his half-formed hopes in chains and sinking them fathoms deep. "We will always be friends, Goddess," he said, some of the ice in his heart leaking into his voice despite his best intentions.

Susan blinked rapidly and her own face stiffened, her bland Society hostess expression forming between him and what she really thought. "Of course, we will, Rutledge. I am so pleased we have had this time to get to know one another again."

Gil cast about for something to say. Something that would ease the parting. "Thank you for coming with me to meet Chloe, Susan. I don't know what I would have done without you."

It was the right note. The tension in her eased a little, though the mask was still in place. "Your nieces are delightful, and Chloe is stronger than she thinks. You will all do very well, I think."

"I would have made a ham-fisted mess of it without you." As he would, undoubtedly, the rest of his life. She must have heard the wistful note he could not repress, because she hesitated, examining his face.

Behind her, Chloe appeared at the door. "Susan? The little girls hope you will come up and say goodbye before you go."

Susan considered Gil for a moment more, then looked over her shoulder at his sister-in-law. "Yes, Chloe, I'll be right there."

Chloe withdrew and Susan faltered and then seemed to make up her mind, crossing the room at a rush and bending to kiss Gil's cheek. He clutched the rug to anchor his hands, which threatened to break free from his control and seize her, and never let her go.

"Come to me, Gil," she commanded, her voice ragged. "This cannot be finished."

"If you need me, I will come," he promised, even as he shook his head.

She straightened, biting her lips until they were white, then turned and hurried out of the room, but not before he had seen the tears in her eyes.

What a bastard he was, making her cry.

24

The family had delayed their usual removal from the heat of London's summer, waiting for Susan to re-join them, though she was too late to farewell the Grahames, who had toured the sights of London and departed again for Edinburgh.

The children greeted her with joy. But listening to their accounts of what they'd been doing and what they planned, Susan could not help but feel that even Michael, her youngest, was growing past the need of her, since all his talk was of the adventures he was going to have with his cousins closest in age, her brother Rick's sons, John and Andrew.

Rick was briefly on shore leave while his ship was being repaired and had taken a house at Bognor. It was close enough to Portsmouth for Rick to watch over repairs, far enough away that he could enjoy a few weeks leave with Mary and his children, and large enough to find room for his brothers, sister, cousins, and assorted offspring, so the entire family planned to descend on him, and Susan's girls were as excited as Michael.

"For the Chirburys are coming for a few days, and I have not seen Daisy in months, Mama," Chrissie explained. "I want to know if I am taller than her. I have grown, have I not?"

Susan's brother Alex and his family had already made the trek to Bognor, and Amy was excited about seeing her favourite aunt. "I have so much to tell Aunt Ella. And I cannot wait to see the new baby."

All three wanted to be off the next day, or that afternoon, if possible, but reluctantly accepted their grandfather's edict that duty to the Crown came first.

The following morning, Susan was escorted by her father to a meeting with officers of the Horse Guard and officials from the Home Office, gave her account and answered their questions. And later that afternoon, David Wakefield escorted her to an anonymous office in a large unidentified building just beyond Westminster, where she was questioned again, this time by three gentlemen who identified themselves as Mr Smith, Mr Brown, and Mr Taylor.

She recognised Mr Taylor. He was some kind of connection to the Haverford ducal family, and she had seen him at events run by the duchess, usually hovering quietly in the shadows, observing rather than joining in. He did that today, leaving most of the interview to the other two men. The questions he did ask seemed almost beside the point, until she realised he was using her observations to take the pulse of the people she had met on her journey north and back again.

It was hours before they let her go, asking her to remain in London for one more day in case they had further questions.

"I'll call for your carriage," Wakefield said. He'd stood by through the whole interview, occasionally fielding a question of his own. "You must be exhausted Susan, but you have done your country a great service."

"I felt I was on trial," she complained, "much more so than at the Horse Guard."

The enquiry agent smiled. "For those three, everyone is on trial. You did well."

He reassured her again when he left her at Lord Henry's townhouse. "As soon as I can, I will send a message to let you know if they are satisfied," he promised. With that, she had to make do, and went up to refresh her soul by joining her children for nursery tea.

"I have a letter from Pat," Amy reported, holding it up and waving it, "and you will never guess!"

"I hope she likes her new home and that she and Clementine are both well," Susan said, happy to be diverted from the pressures of the day.

"Yes, yes, but just listen, Mama." Amy opened the folded sheets and scanned them. "Here it is.

'Uncle Simeon took us to visit Mademoiselle, and your cousin, Mr Cunningham, was there. She addressed him as 'Hamish' and he called her 'Lisette'. Do you suppose it means what I think it means?'

What do you think, Mama? Is it a romance?"

Very probably. Susan had seen the first shoots of it herself, in Hamish's gallantry and Lisette's blushing response. "Does she mention Mademoiselle's brother?" she asked Amy, refusing to enter the speculation.

"Yes, he continues well, Mademoiselle told Pat." She folded the letter again. "I think it is a romance," she declared.

David delivered the message from her inquisitors the following afternoon. Both the official enquiry and the secret enquiry had the information they needed from Susan, and she was free to leave London. "You mean they have checked what I told them and found it to be true," she corrected, which made Wakefield laugh. "You have them exactly, Susan. Don't take it personally. It is their job to trust no one."

Susan went to tell her father, feeling oddly flat with nothing left to accomplish. Which was silly. Moving her family to Bognor would be no mean feat, and she had a reunion with her brothers and their families to look forward to.

She thought of writing to Gil to tell him about the interviews, but she was reasonably certain that the triumvirate of steely-eyed men would not want anything committed to paper. Besides, what could she say? *I told them what I knew?* It would just be an excuse to make contact.

Instead, she busied herself checking on the packing the servants had already completed, adding some items and removing others, so that she felt she was not entirely superfluous in her children's lives, as she clearly was in Gil's.

And when she went up to bed that night and found herself shifting restlessly across the vast empty expanse of sheets, foolishly missing the warm body from that one glorious night, she refused to cry. As she had learned early in her marriage, no man was worth crying over. If he didn't want her, so be it.

Her future had not changed since she first met Gil in Cambridge, and she had been content then, and would be again. She had her family. She had her independence and the wealth to enjoy it. She would devote herself to seeing her daughters well married and her son established. She would continue to enjoy the social scene. She would do what good she could in the world and find satisfaction in that.

Stupid man. Susan cried herself to sleep, and woke heavy eyed, pasting on a smile as she went down to begin the journey to Bognor.

Gil was returning to Gloucestershire in style, in a carriage from the Selby stables. He argued that he was almost fully recovered and preferred to ride, but Chloe insisted.

"I would worry about you, Gil. And what would I say to Susan if you came to any harm!"

Susan would be upset if his fever returned, beyond a doubt, but why would Chloe feel the need to answer to her? His face must have spoken the question, because she said, "Susan? Your betrothed?"

"Not really," he said. "She said that so the doctor would not be shocked when she nursed me."

Chloe frowned, narrowing her eyes. "Why not. She loves you. Do you not want to marry her?"

Loved him? Gil shut his eyes to hide his hopeless longing. "She has her mind set against marriage, Chloe. And even if she didn't— You of all people know how impossible it would be. Her children and my mother?"

Chloe considered that. "So she refused you? Poor brother. I

would have thought–” The compassion in her eyes faded as she opened them wide. “You have not asked her. You have made up her mind for her without giving her a say. Have you even told her how you feel?” She didn't wait for him to speak, clearly guessing his answer from his face or the droop of his shoulders. “Gilbert Rutledge, you must. She has a right to know.”

And in the end, he promised he would try.

The holiday should have been wonderful. Would have been, had Gil's continued absence not been a constant seeping wound in Susan's heart.

Rick and Mary had rented a large house a short walk from the beach, and Susan threw herself into an endless succession of family activities, determined not to give way to her melancholy. Every fine day saw them sallying forth on foot or in a parade of ponies, horses, and carriages: picnics, bathing parties, expeditions to Chichester or to local beauty spots, walks and rides.

In the evenings or on wet days, they played charades, or entertained one another with songs and stories, or put on plays, or ranged all over the house with riotous games of blind man's bluff or hide-and-go-seek.

Susan felt like two people—the outer mask joining gaily in all the activities, the inner self huddling in a corner grieving for the love she had somehow lost. She had been so confident after that one glorious night, but he did not ask her to marry him. He did not even ask to continue their liaison. She would have refused to bring such scandal on her family, of course, but he did not even ask. Instead, nothing. No Gil. Not even a letter.

The Redepennings largely ignored the few events put on by the town's social committee. This was a family holiday, with the children at its centre and the adults reliving memories from their own childhoods as they planned yet another activity to delight the young ones.

Rick and Alex set out to make sure that all the children could swim, and a fleet of sail boats proved an instant hit, with the children in two fleets, one under each uncle, an older child as captain of each two-person crew. They were out on the water most days, dancing across the bay in an endless succession of races and challenges, scandalising the neighbours by giving the girls the same sailing lessons as the boys.

Relatives came and went. Lord Henry could spare little time from London, and the Chirburys stayed only a week before returning to their country house in Gloucestershire, carrying Chrissie off with them to be company for Daisy. Susan's eldest brother, Harry, back in England from the Peninsular for a bare fortnight, managed to post down for a day and night, avoiding all talk of the war, abetted by his brothers and their wives who were troubled by their own ghosts of conflict.

He left for Southampton and a ship back to Spain looking more relaxed, though they had sat up all night talking.

Gil kept intruding. He was part of their childhood memories; the lonely boy from the neighbouring estate who had been gathered under Lady Henry's maternal wing to be included with her own brood. He was part of her brothers' war stories, too. Major Rutledge, and later Colonel Rutledge, specialist in snatching unlikely victories out of probable defeats. At a cost, Susan knew, for she had seen the scars, and at night in her bed she retraced them in her imagination, reliving the night in which he had, for one brief space out of time, been hers.

A hundred times a day, Susan thought of something that would amuse him, or heard an opinion he would refute and imagined his response, or saw one of her happily married brothers in a tender moment with his wife and yearned for the same connection.

She almost wrote to tell him about the letter from Hamish, a typical laconic Hamish missive that announced the dry fact of his betrothal and imminent marriage to Mademoiselle Cornillac—the event to be held within the prison camp at Penicuik, by special permission, so the bride's brother could attend. The only uncharacteristic note was the slightly wistful, "I hope you will wish us happy, cousin." She did. Of course she did, and especially after she read the more effusive note from Lisette that Hamish had included inside his own.

She was very happy. She was more fortunate than she deserved. She would be a Scot now, and a loyal wife, and Susan had made it all possible with her kindness and her forbearance. Lisette had signed herself 'Your loving soon-to-be cousin', which made Amy laugh when Susan showed her the note.

Gil, too, would be amused at the unlikely outcome. Twice she picked up a pen to write him a letter, and then put it down again. Women didn't write to men who were not related. And she had enough scandal to live down without adding to it. Besides, if he wanted to be in touch with her, he would come.

He did not come, though a letter arrived from Chloe in which she said he had recovered from his injuries and left to return to his estate.

The dowager Lady Rutledge was as difficult as Gil had expected, horrified that Gil had returned home without Gideon's daughters. He needed to return to wherever That Woman had taken them and fetch them immediately. Or, better still, give her the widow's direction, and the dowager would accomplish the task herself. She should not have left it to him. He was useless, and always had been. Why, oh why had God taken the good son and left her the stupid one, fit only for cannon fodder and not even able to get himself killed?

Gil let it wash over him. He had heard it so many times it was almost devoid of meaning. And after spending several weeks listening carefully to what Chloe did and didn't say about her marriage, he had no sympathy with anyone who had watched Gideon's treatment of his family and could still refer to him as the good son.

Lady Rutledge expected capitulation. Gil gave her his granite obduracy. "No, Mother," to every demand. Explanations would be a waste of time. She and reason had parted company years ago, perhaps before he was born.

Not that a simple 'no' put an end to her ranting. She nagged. She scolded. She screamed abuse. And when none of that worked, she resorted to hysterical tears, which coursed down her face, carving grooves in the thick plaster of makeup with which she attempted to deny the lines drawn by time. Presumably she preferred Gideon because he had never refused her. Certainly, their father had, because Gil remembered the beatings.

She did, too, because she flinched at his convulsive movement when an arrow cast at random struck too close to the bone. "Rutting Redepenning's slut of a daughter up and down the North Road instead of attending to your duty," she said, which meant that the rumours were worse and had travelled further than he had imagined.

Perhaps he should threaten to beat her, just to shut her up, for after his reaction she didn't mention Susan again, but continued on to other imagined wrongs, all of which were Gil's fault or his responsibility to fix. But she wouldn't believe his threats, and she would be right. He couldn't raise his hand to someone so much smaller and weaker.

Gil finally managed to hand her over to her maid, and went to send for Barton, his steward, whose name had been included in the long litany of those Gil needed to dismiss for not paying her the respect she was due as a viscountess. By which, Gil guessed from her complaints, she meant that Barton had refused her the rents from the river flat properties, which she had been using as her personal purse to supplement her allowance until Gil found out and put a stop to it.

The man appeared in a remarkably short time, pinch-lipped and brow furrowed. "You sent for me, my lord. I was on my way to see you, in any case. I have my resignation here."

He tried to pass Gil a folded sheet of paper.

"Whoa!" Gil said, putting his hands up, palm side out. "Your resignation? Have I put you in such an impossible position then?"

Some of the tension went out of Barton's shoulders and he let the hand with the letter drop. "Your mother said she would have me thrown off the estate, but no one would obey her without your orders."

Gil nodded. "Quite right, too. I left you in charge here, not my mother."

The steward's response was dry, but he relaxed still further. "Her ladyship did not appear to be aware of that fact."

Gil waved to a chair. "Sit down, man, and I'll pour you a drink. Brandy?"

Barton took the offered seat. "Am I going to need a drink?" he asked.

Gil didn't answer until he had passed a glass of brandy to the man and taken his own to a matching chair on the petitioner's side of the huge desk, rather than the grotesque monument to pomposity that held pride of place behind it. He'd have to get rid of that thing. Yet another job.

"I have been a soldier—an officer—since I was little more than a boy, Barton. If I give orders, I expect them to be followed. If they are ignored, I expect a damned good reason for the disobedience, and 'your mother told me to' is not a good reason."

"She is accustomed to ruling here, my lord. Your brother—" Barton stopped and seemed to pick among words before saying, "questioning her decisions to him did no good."

Gil had read the estate's books until his eyes crossed. He would have been willing to bet that understatement covered a multitude of despairing attempts to make the viscount see reason. "Gideon wouldn't care what happened here as long as he had money for his horses and his women," he replied. "I am not my brother, Barton." He sat back, his long legs stretched out in front of him, and looked up at the ceiling. A riotous and bawdy mural with some disturbing images he couldn't now unsee. He hoped that Gideon never paid the artist, who didn't deserve to profit from such nightmares. Another item on his mental list. Lime wash the study ceiling.

He sighed. The list never grew smaller. "I have no idea what I am going to do about my mother, Barton, but that is not your concern. I hope you will stay on as my steward and help me turn this into a profitable estate. Rest assured you will not now, nor will you ever, be expected to take orders from her."

He and Barton parted on good terms, and then Gil had to deal with a succession of other servants who had been trapped between the dowager's demands and his own orders. The housekeeper, Mrs Glossop, had been abused for putting up unused bedrooms in dust cloths to save the servants' work. The cook had followed Gil's directions about basing their meals on food grown or caught on the estate, or purchasing locally, and had been threatened with dismissal for not including expensive imported delicacies. The head gardener had been ordered to plant flowers in the kitchen garden to replace the growing vegetables the cook had requested so she could follow Gil's instructions, and not just any flowers but delicate new arrivals from the East that would come with a hefty price tag and their own gardener.

The butler did not appear. Gil made a note to find out whether the man had folded to Lady Rutledge's instructions. If so, he would be in need of another job. Gil had run from his responsibilities for long enough, and if he could not have the future he wanted, he could at least have peace under his own roof.

On the whole, he would be replacing fewer servants than he expected, and some cautious questions to Mrs Glossop made it clear Chloe still had many sympathisers in the household.

Susan would have organised the place in no time, if he had been able to overcome her aversion to marriage. If he could have thought of a solution to the problem of his mother. If he could be sure they would have no children, or that any children would take after the Redepennings and not the Rutledges.

"My lord?" It was the chief groom, dancing from one booted foot to the other and twisting his cap around and around in his hands.

"Yes?"

"My lord, you told us to let you know if Lady Rutledge ordered a horse or carriage, my lord. She has sent down orders to prepare the travelling coach for a trip to London, my lord."

"No coach," Gil commanded. "Lady Rutledge will not be travelling."

The man looked down at his hands, still turning the cap. "Would you tell her ladyship yourself, my lord? Only…"

Gil reassured the man and sent him off to the stables again, then wearily climbed the stairs to confront his mother.

He had been right to walk away from his Goddess. What had he to offer her? A rundown estate, empty coffers, and a termagant of a mother, who made his house into a prison with her complaints and her rages. A temporary relationship would never be enough, but to marry her would be cruel —even if she consented, and why would she?

But he would write. He had yet to keep his promise to Chloe.

25

Susan lingered in Bognor through July. Michael was having such fun with his cousins and uncles, and she and Amy treasured the time with her brothers' wives, Mary and Ella, who were her dear friends. Mary and Susan had been young wives together, both facing the birth of their first children when their naval officer husbands were overseas. When Alex brought Ella home five years ago, Susan had helped her to face down accusations of wantoness and insanity, at first for Alex's sake and later for her own.

"I come to Longford when Ella and Alex go," she wrote to Anne Chirbury, in response to a letter that reassured her that Chrissie was well and having a wonderful time with a houseful of girls collected from friends and relatives.

Ella and Alex would be leaving soon for their home in Lincolnshire, where they ran a breeding farm for carriage and riding horses. The Horncastle horse fair in August was the highlight of their calendar, and Amy was agitating to go home with them and enjoy the fun. Dinner for the last few days had been enlivened by the couple's descriptions of the young herd they had for sale, many the offspring of the stallion Gil had sold them.

Susan, thinking about Gil, almost missed Ella's increasingly urgent signals to her husband, catching them only a fraction before Alex, who fell suddenly silent and then changed the subject to the other lead Renshaw stallion, one of Ella's own breeding.

Come to think of it, the whole family conspired to change the subject whenever Gil came into the conversation. Was Susan so obvious, then? She would have to be more careful not to let her feelings show.

The resolution lasted until the post arrived the following morning, a letter in Gil's distinctive hand conspicuously on top.

Susan was not alone in the breakfast room, but she ignored Ella and Mary to tear open the letter.

"My dearest Goddess," Gil had written. That was promising, surely?

"I know it annoys you when I address you by that honorific, and can only hope you will forgive me once again, as I take this last opportunity to pour out my heart."

Last opportunity. Not so good.

"My Goddess. How prophetic I was, all those years ago, when I met you and realised straight away you embodied the names you had been given at the baptismal font, however much you disliked them. In all the years since, this has only become more true.

"Joan, the general and saint. Yes, for you have the analytical brain of a general, and the patience and dedication of a saint.

"Boadicea, the warrior queen. That fits too. Courage like a flame. I would follow you anywhere, my queen. As I have on more than one battlefield, sending my heart over the wall with your image a bright flame before me.

"But above all, Athene, The Goddess of wisdom and war. My Goddess, not that I ever hoped to possess you, but because you own me, and have since the first day we met. I had never known a girl could be so bold and so clever, leading the younger nursery party in the snow fight Harry had organised, and winning all by sending a feint to disguise your move to capture our fort when we sallied forth, full of confidence in our superior male skills.

"You stood on our ramparts, bombarding us with our own reserve snowballs, laughing at our surprise. And you shone like the sun itself, my Goddess. I was lost from that moment. Or found.

"I came to Longford Court bruised from a home that was no home at all.

Your mother gave me sanctuary. Your father showed me what a man should be. Your brothers welcomed me into their circle. You—Goddess, you gave me a creed to live by.

"*The first time I spoke roughly to my sisters in your presence, as I had been taught, you looked at me in such a way I never did it again. Ever since, I have measured myself by 'what would The Goddess think', almost always falling short, but I am a better man for it.*"

"Susan?" Mary's voice interrupted the reading, and she looked up into her sister-in-law's concerned eyes. "Is it bad news?"

Susan dabbed at her eyes with a handkerchief, impatient with the tears that blurred the page. "I am not sure, Mary. Give me another minute, would you?"

"*Ah, but I am rambling. Avoiding the point, as I have been for weeks.*

"*Goddess. Queen of my heart. My beloved. You have privileged me beyond all my deserving and I will never forget the glory we found together. Nor will I presume on it, my Goddess. You need not worry that I shall importune you, or embarrass you in any way.*

"*You, in your wisdom, withdrew after that one night, knowing as well as I that we had no future and too kind to offer false hope to your helpless worshipper. A woman of your virtue does not have affairs, which makes your gift to me even more precious.*

"*I am not a fit mate for any women. Quite apart from the dark strain in my blood, I have nothing to offer but a broken estate, an estranged family, a mother whose sanity is seriously in question, and a foolish dreamer of a man with few —if any—redeeming qualities.*

"*No. I insult you with that assessment of myself. I must have some features that are pleasing, because my Goddess allowed me to worship her. And I shall carry the memories all my life.*

"*I love you, Goddess. I love Susan Cunningham. I love Joan Athene Boadicea. I have, and always will. I love you, and I wish you every happiness.*

Ever yours, Gil."

Susan, the tears still running down her face, crumpled the last sheet and then smoothed it again, catching back a sob when a corner tore. "That stupid, bone-headed, prideful, arrogant, lummox."

Mary raised her brows. "Rutledge, I take it."

"Good guess." She dabbed at her eyes and took a deep breath.

"No one else ever provokes you to such rage, Susan," Ella said. "When I told Alex the two of you had gone off to Scotland together, we were convinced you would either kill him along the way or bed him." Her eyes sharpened as Susan blushed. "Susan! You did!"

"He is not dead," Susan said, dryly.

"No, clearly not, if he is writing a letter that provokes you so."

Susan flapped the pages at Ella, exasperated beyond her usual reserve. "He says he is not fit for a wife, and I deserve better than to be his mistress."

Ella sat back and sipped from her cup of tea. "That bone-headed, prideful—what was the rest of it? Lummox, I remember."

Susan was nodding when Mary commented, "You make a good pair."

"I beg your pardon? Whose side are you on?"

Mary smiled. "Yours, of course." She exchanged glances with Ella and spoke for them both. "We want you happy, Susan."

They didn't understand. "If he will not come to me, what can I do."

"Go to him?" Ella suggested.

"I have never run after a man in my life." Although she had, hadn't she? She had gone to Gil, when it was clear he would not come to her. Could she do it again? With so much at stake?

"That's pride talking," Mary insisted. "And what good is it doing you, may I ask? He wants you. You want him. What is stopping you from taking him?"

Susan's lips curled into a contented smile. "I did, and it was wonderful."

"Was it enough?" Ella asked. "Will the memory keep you warm for the rest of your life?"

No. No it was not enough. She wanted Gil for her husband. But… take him? How? When he was on his estate and she was here in Portsmouth? "You think I should write back?"

Ella refused to give instructions. "What do you want to do?"

That was easy. "I want to shake him until his teeth rattle. And then kiss him until he can't stand up."

"Difficult in a letter," her astute friend observed.

Susan stood up, with a decisive nod. "You are right, of course. Will you and Alex take Amy home with you, Ella? She will be thrilled, and Mary, if you and Rick will keep Michael…"

The other women agreed, and Susan hurried away to set arrangements in place for a hurried trip to western Gloucestershire. *Brush her off with a few compliments, would he?*

This morning Gil was working in the fields, still feeling a grip where the bullet had carved its hole but rejoicing in his returning strength. He had fled the house with his mother's abuse wringing in his ears. Gideon never so demeaned himself. Gideon kept a distance between himself and the labourers. Gideon would have stayed home and taken her into Chipping Niddwick, for she needed a new bonnet.

Goaded beyond endurance, he had told her that Gideon had spent the viscountcy into near bankruptcy and she could expect no new bonnets, perhaps for years. Which had brought the expected flood of tears, until he had to call her maid to deal with her hysteria.

Was she quite mad? Should he have her confined? Usually the physical labour and the undemanding company of the men brought him peace, but today his mind was a squirrel in a trap, going around and round.

Life stretched before him as an aching emptiness where, for a short time, The Goddess had warmed his heart. The first time, when Gideon had him transferred overseas, and then sent him a clipping with the announcement of her wedding, he had thrown himself into battle hoping to die. Unscathed and covered in glory he had, in time, made some peace with that loss.

This time was much worse. He had glimpsed Heaven and had it torn away; had thrown it away.

A footman was running through the field. Trouble at the house? He braced himself for whatever disaster his mother was originating now. "My lord? A visitor, my lord. A lady. Mrs Glossop asks that you come quickly." A visitor to his mother? Or to him?

He came in through the mews, where the carriage put a hitch in his stride and hope in his heart. He knew that dark blue paint with the thin gold stripe and the cheerful red hubs to the black wheels.

He leapt the stairs to the side door two at a time and was halfway down the hall to the front of the house before he heard his mother's voice, raised in a full-scale tantrum.

"Throw her out, I tell you. I'll not have that woman in my house. They stole my son, my baby, my little Gilbert. I hate them. I hate them all, and her I hate the worst. Gideon understood. Gideon would have known what to do with the whore. Why did he have to die, and leave me with the traitor? Treachery, all around. Throw the woman out, quick, before my son gets home. He'll take her part, but she'll not have him. You'll not have him; do you hear me?"

Inside the drawing room, Susan stood calmly by a side table where her bonnet already lay, removing her gloves, while the dowager darted about, her hands in claws ready to strike, trying to reach Susan past two footmen who moved to block her. Mrs Glossop and the butler stopped mid argument to stare at him, and Susan looked up and smiled.

He stood in the doorway and grinned back like a fool, and only the reactions honed by years of battle came to his rescue in time to catch his mother's wrists before she could scratch at his face. His eyes. She had been aiming for his eyes. As he held her, he felt the bile rise in his throat.

"Who looks after Lady Rutledge?" Susan asked the housekeeper, her calm voice soothing his mind. "Send for her, please, and tell her to bring whatever medicine her ladyship uses."

"She can't have you," Lady Rutledge raved. "She would never let me have my grandson to raise as a Rutledge should be. All my plans…"

Gil looked down at her, twisting and turning, trying to break free. No chance of that. He had her stick-thin wrists firmly held, his fingers locked but loose enough not to bruise if she would only stay still. Her face was distorted in her rage and her eyes were wild as she kicked at him with her slippered feet, doing no harm.

The housekeeper and butler had departed on Susan's errands while the footmen hovered uncertainly. "Gil, I've asked Mrs Glossop for a blanket to wrap around your mother. If you hold her for a short time more, I think we can make her more comfortable."

In minutes, she had it all arranged; a blanket wrapped and tied so that Lady Rutledge could not move her arms, the maid with a bottle of syrup. Gil sniffed the sickly-sweet odour. "Laudanum?" How did he not know his mother was a laudanum dreamer? He'd seen the sickness before.

"Heavy on opium, I think. Your brother used it, I know."

Lady Rutledge spat out the first spoonful, then changed her mind and tried to lap it back. She took the second eagerly.

"There, my lord, she'll be calm in no time," the maid told him.

Gil felt a vast weariness. Susan had seen the worst now. She had —with her usual calm efficiency—managed him, his mother, and his servants, but she could not possibly want to do so for a lifetime. He watched the servants remove a drooping Lady Rutledge from the room, and waited for Susan to tell him her errand, and to leave.

As the last footman exited the room, she crossed to the door and closed it firmly, then turned the key in the lock. The part of his anatomy that was seldom in full control in her presence approved the action, and suggested assault and pillage. He told it to shut up. Whatever she had in mind, her glare as she turned to face him suggested she did not intend to indulge his rampant manhood.

"I am extremely angry with you, Rutledge," she began.

"I am sorry, Susan," he said. "I had no idea she would behave like that. I didn't even know about the laudanum." He held up a hand to stop her obvious rejoinder. "Yes, I should have. I have no excuse."

Susan gave a deep sigh. "Of course, you have an excuse. Or at least a reason." She took two quick strides until she could reach him to poke him in the chest, punctuating her points. "You are a stubborn, prideful, male, trying to do everything yourself instead of asking for help." To his dismay, tears welled in her eyes, and she blinked to dispel them. "That letter. Oh Gil, that wonderful, wrong-headed, annoying letter! How dare you turn down my offer of marriage when I am exactly what you need?"

Eh? Gil blinked hard and shook his head. *He must be hearing things.* "Offer of marriage?" he asked.

"I came to your bed, you silly man. What did you think I was doing? Having a widow's fling?" Suddenly, she stepped closer, wrapping both hands around him and laying her head on his chest, and his own arms moved of their own accord to hold her in an iron embrace.

"Of course you did," Susan murmured, but not so quietly that he couldn't hear every word. "Ella and Mary say we are each as bad as the other, and I didn't tell you how I felt because I was afraid you would send me away."

"Goddess," he managed to choke, terrified that this moment of heaven would end in hell, as had all others before it. "Don't say any more. Not unless you mean it."

She pulled back. "I want to be your wife, Gilbert Rutledge. And you want me, as you said perfectly clearly in your letter. Together, we can face anything."

"But my mother… My estate…"

She put a finger up to cover his lips. "Anything. Yes or no? Will you do me the inestimable honour of accepting my hand in marriage?"

It was to be heaven, then. Against all the odds, with his troops in disarray, his powder wet, and his battle plans all focused on chasing mirages in precisely the wrong direction, Forlorn Hope Rock Ledge had won again.

"Goddess," he groaned, before covering her mouth with his own.

26

Gil waited for his bride in the foyer of the little church in Chipping Niddwick. They would progress up the aisle together in the old fashion, they had agreed, escorted by her children and his nieces. Michael had dressed with the groom's party and was currently doing his nine-year-old best to stand still, as befitted the solemnity of the occasion, but could not help running a finger between his adult miniature of a fashionable cravat and his neck.

Gil shot him a sympathetic glance. His cravat was tight, as well. And his throat was dry. And the happiness that had been bubbling out of him at odd moments for the past ten weeks was buried under a load of totally pointless fear.

Of course, she would not pull out at the last minute. Nothing had changed her mind in the ten weeks since she ambushed him with her proposal and accepted his total surrender.

She had read the estate's books, and praised his dispositions, while suggesting several changes that she'd tried successfully for herself or Michael. She had reluctantly accepted his unwillingness to follow custom and the law, and make her private wealth his own. Instead, she had proposed a loan, with fair repayment terms, the interest to her and the principal in trust to be split between her daughters and any children she and Gil might have together. Gil had appealed to Lord Henry, who advised Gil to fall in with Susan's plans, since she had an excellent head for business.

She had entered into vigorous correspondence with his sisters and Chloe, mostly about the wedding, but also about the estate and its servants.

She had commanded Gil to fire the butler and one or two others who were under his mother's thumb and had found him replacements. She had made arrangements for his mother to be closely nursed, with three sturdy but kindly keepers to supplement the services of the maid his mother trusted, whose wages Susan doubled.

Gil had thought she might want Lady Rutledge sent away; had even suggested it. "She should not be near children," he warned. Susan agreed, especially after the first time that Moffat came running to fetch Susan because Lady Rutledge had Amy cornered in the library and was spewing a cart load of venom about the Redepennings in general and Susan in particular.

"We could have the old gatekeeper's cottage made into a haven for her," Susan suggested. "It is walled on three sides, Gil, and far enough from the house that if she escapes her attendants again, they will have time to send up the alarm."

When Lady Rutledge refused any involvement with the project, Susan ordered the repairs and redecoration herself, and made a cosy house for her future mother-in-law, entirely suitable to the needs of an elderly and infirm widow. Which the woman was, though she still dressed as if she was in her twenties. Yes, and painted, too, finishing the mask with red lips as if the admirers of years gone by would appear on her doorstep at any moment.

Lady Rutledge had been invited to the wedding, but had refused, to Gil's relief. Undoubtedly, had she come she would have made a scene. And undoubtedly, had she made a scene the Redepennings, who were here in force to support the happy couple, would have stopped her without making any fuss, and without showing in word or deed that anything was wrong.

Hamish and Lisette had been invited but had sent their regrets and a large silver tray embossed with thistles. Lisette confided in a note to Susan that she was uncomfortable travelling in her current condition, which prompted another flurry of present buying and letters.

Gil walked to the door and looked out again. Still no sign of the carriages from Longford Court, where the ladies had gathered to prepare for the wedding. "We were twenty minutes early, Rutledge," Alex reminded him. "She'll be here."

Rick clapped him on the shoulder. "Soon enough, the waiting will be over."

He had been waiting all his life, since he was twelve. And knowing she really would soon be his had made the waiting harder.

Michael had taken over his watching post at the door. "They are coming, sir." And sure enough, a succession of carriages drove crisply up the lane, deposited a bevy of ladies and girls at the lynch gate, and drove on. First, Rede's countess, Anne Chirbury, and her sisters and eldest daughter. Then Rick's Mary and Alex's Ella, with Amy and Chrissie, and the senior Mrs Cunningham, mother of Susan's first husband.

The two girls, soon to be his daughters, came to him for a kiss on the cheek and then waited with him in the foyer while the other ladies went to sit down.

Mina, Flora, Chloe and his nieces were in the next coach. All of them were staying with the Chirburys rather than at Thornbury Hall, but he was beyond grateful to have his family at his side, though Mina's children had not made the long trip.

Finally, the coach he had been waiting for. Lord Henry descended first, then turned to give his hand to his daughter, who balanced for a moment still in the carriage, her eyes searching for and finding Gil.

He met her radiant smile with his own, and time, which had been dragging its heels all day, suddenly stopped altogether, so he was conscious of nothing but The Goddess's smile; nothing but her hand placed in his by Lord Henry who had somehow crossed the churchyard in a flash.

Gil stood smiling down, fathoms-deep lost in her beautiful eyes until Michael told the others, impatiently, "You all need to go and sit down so that my Mama and my new Papa can walk into the church."

And they did. And Gil woke enough to himself and his surroundings that he could offer Susan his arm, and follow in the wake of the children, his new son leading the way and each of his new daughters holding hands with a little niece. They processed slowly up the centre of the church to the altar where he would promise himself to Susan for a lifetime, and she to him. Superfluous, on his part. His vows had been made, long ago. He would repeat the formal ones here, in front of the vicar and the congregation, and be proud to do so. But he and God knew he had always belonged to The Goddess.

Their carriage—Susan's cabriolet-phaeton with Gil driving—was the centre piece of a noisy and joyful cavalcade on the road back to the Hall. Carriages, people walking, adults on horseback and children on ponies—it was hardly the private moment with her husband that Susan craved, but that would come. Meanwhile, she had his ring on her finger, her hand tucked in his arm, her head on his shoulder, and no duties at all for the next two hours. And beyond, because what happened after the guests left would be no duty.

How she had craved sisters when growing up in a house full of boys, and now she was blessed with so many, not all here, but the four who were—Chloe, Mina, Mary, and Ella—had firmly instructed her to leave any petty household crises to them, and just greet the guests and enjoy their company.

Susan looked at the carriage behind them, where Chloe and Mina travelled together. Neither had been back to Thornbury Hall since arriving in Longford. "Will they be all right?" she wondered.

Gil must have been wondering, too. He didn't have to follow her eyes to understand her thinking. "Chloe is much stronger than we thought; stronger than she thinks herself. And Mina is a rock. I think asking Anne Chirbury to have them to stay was a good plan, but a visit to the Hall will be good for them. Put some old ghosts to rest, especially with all the redecoration you've done."

Susan waved a hand in dismissal. "A lick of paint, and some furniture and ornaments changed for better ones from the attics."

He pushed her bonnet back slightly so he could kiss her, prompting hoots from those riding in escort. "It feels like a home," he said.

But as they pulled up before the front steps, she sensed a ferment bubbling within. The servants lined up to welcome them looked anxious, and Mrs Glossop and the butler Susan had hired to replace her mother-in-law's minion hovered frowning, stepping forward as soon as Gil brought the cabriolet-phaeton to a halt.

Before Gil could climb down and come around to assist Susan, Chloe rushed up from her own carriage, and intercepted the two servants.

Gil had missed the byplay. He was focused on his own plan, clearly, which was to lift Susan from the cabriolet-phaeton and carry her up the steps. From his arms, she looked anxiously at Chloe, who smiled back and mouthed, "No duties!" before taking Rick by the arm and whispering something to him.

So Susan relaxed, and let her new husband carry her past the clapping smiling servants and into her new home.

"A guinea says he can't carry her all the way to their rooms!" Rick shouted, and several of the other men took that bet. Gil smiled into her eyes, lifting an eyebrow. "I need to take my bonnet off," she said, and he laughed and headed for the stairs and up to the next floor, with the children and many of the guests hooting along behind.

Not, she noticed, most of her brothers and sisters, who had disappeared through the double doors that led onto the series of reception rooms where the wedding feast lay waiting.

They were no more than twenty minutes, even with the kiss Gil demanded as payment for his services in helping her with her bonnet and her hair, in lieu of the maid he had sent away, and they were cheered and pelted with rice as they came through the doors.

"What happened to the special cake?" she asked, a little later, when she realised that several of the items on the menu for the spread were unaccountably missing.

"A minor problem in the kitchen," Mina assured her. "Cook has something else coming, and it will be here shortly."

"This isn't the wine I chose," Gil murmured, frowning, after a sip.

"An accident," Ella informed him. "But this one is very nice."

"Was anyone hurt?" Susan asked. Two of the footmen were limping, and she had seen a maid with a black eye.

"Nothing to speak of," Mary said. "Now stop worrying and enjoy yourself."

"Have you seen Chloe?" Susan asked Gil, as it drew near time for the speeches, and he nodded to the back of the room, where Chloe was just entering. Mina, Mary, Ella, and Flora converged on her and spoke briefly before turning back to smile across at Gil and Susan just as Lord Henry shouted for order.

Susan pushed her suspicions to the back of her mind. Whatever was going on, her sisters had it under control, but they would certainly explain it to her later.

"Lady Rutledge staged a scene," Chloe reported, when most of the guests were gone and only family remained. "She escaped her attendants, locked herself in the reception rooms, destroyed as much of the food and broke as many of the bottles as she could, then took laudanum and composed herself to die in the wreckage."

"She misjudged the amount," Ella continued. "And was emptying the contents of her stomach when the servants managed to break in."

"Chloe was marvellous." Mina gave her sister-in-law a hug. "She calmed down the servants, gave us all tasks to do, and tipped your brothers the wink to get you out of the way while the rooms were set up for you."

"And Ella sent for a brine solution, which we gave to Lady Rutledge until the doctor arrived," Chloe said.

"He says she is in no danger, Gil," Ella reported, "but she is quite miserable."

Gil couldn't dredge up any sympathy. "I am sorry our day has ended on so sour a note," he said to Susan, but she beamed back at him.

"I told you months ago, my dearest love, that you didn't have to do everything yourself, and today proves that the lesson is for me, as well. We are not alone, Gil. We will never be alone."

And she kissed each of the sisters in turn. "Thank you. Thank you for a wonderful day, full of precious memories."

EPILOGUE

The Honourable Henry Gilbert Michael Alexander Rutledge
was celebrating his acceptance into the Christian fold in the
time-honoured manner, by roaring his outrage at the water poured
over his tiny head.

His youngest godfather and half-brother, an experienced baby-
handler as the oldest male child in a family with two babies, lifted him
against a shoulder and patted his back with precisely the right pressure,
until Hal let his head drop and stuffed a fist into his mouth for sucking.
Gil grinned at his step-son over the baby's head. No one could be more
delighted at Hal's birth than Michael, who dearly loved little Joanne
but had told his mother firmly that the family needed more sons.

"You now have three girls, and Aunt Chloe has two, and I'm all
on my own," he complained, though no one was more popular than
Michael in the house that had been home to Gil's mother for the
last two years of her life, and was now flooded with light and happiness since Chloe and her daughters had moved back to the estate.

Amy, fresh from the triumphs of her second London Season,
was holding her two-year-old sister Joanne, heedless of the hands
that twisted the ribbons knots on the shoulders of her highly stylish

jacket. Not one to have her head turned, their Amy. He could not be prouder of her if she was his own blood, and not merely the eldest daughter of his heart.

She had been kind to his mother, striking up an odd sort of friendship in visits to the old lady. Gil had worried at first; had insisted on an attendant being present at all times. But the dowager had faded since her failed attempt to spoil his wedding and spent her time with Amy looking at fashion plates and reminiscing about social triumphs half a century in the past.

"Which is very useful, Papa Rutledge," Amy told him, caustically, "for if I am in doubt about how to behave once I am out, I shall just do the opposite of what her ladyship recommends. She has a good eye for colour and cut, though."

His mother helped choose the pattern and fabric for Amy's presentation dress and the gown for her first London ball, grumbling all the while about Susan having them made in Longford instead of London, as was proper. She was in bed with what the doctor called a mild cold when Amy went over to model them both for her. She ignored Gil and Susan, as she always did, but tears stood in her eyes as she looked at Amy.

"That village dressmaker did well enough," she grumbled, reluctantly. "You look pretty, Amelia. Remember. Carry your head high. Never let them know you are afraid."

Gil felt a twist in his heart at the depth of pain underlying that advice, but his mother had not finished surprising him. "Gilbert! When you wrecked my rooms redecorating, did you find the loose floorboard in the corner by the dressing room?"

Gil and Susan exchanged glances. "No, mother," he replied.

"Three out from the wall. I hid the Rutledge jewellery there when we first moved to this place. I suppose you should have it. You can sell them. You won't bet it all on a horse race or give it to a wanton woman. But keep the pearls. I want Amelia to have them and to wear the pearls with that ball gown. They will be just the thing." She turned her shoulder, clearly dismissing Gil again, and spoke to Amy. "I wore them at my wedding, but don't let that bother you, girl. Men are not worth the grief they cause, but the pearls are pretty."

They stayed another ten minutes, leaving when the old lady fell asleep. The jewellery was exactly where she said it was, and more extensive than Gil had expected. It was his mother's final legacy, for in the morning the servants came to tell them she had died in the night, and though much of what they had found under the floorboards proved to be paste, a fine diamond set paid off the last mortgage, an emerald parure refurbished the stable roofs, and Amy faced the *ton* for the first time wearing the exquisite pearls, with matching necklace, earrings, and combs.

That had been eighteen months ago, when Joanne was just beginning to shuffle around the nursery on her bottom. The family had gathered to support him at the old lady's funeral, joined together again in London to make sure that Amy's social debut went flawlessly, and here they were once more, in the church at Chipping Niddwick, surrounded by friends and neighbours, to celebrate the wetting of his son's head.

Chrissie, his other girl, was arm-in-arm with Daisy Redepenning. As usual. The pair of them would be presented in only a couple of years, and he and Rede had agreed that the fathers would need a stout pair of sticks to beat off the admirers.

The two girls with them would have their suitors, too. Respectful ones, with proper proposals of marriage, for all the menfolk of the family would be on hand to ensure it, even though their parents had not been wed. They were Jules' daughters by his mistress, their ivory skins and almond eyes a complete contrast to the golden good looks of their friends. Jules' wife Mia had brought them home from the Cape of Good Hope not long after Gil's wedding, and the Redepennings had taken the two illegitimate children into the family and their hearts without a question, just as—long ago—they had accepted a lonely boy from the neighbouring estate, given him a refuge and a creed to live by, and made a man of him. A man who now had everything he could ever want.

On an impulse, as the psalm singers in the West Gallery raised their voices in the last song, Gil put his arms around his Goddess and captured her lips with his. She responded as she always did, ignoring the grins and nudges of the family.

"What was that for?" she asked, when he let her breathe again.

"Luck," he told her. "I have so much luck that I wanted to share."

"Share again," she advised. And so he did.

THE END

ABOUT THE AUTHOR

Jude has been trying to be a novelist since she was fourteen. She was a good enough reader to see that the first two attempts (one when she was fourteen and one in her early twenties) weren't good enough to publish. Then along came life. A seriously ill child who required years of therapy; a rising mortgage that led to a full-time job; her own chronic illness… the writing took a back seat.

As the years passed, the fear grew. She'd waited so long. If she never finished any of the dozens of novels she started, no one would ever judge them.

Jude's mother believed in her, and on the way home from that great lady's funeral, Jude realised she'd left it too late for her Mum to ever hold a print copy of one of her books. So she replaced the fear of finishing with the fear of not finishing, by telling everyone she knew that she was writing a novel.

In the five years from publishing her first fiction book in 2014, Jude published seven novels, thirteen novellas, a heap of shorter stories, and more novellas in group anthologies. She plans to keep going till she runs out of years.

Jude writes historical fiction with a large helping of romance, a splash of Regency, and a twist of suspense.

She then tries to figure out how to slot it into a genre category.

She's mad keen on history, enjoys what happens to people in the crucible of a passionate relationship, and loves to use a good mystery and some real danger as mechanisms to torture her characters.

In her other identity as Judy Knighton, she is a plain language consultant specialising in contracts, insurance policies, and financial disclosure statements. Fiction is more fun.

Website and blog: http://judeknightauthor.com/
Book blurbs and links: http://judeknightauthor.com/books/

Do you like news before anyone else, plus discounts, and free stuff?

Sign up to Jude's newsletter. The main newsletter goes out once every two months, and includes news about coming books, discounts, contests, and events. Every newsletter also has news abut books from Jude's author friends, and a free story that Jude writes just for newsletter subscribers.

In between newsletters, if Jude has something exciting to share she occasionally sends a one-topic email.

Free book as a thank you

As a thank you for subscribing to Jude's newsletter, you can expect a series of three emails, the first offering a free copy of one of Jude's books, and the next two with links to other free stories. So why not subscribe today?

Subscribe to newsletter: http://judeknightauthor.com/newsletter/

ALSO BY JUDE KNIGHT

Regency books

The Golden Redepennings series

True love is rare and elusive, but they won't settle for less

Candle's Christmas Chair (A novella in The Golden Redepennings series)

Candle and Min are separated by social standing and malicious lies. He has until Christmas to convince her to give their love another chance.

Gingerbread Bride (A novella in *The Golden Redepennings* series)

Mary runs from an unwanted marriage and finds adventure, danger and Rick, her girlhood hero, coming once more to her rescue.

Farewell to Kindness (Book 1 in *The Golden Redepennings* series)

Love is not always convenient. Anne and Rede have different goals, but when their enemies join forces, so must they.

A Raging Madness (Book 2 in *The Golden Redepennings* series)

Their marriage is a fiction. Their enemies are all too real. Uncovering the truth will need all the trust Ella and Alex can find.

The Realm of Silence (Book 3 in *The Golden Redepennings* series)

Gill has a list. Rescue Susan's daughter, destroy her dragons, defeat his demons, return to his lonely life. How hard can it be?

Unkept Promises (Book 4 in *The Golden Redepennings* series — published July 2019)

Mia hopes to negotiate a comfortable marriage. Jules wants his wife to go home to England, where she belongs. Love confounds them both.

A Baron for Becky

Becky was a fallen woman. How could the men who loved her help set her back on her feet?

Revealed in Mist

As spy and enquiry agent, Prue and David worked to uncover secrets, while hiding a few of their own.

A Suitable Husband

Marcel knows that a chef from the slums, however talented, is no fit mate for the cousin of a duke, however distant. But Cedrica can dream.

Lord Calne's Christmas Ruby

Lalamani is a wealthy merchant's heiress with an aversion to fortune hunters. Philip is an impoverished earl with a twisted hand. Combating a villainous rector to save her aunt, they find that their differences count for nothing.

House of Thorns

Bear's rose thief bride comes with a scandal that threatens to tear them apart.

Paradise Regained (novella in the Bluestocking Belles collection *Follow Your Star Home*)

In discovering the mysteries of the East, James has built a new life. Will unveiling the secrets in his wife's heart destroy it?

The Beast Next Door (novella in the Bluestocking Belles collection *Valentines from Bath*)

In all the assemblies and parties, no-one Charis met could ever match Eric, the beast next door.

Lunch-length reads: story collections

Hand-Turned Tales and Lost in the Tale

A double handful of short stories and novellas, free from most retailers. Try the range of Jude's imagination one bite at a time, in a lunch-length read.

If Mistletoe Could Tell Tales

A repackaging of six published Christmas stories: four novellas and two

novelettes. Because nothing enhances the magic of Christmas like the
magic of love.

Hearts in the Land of Ferns

Five stories all set in New Zealand: two historical and three contemporary
suspense. *All That Glisters* has been published in *Hand-Turned Tales*. The
other four have all been published in multi-author collections, but never
before in a collection of Jude Knight stories.

Victorian books

Never Kiss a Toad (with Mariana Gabrielle)

Caught together in her father's bed, Sally and Toad are wrenched apart, to
endure years of separation. But neither distance nor malice can destroy
true love.

God Help Ye, Merry Gentleman (with Mariana Gabrielle)

A Christmas collection: two purpose-written short pieces in the world of
Never Kiss a Toad, showing Sally's and Toad's childhood and youth. Plus
some other published pieces from blogs, newsletters, and books set in the
same world.

Forged in Fire (novella in the Bluestocking Belles collection *Never Too Late*)

Burned in their youth, neither Tad nor Lottie expected to feel the fires of
love. Until the inferno of a volcanic eruption sears away the lies of the past
and frees them to forge a new future.

Post-apocalyptic fiction

A Midwinter's Tale (novella in the Speakeasy Scribes collection *Resist and Rejoice*)

Verity Marchand is an orphan of time, her family tavern under the ice that grips Boston. When Verity's dreams lead her into a nightmare, she'll need a miracle—or the family cat—to save her.

Contemporary

A Family Christmas (novella in the Authors of Main Street collection *Christmas Babies on Main Street*)

Kirilee is on the run, in disguise, out of touch, and eating for two. Trevor is heading home for Christmas, after three years undercover, investigating a global criminal organisation. In the heart of a storm, two people from different worlds question what divides and what unites them.

Abbie's Wish (novella in the Authors of Main Street collection *Christmas Wishes on Main Street*)

Abbie's Christmas wish draws three men to her mother. One of them is a monster.

Beached (novella in the Authors of Main Street collection *Summer Romance on Main Street*)

The truth will wash away her coastal paradise

ACKNOWLEDGMENTS

I owe thanks to so many people for this book. My beta readers, of course: My sister Sue, and also Doreen, Tray, Sandy, Jan, Angela, and Carol. Especially Carol, who commented on the beta version then reread scenes as I rewrote.

Thank you to Dr Jacqueline Reiter, who checked the scenes with the Martello Tower, and to other experts in their topic who answered my random questions about all sorts of things that cropped up as I was writing.

Thank you to Andra Jenkins, whose editing suggestions made me dig deep in the rewrite. Andra, I owe you some of my best scenes.

Any errors in fact or language are my own, but you would find more of them if not for my excellent friends, without whom I could not have written *The Realm of Silence*.

Thanks also to my beloved husband for putting up with a wife who keeps running off to the nineteenth century. I love you, darling.

And lastly, thank you to the readers who kept asking for the next in *The Golden Redepenning* series. And yes, Mia and Jules are next.